Compromised

A Stephanie Chalice Thriller
#6

By

Lawrence Kelter

Street Books

Editing by
Pauline Nolet

Interior book design by
Bob Houston eBook Formatting

For

The insatiably curious

Acknowledgments

The author gratefully acknowledges the following special people for their contributions to this book.

As always, for my wife, Isabella for nurturing each and every new book as if it were a newborn child, and for her love and support.

Compromised

A Stephanie Chalice Thriller
#6

Lawrence Kelter

Chapter One

I stared down at my corpse and it stared back at me, two cold and lifeless eyes that would have otherwise been fixed on the funeral home ceiling had I not intersected their gaze. Dead Stephanie Chalice was wearing a navy blue dress, one that was customarily trotted out of the closet for occasions like confirmations, christenings, and baptisms. I instantly recognized the silk charmeuse fabric and the ruffle that cascaded from the shoulder to the waist. *Funny, I never thought I'd be buried in that one,* I mused. My husband, Gus, was, or should I say had been, a big fan of frenzied undress, and I'd often found myself in states of being partially undone after recovering from bouts of spirited spontaneous sex. *Ha! I think this may be the first time I've ever been horizontal in that one. Hey, I'm laughing about this,* why?

There were no visible clues—the cause of death appeared to be outright unrecognizable. *No bruises or contusions, puncture marks or ... If I'd taken a beating, the mortician certainly did a great job of covering up any discoloration and marks.* I guess I could've died of natural causes, but then again, when a thirty-year-old homicide detective takes a dirt nap ...

Suspicious.

So how did I end up dead?

In most cases a cop falls when he or she has lost their edge, they've underestimated the perp or the danger of the situation, or there was a distraction, or the cop was otherwise compromised. Most of us NYPD types are pretty savvy and don't just walk toward the grim reaper with our arms spread wide open.

How'd you screw up, jackass? You left behind a son and a husband. Speaking of which, there's the handsome devil now, but … Christ, he looks like hell. Gus usually looked dapper, but today his suit hung uncharacteristically from his square broad shoulders. His eyes were bloodshot and glassy, and his face looked strained and tired.

"How'd I get here, Gus? How'd I end up in a box?"

He used to be my partner, but tying the knot put an end to that. My new partner was green, green as in wet behind the ears, and green as in by-the-book, but he was a good kid and didn't mind taking direction. "Does Yana know what happened to me? Was he there when I bought the farm? Did you talk to him? Did he tell you how it went down?"

Gus remained silent while he stared at me lying in the casket, looking despondent, his head bowed as if the weight of the world were pressing down upon it.

I suddenly felt hollowness in the pit of my stomach. An icy chill began in my arms and ran through me. *Oh my God, this is for real. Dummy! Risk taker! What in God's name did you do?*

I tried searching my mind for the details of my death, but my thinking was fuzzy and I was unable to string my thoughts together. *Think, damn it. What is wrong with you? Are you on drugs? What is it? Why can't you remember?*

"Oh my God."

Who said that? I felt someone take hold of my hand. My eyelids fluttered. Bright light caused my eyes to water. I heard someone gasp.

"Come on, Stephanie. Come on back to us."

That's Gus. It has to be, but ... come back from where? I was no longer looking down at my corpse. White billowy clouds surrounded me and I felt as if I were floating upon them.

He pleaded, "Wake up. Please wake up."

Gus, where are you? I looked all around, but there was no one in view. It seemed that I was completely alone.

Someone stroked me lightly on the cheek. "Ms. Chalice, can you hear me? It's Dr. Efram. Your husband is here with me. Can you open your eyes?"

My eyes are open, but there's no one here. I began to feel anxious, but then a drop of water fell on my cheek and I gradually understood that I needed to transition out of a very deep and all-encompassing sleep. I opened my eyes, this time for real. Gus was standing over me. He was crying. His eyes were red and his throat tightly clenched. I touched my cheek and realized that he had awoken me with a solitary tear, pulled me back from the abyss in which I'd been lost.

"Oh, thank God!" Gus put his hands on the sides of my face and kissed me long and hard. When he pulled away, I could see that he was panting and seemed to be emotionally exhausted.

I was completely disoriented and wasn't quite sure of where we were. "What's wrong with you, Gus?"

He smiled as tears continued to roll down his cheeks. Then he pressed his lips to mine and kissed me again. He sighed and looked toward heaven. "Thank you, God. Thank you."

A doctor turned to Gus and politely stated, "I need a moment with the patient."

Gus pointed at the doorway. "Do I have to..." he asked reluctantly.

"No. Just give me a little room," the doctor replied. "You can stay here."

Gus stepped back, giving the doctor the room he needed. "I'll be right here, Stephanie," he said in a reassuring voice. "I'll be right here in the room with you."

Gee, clingy much? Uneasy insecure Gus was causing me to worry.

The doctor held up a small illuminated flashlight and checked each of my eyes. "Good," he exclaimed in a professional tone.

"What's good?"

"Fundus on both sides appear to be normal."

What the hell is a fundus? It finally dawned on me that I was lying in a hospital bed, but so much unexplained activity was going on around me that I still felt confused. "What is going on here?"

"You were out for quite some time," the doctor advised and held up his finger. "Please follow my finger." He began moving it around without offering further explanation. I followed it with my eyes. Again he said, "Good."

"'Out for quite some time?'" I turned to Gus. "Babe, what am I missing?"

I saw his throat tighten, but he didn't reply.

"You were unconscious," the doctor said. "I'm glad you finally came back to us."

'Glad you finally came back to us?' "Was that ever in doubt? Gus? For the love of God, what happened? What's going on?"

"Just another moment," Dr. Efram said, interrupting Gus before he could answer. "Stick out your tongue."

If you insist.

The doctor barked instructions in rapid succession and I followed along. "Touch your nose. Touch my finger. Touch your nose ..." and on and on. He felt my face and tested my hearing with a tuning fork. "You seem neurologically sound. I'll call a neurologist for a consult and arrange for further testing but for the moment ..."

"For the moment what?" Gus asked anxiously.

Dr. Efram smiled warmly. "For the moment feel free to kiss your wife again, and again and again if you wish."

Gus willingly obliged.

It was wonderful to feel his warm lips pressed against mine, but I just couldn't stand not knowing what had happened. "When did I get here? Can someone please tell me what the hell happened?"

Efram glanced at me with expectation. "We were hoping you'd be able to tell us, Detective Chalice."

My eyes opened wide. *"Me?"* I strained to remember what had happened that might have put me in the hospital, but there just weren't any recent memories. I knew who I was and what I did, but the latest events ... I shrugged and felt my facial muscles stiffen. I felt as if I was going to cry.

Dr. Efram must have sensed that I was emotional. "It's all right," he said. "Cry if you feel you need to. It's not uncommon to feel sad or disoriented after awakening from a coma."

"What? Did you say that I was in a coma?"

Gus sniffled. "You were out for five days, Stephanie. We were worried that—" Gus stopped in mid-sentence and turned away. I saw his chest rise steeply and then fall before turning back to me, fighting back tears. "I'm just so happy you're all right."

"But why can't I remember anything, and why won't you tell me what's happened?"

It looked as if Efram was about to speak, but he stopped when he saw me reach for the back of my head. I felt a sharp twinge where I touched it and felt that my head was heavily bandaged. I held out my hands imploringly. *"Gus?"* I could see that he was unable to speak, and in the next instant he covered his eyes and bawled like a child.

Chapter Two

Gus was chased out of the room, then doctors and nurses paraded in one after another, all eager to have a crack at me, pinching, poking, prodding, squeezing, testing, and annoying me to death.

"Five days?" Gus' words ran through my mind over and over again. Dr. Efram had subsequently explained that I'd been brought in by ambulance on Monday evening and it was now late Saturday afternoon. *Five days. Dear God. No wonder Gus is such a basket case. Can't imagine what he must be going through. I can't believe I haven't seen my little baby boy Max in five days. Jesus.* A tear popped out of my eye. I shook my head while medical staff tested me like a lab rat. I had been unconscious five full days. Still, the question remained, what had happened?

More than an hour passed before the hospital staff was finished with their initial examination and Gus was allowed back into the room. He looked better when I saw him again—relieved was a better word. Folded blankets and a pillow rested on the recliner near the window. It didn't take a detective to figure out that Gus had slept by my side all week long. "How's your back?"

He seemed surprised by my question. "My back? You've been unconscious for days and you're worried about *my* back?"

"Well, I mean, sure. You slept in a chair all week, didn't you?"

He nodded.

"That spine of yours is probably twisted up like a pretzel."

Gus shrugged, but his expression was buoyant all the while. He didn't answer my question but instead sat down alongside me on the bed, leaned over, and hugged me with his cheek pressed firmly against mine. "Thank God," he whispered.

"You're smothering me, you big lug." I pushed him away good-humoredly. "Enough with the melodrama already. What does a girl have to do to get a straight answer?" I winked a sultry wink. "And by the way, sailor, I'll do just about anything to get what I want."

"We don't have any answers." He looked into my eyes lovingly. "*I* don't have any."

"Well, what do you have for me? Tell me something, will you? Tell me something before I go completely bonkers."

"You don't remember *anything*?"

"I already went through this with the doctors. My mind is blank. They think it's probably confusion as a result of the weeklong snooze."

"Maybe."

"What does *that* mean?" I asked unhappily.

Gus wore a rare sheepish expression on his face. "You may have amnesia, babe. Doctor Efram said it's not uncommon in cases of severe head trauma."

I touched the thick bandage on the back of my head. "This, huh?"

"It appears that you were slugged with a blunt object and that you have a severe concussion. Your brain really swelled up and we were afraid ..." His hand went to his mouth, but he removed it after a moment. "The point is that you're all right. I called Ma to let her know you're awake. She'll come down to the hospital as soon as I get back to watch Max."

"But what about Yana? He doesn't know what happened?"

Gus cringed. I could see by his dire expression that something was terribly wrong. As mentioned, Tadashi Yanagisawa had been my partner for about a year, ever since our CO had deemed that it was a violation of department policy for Gus and me to operate as a team.

"Gus, what happened?"

He shook his head with despair. "I'm sorry, Steph. Yana ..." He looked away and drew a deep breath. "Yana didn't make it."

"Oh my God." I strained to remember what had happened, but there was a wide and jagged rift in my memory to which I had no access. *Yana didn't make it?* I gasped, filling my lungs with air, and tears began to drizzle down my cheeks. "Gus, what are you talking about? Is Yana dead?"

Gus nodded. "I'm so sorry."

I grabbed a tissue as the horror of my partner's death washed over me. I squeezed my eyes shut, trying to force my memory to return, but it just wasn't there. The damn thing just wasn't there. "What the hell happened? The last thing I remember is ..." I had a vague recollection of that Monday, the day I was told I was admitted into the hospital. I remembered rushing around the apartment that morning, getting Max ready for the day and Ma hitting me with one of her requisite zingers as soon as she walked through the door to babysit. It was something about me never having Max ready for her on time. I remember that she had laid into me pretty good, going on and on about how I never go to bed at a reasonable hour and how I was going to run myself into the ground. She was always full of motherly advice and complaints about me not listening to any of her sage wisdom.

"What do you and Gus do all night?" she'd asked.

"Duh!"

"All night? Is he Superman or something? My God, the two of you must be insatiable."

"Well, not *all* night, but we can hardly play hide the salami before the little one goes lights out for the night, now can we?"

"'Hide the salami?' That's disgusting. I'm going to wash your mouth out with soap. I'm still your mother."

I snickered. "I'm well aware," I'd said and gave her a respectful peck on the cheek.

I recalled feeling that familiar pang I always got when I kissed Max goodbye before leaving for work.

Fast-forward a bit and I vaguely remembered that Yana and I had spent the day questioning relevant parties on the Serafina Ramirez homicide case, but when it came to the specific interviews, and the sequence of the day's events ... I looked out the window and could sense that I wore a vacant expression on my face. "Christ," I barked. "What's wrong with me? I can't remember anything."

"You will," Gus assured me. "You've been in a coma all week. Give it a little time to let the cobwebs clear."

"I know, but ... shit." I felt a frown pulling at the muscles in my face. "Jesus. I can't believe that Yana's dead."

Gus leaned forward and put his arms around me. "I'm sorry. I didn't want to tell you so soon, but I knew you'd ask."

"I want to remember so badly, but it's just not there. It's as if my head is empty."

"Far from it. It's just short-term memory loss. It's like getting a cold—you just have to let it run its course."

"Short term? How long is short term?"

"The doctors can't be sure—a few days or weeks." He shrugged. "It's the brain, Stephanie. You know how complicated the mind is. There just aren't any absolute answers."

"I need something to jog my memory. I need ..." My eyes flashed with revelation. "My notebook. You know how I ..."

"I know, you're a meticulous note taker. It's with the rest of your stuff in the evidence room."

"Why there?"

"Shearson's orders. She said that your notebook would help to establish a timeline leading up to the altercation. I couldn't argue. Not that she would've listened to me anyway."

Pamela Shearson was a deputy commissioner. I didn't love her or her overly ambitious agenda, but she had good instincts and was rarely wrong. "I need it."

"I'll request it and see if I can get my hands on it before the next time I come to visit."

"How?"

"'How?' What do you mean?"

"How, Gus? How was Yana murdered?"

"He was shot in the chest. No witnesses to the actual shooting, no video, and you ... well, I'm sure your head will be clearer tomorrow."

I couldn't remember what had happened, but my skill set was still intact and I began calling on it immediately. "But we have forensics, don't we? There's a bullet slug with markings we can run down, and possible DNA, and—"

Gus held up his hand, cutting me off before I could finish my diatribe. "Easy now. It's a cop killing. A dedicated task force has been established, rewards offered ... No one is taking this lightly, and five days is a long time. The slug has been analyzed. It came from a thirty-caliber rifle."

"What kind of gun?"

"We're not sure yet. Ballistics is still trying to match the rifling marks on the slug to a specific weapon."

"From what distance?"

"A nearby rooftop."

"But then how ... " I felt my face muscles tightening and my head throb painfully, so painfully that I had to squeeze my eyes shut to deal with it.

"You all right?" Gus asked with urgency. He waited a moment and then pushed the call button.

A nurse rushed into the room and glanced at the heart monitor. "You have to calm down," she said firmly. "Your blood pressure is way too high." She called to a second nurse who had just entered the room. "Page Dr. Efram and bring me five milligrams of Valium." I had an oxygen tube in my nose. She turned up the flow. "Deep breaths, honey. You have a head injury. The last thing you need is more bleeding in your brain. Come on, slowly in and out. Fill your lungs. Hold it ... Let it out slowly. Again." The second nurse returned and handed her a syringe. "I'm going to give you a small amount of sedative, just enough to calm you down." She injected it into my IV line.

I felt the sedative take hold. My eyelids felt heavy and I could sense my tension floating away.

"We have to clear the room," the second nurse said to Gus.

He looked terrible as he backed toward the door. "You'll be fine," he offered in a soothing tone, but the worry I saw on his face made me think otherwise. *How could someone have shot Yana from a rooftop and knocked me unconscious too?* Something just didn't add up, but the medication was having its way with me, eradicating worry, removing doubt, and lulling me gently to sleep.

Chapter Three

Ma looked surprisingly good for a woman who had lost her NYPD husband and had now come uncomfortably close to losing her only daughter. She had taken Dad's death really hard. She'd mourned deeply and had never truly felt alive until ... My marrying Gus had reignited her pilot light, but it wasn't until Max's birth that the flame truly breathed oxygen again and began to burn brightly—and thank God because she was going down that road of those old Italian widows who dressed in nothing but black all of their remaining days. You know the ones I'm talking about, those women who looked like they were a hundred and twelve when in fact they were only fifty.

One of her friends had recently become a widow and was on one of those antidepressants. It wasn't Paxil or Lexapro. It was one of the newer miracle drugs. I think it was called Darnitol or Screwitol or Hellwithitol, or something equally hopeless sounding.

Ma scrutinized my face carefully. "You look okay," she said in a motherly, emotionally fortifying manner. "I told you that all you needed was a good night's sleep. So, how do you feel?"

"Like I was hit by a semi that backed up and rolled over me again."

"That sounds like an improvement," she quipped.

I grinned awkwardly and opened my arms to pull her in. "Come here, you old pain in the butt." I'm not sure which of us began to cry first, but I think I edged her out by a nose.

Ma gave us a moment to indulge in emotional catharsis before insisting, "That's enough of that." She wiped away her tears. "Are you a cop or a baby?"

"Right now?"

She smiled sympathetically and sat down on the bed next to me. "Don't be so hard on yourself. You took one hell of a blow to the head. You scared the shit out of all of us."

"I feel so hopeless. I can't remember anything, not what happened to me or ..."

"It'll come back to you, sweetheart. The doctors said that it would take some time for your memory to return."

"I don't have time. Someone shot my partner. Do you understand how that feels?"

"Not entirely, but I have some idea. I know it must be eating at you, but at the moment ... well, honey, there's nothing you can do about it."

"I've got to pull myself together and figure out what happened. Some cop killer is walking around free as a bird."

"I don't think you can force yourself to remember, Stephanie. You've got to try to relax and give yourself time to heal. You're no good to yourself or Yana while you're lying here, and the doctors said you could be here at least another week. That's my best advice," she said with a weak smile. "Not that you listen to anything I say."

My first thought was to check myself out of the hospital, but department protocol had to be followed and I knew that it would be quite some time before the department doc okayed my return to active duty. "This blows! It really does. Someone shot my partner and—"

"Yes, sweetheart, it blows, but you're alive and well, with a handsome husband and an adorable little son. Things could be worse, a hell of a lot worse." She patted me on the leg. "I made a delicious eggplant parmigiana. I'll bring you some as soon as the doctor says that you can eat normally."

"That sounds good. I hope you didn't cheap out on the mozzarella."

"Of course not. Why would you—"

"Did you use Polly-O?"

"Yes, Stephanie, I paid full price for Polly-O even though the store brand was on sale for half the price, just because I know you're such a pain in the ass."

"I'm not a pain in the ass. I have a discriminating palate."

"Of course you do. Anything that makes you happy makes me happy."

"Stop patronizing me."

"I'm not."

"The store brands aren't as good as Polly-O."

"Eaten fresh, yes, I agree, but melted and covered with my homemade sauce ... I can't taste the difference."

"I guess your palate isn't as refined as mine is," I said snobbishly.

"Ha! My palate's not refined says the girl who eats from street carts. You've got a lot of nerve."

"What about the Romano cheese?"

"What about it?" she asked cynically.

"Did you buy that pre-grated sawdust the supermarket tries to pass off as a dairy product, or did you buy the imported stuff?"

"Honey, where is this coming from? When do I ever scrimp on my ingredients? I got a nice fresh chunk of Locatelli. I'll grate it when I need it. My goodness, you're certainly in a bitchy mood.

Maybe the doctor should check to see if that head injury threw your hormones out of whack."

"Gus won't talk about the shooting," I griped.

"*Ah,*" she emoted with revelation. "So that's what this is all about."

I shrugged.

"Well, of course he won't. The last time it was brought up you had to be sedated. Are you crazy, Stephanie? You were out cold for a week. Put your health at greater risk, why don't you? I mean, my God, how stubborn can you be? The city is literally crawling with police officers looking for the shooter and the story is running on the news day and night. Let your colleagues do their jobs."

"I'm impatient."

"'I'm impatient,'" she parroted. "You know what? How about if I tell you a story."

"You mean like when I was a little girl?" I asked in a childlike voice.

"Yes. Exactly like when you were a little girl, you ornery kid."

"Will it help me get out of here faster?"

"Yeah, of course it will," she replied with a healthy dose of sarcasm. "Dream on, princess."

"Then I'd like a better offer."

"I could sing you a lullaby."

"On second thought ... I'll stick with the story."

"Rotten kid." She showed me the back of her hand. "It's a true story. It's why your father became a policeman."

I searched my memory, the portion of it that I could access, anyway. My father had told me so many stories about his early days on the force and I knew how very strongly he believed in the criminal justice system, but the catalyst that had made him become a cop in the first place ... "I've got to hear this."

Ma helped me to prop myself up and fixed my pillow. "Comfy?"

"Uh-huh. Got any popcorn?"

"I think I have some Altoids."

"Pass."

"Ha." She smiled happily. "I'm glad that ka-nock on the head didn't knock the *pain-in-the-assness* out of you."

"You've always said that I'm hardheaded."

"All right. Settle in. This may take a bit."

"Ready, Mommy," I said in a baby's voice before suddenly barking a demand, "This better be good."

"So your father and I had been married about three years and—"

"Ma, is this the adoption story? Because if it is, I'm not sure I want to hear it again."

"But the story has such a wonderful ending."

I had not learned that I was adopted until I was an adult, and when I was finally told … well, it wasn't under the best circumstances. I love my parents dearly, but being reminded of the story, well … it was just something I went out of my way to avoid. "I love you, Ma, and I understand that you and Dad waited a long time to adopt but …"

"I'm just trying to say that good things come to those who wait." She hugged me. "Your father and I waited a long time, but we got the most precious little girl and …" Her tears wet the side of my face.

"Okay," I began in a lighthearted tone. "This is no time for waterworks. I get the message—I can't just sprint out of bed and pursue Yana's shooter. I get it. I'll have to wait."

She reached for a tissue. "Let your colleagues do the work this time, sweetheart. I know it's not your style, but challenging yourself with a task that you're not equipped to complete, well …

it won't help you heal any sooner. You've got to concentrate on getting better and being there for Gus and Max. Everything else is meaningless at this point." She dabbed at her eyes with the tissue. "Look around and smell the roses, damn it. Do you know how lucky you are? How lucky we all are that you're okay?"

Ma was still sobbing, so I waved the white flag and took her in my arms just to make her stop, but asking me to look the other way and forget about a felon who'd killed my partner just wasn't going to happen. "I thought you were going to tell me about why Daddy decided to become a cop."

"Oh that," she said dismissively. "That's a very long story."

Chapter Four

Ma was still waxing nostalgic about my days as a little girl and the joy I'd brought to her and my father. She had gone through an entire box of those hospital-sized mini boxes of tissues.

Her melodramatic old stories were beginning to drive me bonkers. "*Christ.* Where's the call button? I need some morphine. STAT!"

"*Yeah?* Make mine a double," she snapped. "You rotten kid, you mean the world to me. What's wrong with me getting a little emotional?"

I told myself, *Let it pass. You can't blame the woman for being a little bent out of shape.* "Okay, let's hug it out, but then can we please change the subject?"

She smiled and leaned in for a tight squeeze.

We were still in each other's arms when I heard the sound of a man clearing his throat. I looked up and saw Gus at the door, holding Max. My eyes lit up. Max's did likewise. I threw my arms open and the little guy went nuts. Gus handed him to me. I smothered him with kisses and blew raspberries on his cheeks and neck.

He giggled for all he was worth and gave me an enthusiastic chorus of, "Ma, Ma, Ma, Ma," the only word in his vocabulary.

"Oh my God, I missed you. I missed you so much." A second round of kisses, tickles, and raspberries pushed every ounce of

Ma's melancholy tales out of my head. "Were you a good boy for your daddy?"

"Ma, Ma, Ma, Ma."

I glanced up at Gus. "He said yes."

Gus sat down, bringing the total number of people on my bed to four. The bed was definitely crowded, but it felt wonderful to be surrounded by family. Gus leaned in and gave me a big warm kiss. For a very brief moment I began to feel like myself. I grabbed Gus and pulled him back for a second smooch, then put my arms around the three of them and pulled them all close.

"It's so good to have you back with us." There was something in Gus' voice. He sounded grateful, of course, but there was something more, a hint of desperation I found unnerving.

I looked into his eyes and saw that he was on the verge of tears. "Hey, cut it out. I woke up, right?"

Ma interjected, "Just like Sleeping Beauty."

He nodded with his eyes closed.

"Hey, what's wrong?"

"Nothing," he replied. "I'm just so—Stephanie," he began in an alarmed voice, "are you okay?"

"Yeah. Why?"

"Your eye. It's ..."

And then I felt it. My right eye felt weird, as if it were wandering. My focus went out of control. "That's not good," I said in a comical voice belying the true extent of my worry. I sensed that something bigger was coming, something far worse. My head began to shake. "Oh God." I tried to lift Max but couldn't. My arms felt stiff and they began to shake as well. "Take Max," I said with urgency.

Ma gasped. "Oh my God."

Gus quickly plucked Max out of my arms and handed him to Ma. "Take Max out of the room," he said in a tone so emotionally charged that it made me worry all the more. "Get a doctor, *quickly*." He grabbed the call button and pressed it.

I felt tremors build in both of my arms. "Hold me, Gus. What's happening? I'm s-s-scared." My throat tightened and began to ache terribly. It became an effort to breathe. I heard footsteps racing toward me as my body began to rock with spasms.

I was gasping for air as Dr. Efram came into view in front of me. He placed his hands on my shoulders and turned me on my side just as my arms began to thrash. "Easy now. Try to relax. This should pass in just a moment."

A nurse grabbed my arms and pressed them firmly against the bed. A second nurse injected something into my IV.

"Easy now," Efram continued in a soothing voice. "Breathe, Stephanie. Breathe."

But I couldn't breathe. My throat was frozen. My head began to spin and I could feel the world ebbing away. I saw Gus' face. He was petrified. Then my forehead became cold and clammy and everything went black.

Chapter Five

A great deal of time must've passed, but to me it only seemed like minutes—the sky had grown dark outside the hospital window. I struggled to open my eyes and saw a cloud drifting by, blotting out the moon.

Gus was sitting in a chair next to the bed, holding my hand and looking into my eyes.

"How do you feel?" he asked.

"Groggy."

"They gave you Valium again. You'll feel lethargic for a while."

I was conscious, but I wasn't myself. I was tired and confused and felt vulnerable in a way I had never felt before. "That was one wild ride. Had no idea I could do anything like that."

Gus smiled to comfort me but didn't speak.

"I guess that was a seizure, huh?"

He nodded. "Uh-huh." Then he got up and hugged me for what seemed like minutes, pressing his face against mine in an effort to make me feel whole.

"Can I expect any more of those rollercoaster rides?"

"The doc will be in to explain in a little while."

"You're not telling me everything, are you? You're a lousy poker player, Gus—I can see it in your eyes right now, and I saw it a couple of times before. Come clean," I said in a groggy voice. "You know I'm tough enough to take it."

Gus took both of my hands and squeezed them, then edged forward and looked deeply into my eyes. He was fighting to maintain a brave face, but a tear plopped on my hand, betraying him. I saw his Adam's apple catch in his throat. He finally sighed with despair. "You didn't take a blow to the head, Steph." He looked deeply into my eyes.

"Oh my God."

He wiped away his tears and inhaled deeply before continuing. "You were shot."

The sedative was still doing its thing. I absorbed the information but didn't react to it. I was still adrift on a benzodiazepine high, confused and somewhat unresponsive. "But ... what do you mean?"

"You were shot, Stephanie. The bullet came from the same gun that killed Yana. We thought it would be a bad idea to tell you the truth right after you awoke from the coma, so we invented a story. We figured you'd have to hear the truth soon enough." Gus squeezed my hands so tightly they hurt. "It's going to be okay, Stephanie. The only thing that matters is that you're alive."

But how alive will I be? And then a revelation hit home as understanding broke through the veil of chemical tranquilizer and the consequences of the injury registered with me all at once. *Seizures. Brain damage.* "Oh Jesus." *Calm down,* I told myself. *Don't jump to conclusions.* But then I saw the expression on Dr. Efram's face as he entered the room.

Glancing at Gus, he asked as if he were walking on eggshells, "Did you tell her?"

Gus nodded and then once again he began to bawl.

Chapter Six

Gus sat silently and listened as the doctor gave me the bad news. A bullet had ricocheted off the sidewalk and clipped the back of my skull. The projectile had entered my brain and damaged the corpus callosum, the neural network that connects the two hemispheres of the brain.

"You're a very lucky woman," Efram began. "Ninety percent of all gunshot head wounds prove fatal. Those who do survive usually have severely debilitating brain disorders, but happily you seem to be the exception, and you're going to live to a ripe old age. You have a wonderful family to support you, and you just can't ask for anything more than that."

I wiped away tears while he held an X-ray film up before the overhead light and pointed to where the bullet had entered my brain. "The bullet didn't shatter and that was very fortunate," Efram continued, "but as you can see, it penetrated the brain tissue."

Gus explained that the bullet hit the ground and ricocheted before hitting the back of my head. The theory the NYPD ballistics unit was going with was that the bullet began to tumble end over end after deflecting off the sidewalk and had lost a great deal of its velocity before striking me.

"According to what they told me," Gus said, "it was the only reason you're still alive."

"Oh my God." I stared at the film and shuddered. It was a miracle that I was still living, breathing, and thinking. "Did you get all of it out?" I asked with concern.

"We believe so," he said with conviction. "You were on the operating table for nine hours and the surgeon was very skilled, very skilled indeed."

"Then why did I have a seizure?"

Efram pressed his lips together. "For the same reason you're experiencing memory loss. In a penetrating injury from a high-velocity object like a bullet, injuries can occur not only from the initial laceration and crushing of brain tissue by the projectile, but also from the subsequent cavitation."

"Cavitation?" I asked.

"The cavity made by the bullet."

"Oh?"

"You see, high-velocity objects create rotations and they can create a shockwave that causes stretch injuries. A cavity can develop that is three to four times greater in diameter than the bullet itself. Though this cavity is reduced in size once the initial trauma is over, the tissue that was compressed during cavitation remains injured. Destroyed brain tissue may either be ejected through the entrance or exit wounds or, as in your case, remain packed up against the sides of the cavity that was formed by the bullet."

"And that's why I had a seizure, because of the compressed brain tissue?"

"Most likely. Now that you're conscious and most of the swelling has gone down, we'll run a battery of tests to better evaluate which area of the brain is causing you trouble."

Intuitively I already knew the answer but asked anyway, "Will it happen again?"

"I'm afraid that's quite possible, but we can control your seizures with medication and the amnesia should resolve itself with time. The brain is very adept at rerouting the neurological pathways. You're a young and vital person, so I'm optimistic that you'll live a full and productive life."

Gus grinned weakly although he was still sniffling.

I smiled at him adoringly before turning back to the doctor and verbalizing what they were both afraid I'd ask, "But my career as an NYPD detective is over, isn't it?"

Efram took a moment before answering, but then he had no choice but to tell me what I already knew to be true. "I'm afraid so," he said in a sad tone. "Most definitely."

Chapter Seven

"Yay!" Ma cheered. "They said you could go home tomorrow. Doesn't that make you happy?"

"Sure," I replied without enthusiasm. *Home to what? I won't be a cop anymore.* The decision might not be made official for months, but it was just a matter of time. Even if I were allowed to return to the force, I'd be chained to a desk somewhere I'd never see action again. The department would control my environment and make sure that I wasn't a hazard to myself or anyone else.

A cop with a seizure disorder was like a pilot with a history of hysterical blindness. No one would put their life in the hands of that pilot, and no cop would be able to trust a partner like that out on the streets. A cop has to have confidence in his partner, and a ticking time bomb doesn't inspire confidence. Everyone would be watching and waiting for me to have a meltdown and go to pieces. You can't be out on the streets under those circumstances.

"I've been cooking for days," Ma said. "I made every dish you can possibly think of. I know you haven't eaten with gusto, not with the dreck they feed you in here. I even baked a cheesecake with pineapple and a graham cracker crust just the way you like it."

"That's sweet of you, Ma. Thanks." I wanted to sound more excited about all the yummy dishes she had prepared, but it just wasn't in me. I took a deep breath and filled my lungs with air before turning to look out the window.

The next thing I knew Ma had plopped down on the bed. She patted my leg. "Did I tell you about Angie Messerole?"

I turned to look at her and gauged that she was exerting herself emotionally in order to pique my interest. "The widow on the top floor of your building?"

"Uh-huh."

"How's she doing? She hasn't looked well since her husband, Rocco, died."

"You should see her now," she explained excitedly. "She took the insurance money and did a complete makeover."

"By makeover, I presume that you don't mean hair and makeup, do you?"

"Head to toe, Stephanie—she did it all, the boobs, the butt, liposuction, tummy tuck, her eyes, her teeth, her nose ... she's unrecognizable."

"Does she look good?"

"She looks *amazing.* She looks like a movie star."

"Good for her. She deserves a second chance at romance. I hope she meets a nice—"

Ma snorted.

"What's that about? Does she have one of those Wayne Newton faces that looks as if it's made of plastic?"

"No." she chuckled. "I already told you that she looks great."

"What, then?"

"She's got a girlfriend," she screeched. "Do you believe it? It took twenty-five years of marriage for her to figure out that she doesn't like a penis? How does that even happen?"

I shrugged. "Maybe it didn't."

"What? What are you saying?"

"Maybe she liked coochie all along."

"But her marriage ..."

"Just saying."

"No. I don't believe it. Either you like men or you don't."

"Some women go both ways. More than you'd imagine. How do you explain that?"

"It's just a diversion, Stephanie. People get bored and they try new things. Trust me. Your mother knows what she's talking about."

"If you say so." I rolled my eyes, then noticed someone standing in the doorway. I knew who it was instantly. "Are you Haruki?"

He nodded. Haruki was Yana's brother. I'd heard that he'd flown in from Japan for the funeral. "I hope I'm not interrupting?" he asked politely.

"No. Please come on in."

Ma got off the bed and met him as he entered the room. "I'm so sorry about your brother. I only met him a few times, but he was a very nice man."

He bowed as was tradition in Japan and many other places in the Far East. "Thank you so much."

It was still an effort for me to move, but I managed to stand and tie my robe. I didn't know how to greet him, but he opened his arms, removing my indecisiveness. "Yana and I were very close. I'm ... I'm so very sorry. There was nothing I could've done."

"I know that, Detective Chalice. I know that you were shot first and were unconscious when my brother was hit."

I grinned sadly. Yana was a rookie detective the lieutenant had assigned to me. He'd emigrated from Japan and had carried with him the rigidness and formality his parents and culture had instilled in him. I had made it my job to get him to loosen up. He was a good student and was learning quickly. I'd even taught him the fine art of police partner banter. "Your brother called me Stephanie. I hope you're comfortable calling me Stephanie as well."

"If you'll call me Harry."

"Of course I will. Yana was a good partner and a close friend. He was one of the most sincere people I ever met."

Harry nodded again. Like his brother, he seemed very formal and traditional. "Thank you. It warms me to hear this because there is a Shinto proverb that reads, 'Sincerity is the single virtue that binds the divine and man in one.'"

"That's a lovely saying."

"I wanted to wait until you were fully recovered before visiting, but I have a flight back to Tokyo in the morning. I'm only allowed a short period of bereavement."

Harry was a law enforcement officer in Japan. In what capacity, I wasn't sure. "I'm really so happy that you stopped by." Yana used to speak of his brother with great fondness. From what he'd said, he and Haruki had been very different growing up. Yana had been very serious and focused, whereas Haruki was more of a free spirit, a wild child.

"I think Yana would've wanted me to tell you that he liked and respected you very much. He said that you were a very good teacher."

"He didn't need very much teaching. Yana had good instincts and that just can't be taught. What happened that night ..." A lump formed in my throat. "It all happened so quickly. From what I was told, the second shot came within seconds of the first. There was nothing he could've done to avoid it."

"Would it be all right if we exchanged phone numbers and email? I would like to hear when my brother's murderer is apprehended, and how he will be punished."

"Of course."

Harry presented his card with two hands and a polite bow. I fished in my purse and, when I found my business cards, presented mine in the same manner.

Chapter Eight

My hands were relaxed and steady as I leveled the small-caliber Smith & Wesson Model 2213 handgun at the target and squeezed the trigger. I was firing a weapon with almost no kick because the doctor was worried about the potential trauma from the kick of a powerful weapon. The feel of the single-action trigger felt like a homecoming, and the small holes my rounds made in the paper target were like old friends who were excited to see me again. It was the first clip I'd emptied in what felt like an eternity. I had three filled clips lined up and waiting, and couldn't wait to go at it again.

Gus smiled at the demonstration of accuracy and pulled the side of his Peltor shooter's muff away from his right ear. "Like getting back on a bicycle, right?"

I pulled off my muffs, placed them on the sill, and ejected the clip. "I love you, Gus, but you don't have to pat me on the bottom all the time."

"I don't," he protested.

I shot him a stink-eye warning. "It's hardly the best shooting I've ever done."

"One day at a time, Steph. You haven't held a gun in your hand in over a month. I'll bet it feels good, though, doesn't it?"

"It's the only thing that still makes me feel like a cop."

"But you are a cop."

"Yeah, in title only. We both know there's no way I'll ever work another case again."

"You don't know that."

I fired off stink-eye warning number two. "Believe me. I know it." We were at the Westside Rifle and Pistol Range, which Gus and I referred to as the 20/20 because the address was 20 W. 20th Street. I was firing one of my own personally owned guns at a private range and not my service-issue Glock at the NYPD range. It wasn't an apples-to-apples comparison, but the experience made me feel a little bit like the way I used to feel. I'd been looking forward to firing a gun for almost two weeks, ever since the doc told me I could give it a whirl if I stuck to my daily dose of Dilantin and didn't experience any new seizures.

"Let's drop the lame-o attitude and let's see if you can tighten up your grouping with the next clip."

"Yeah. Let's see." I slapped the next clip into the gun, pried my muffs apart, and placed them over my ears. I sneered at Gus, extended the gun, and fired off a single round.

"What the?" Gus seemed confused until I reeled in the target and put my finger through the hole I'd just made, right through the perp's junk instead of one of the kill zones. He cringed.

I sneered at him.

"Guess that's my cue to take off."

"It is indeed."

"Carry on. I'm going to grab a soda. Want one?"

"No. I'm good."

"All right. Come find me when you're done circumcising targets."

I gave him a thumbs-up and reeled the target back out.

Gus cupped his balls and slinked away.

~~~

Gus was sitting alone at a table, refilling a clear plastic cup with Coke. He smiled when he saw me approaching. "How'd you do?"

"Not bad for a rookie. I'm surprised you didn't stick around to watch."

He shrugged. "Ah, it's kind of a personal thing. You know, just you, the gun, and the target. I figured I'd only be a distraction."

"I think I scared you off with that crotch cutter I fired off."

"Yeah." he chuckled. "That too."

I placed my lockbox on the table and sat down. "Mind if I take a sip?"

He shook his head. "No caffeine, remember?" He pulled a bottle of water out of his backpack and handed it to me. "Drink up."

"There's nothing quite like the smell of a discharged weapon in the morning."

"My mother always told me to look for a girl who preferred the fragrance of nitroglycerin to Chanel N°5."

"She's a wise woman. Anyway, I needed a little independence. You and Ma have been fussing over me like worried hens. You don't even leave me alone with Max."

"For the time being. Eventually everything will get back to normal."

"If only that were true."

"Babe, let's not go there again. Let's just make the best of it. You know what they say, 'When life hands you lemons, you have to make lemonade.'"

"I hate that expression. Whoever made it up was probably one LSD trip short of a total mental meltdown."

He smirked. "You'll be okay."

"But I won't be a cop."

Gus grabbed my hand. "Hey, whatever you are or aren't is good enough for me."

I forced an accepting smile. "Love you, babe." *But will it be good enough for me?*

Chapter Nine

Despite NYPD's best efforts and a plethora of generous rewards that were offered by the City of New York and the Detectives Benevolent Association, Yana's murderer had yet to be found and the trail was growing colder every day.

The doctor finally agreed to let me use a computer. Likewise with television, he was concerned that the rapid eye movement and hand coordination associated with computer usage might trigger another seizure, but I was now over a month seizure free and was granted a maximum of thirty minutes' usage per day— not a lot of time, but I have crazy-fast fingers on the keyboard.

The very first thing I did was log in to the NYPD mainframe and pull up the report on the shooting. More than a month had passed since my partner, Yana had been murdered, and my future as a New York City cop robbed from me. I was determined not to wait this one out a minute longer. I was on paid leave of absence until a final decision could be made concerning my fitness to serve as one of New York's finest again, so I was not official, but that didn't matter to me in the slightest. I was ready and determined to track down Yana's killer.

My current short-term memory was intact. I could remember the events of each and every day that had passed since getting out of the hospital, but the day the lights went out … well, that period of time was still a mystery, a dark void within which a portion of my past was buried. Somewhere along the line a sniper had picked off Yana and me from long range. There was such a painful and desperate ache within me to remember, to recall the moments before the homicide took place, and put a face on the shooter. The memory was denied to me, a locked vault I was unable to open.

I only knew from reading Yana's recovered notebook and mine that we had just come from interviewing the parents of Serafina Ramirez in their apartment. Our car had been recovered about half a block away from their building next to an abandoned lot, so it was a safe bet to assume that we were walking back to our car when we were both shot. Ballistics placed the shooter on the roof of the tenement building we had just come from. We were about a hundred yards from the building when the first shot was fired.

If the investigator's theory was correct, I was hit first; then Yana turned and took a fatal shot in the chest. Local residents had reported hearing only two gunshots. The shooter had fired off two quick shots in rapid succession from a .30-caliber rifle.

Thank God the shooter had used small rounds. Had the bullet been larger, even after ricocheting off the sidewalk, it might've taken off half my skull, and then it would've been lights out forever.

"Oh no you don't." Gus had crept up behind me and was looking over my shoulder. "You can't do this, Steph. Do you want to get better or not?"

"Of course I want to get better. What kind of question is that?"

"Well, then prove it," he said hotly. "You think this is good for you? You think it's good to get yourself all worked up? You've been complaining that we don't even trust you enough to leave you alone with your own child. Do you want that to change, or do you want to trigger another seizure? The doctor told you that you have to stay quiet and well rested. He warned you about what might happen if you get too worked up. Remember what he said? A cerebral aneurism—want one of those on top of everything else?"

"Easy, Gus. I'm just trying to satisfy my curiosity. You think I can just sit back and forget what happened? You goddamn well know that I'm not built that way." I heard Max crying in his bedroom. "Shit!"

"Looks like you've got a choice to make," he said angrily. "Do you want to be a mother or a corpse?"

"That's crazy talk, Gus. Do you really think a little computer time is going to kill me? I was strong enough to fire a weapon at the range, wasn't I?"

"Weapon?" he groused. "That was a peashooter."

We were both getting worked up.

"The doc gave his permission for you to go to the range, and you damn well know we're talking apples and oranges," he contested. "It's rapid eye movements he's concerned about—rapid eye movements and spikes in blood pressure."

"Did you read the warnings that came with my Dilantin scrip? The medication I'm taking is probably riskier than a little computer time. Don't go all worrywart on me, okay?"

"I'm trying, but we can't take any chances. Can you imagine having a seizure while you're alone with Max? Do you have any idea what could happen?"

Gus' warning froze me through and through. The idea of me hurting my son took all the wind out of my sails. I closed my eyes, shut the laptop, and reached for Gus' hand. "You're right. Max is crying," I said. "Let's go do something important."

Chapter Ten

"Where are you going?" Gus asked.

I was already showered and dressed when he awoke. He'd caught me as I was buttoning my jacket. "Think I can go for a walk on my own? It seems I slept through most of the winter—I'm beginning to feel like a hibernating bear. It's pretty mild and sunny outside—I thought I'd get some fresh air. Max is playing with Ma. I changed and fed him."

"Give me five minutes and I'll go with you," he offered enthusiastically. "We can walk over to the bakery and pick up some fresh bread."

"Listen, you carb hound, I've already eaten."

"I'll keep you—"

I cut him off. "Gus. It's *enough*. There's only been the one seizure incident in the hospital. I took my medicine as soon as I got up and I'm fine. Hear me? I'm fine. I'm thirty years old. If I can't take a walk down the block by myself, then ... I don't want to get into this again, but I can't take being smothered and mollycoddled anymore. 'Don't do this. You'll get all worked up. Don't do that; you might have another seizure. You're still healing. You're still fragile. Your head will explode.'" I rapped on my head with my knuckles. "All better. I'm as good as new, Gus, and I'm ready to spread my wings. Ma and I can more than take care of Max, and it's high time you went back to work." I teased him, "Stop loafing, you slacker." He'd been on spousal leave to take care of me, but I felt that I was well enough to take care of myself. "Stop using your wife as an excuse to lie around and watch basketball. Go back to work," I barked playfully.

"Hey! What's all the noise about?" Ma asked, firing both barrels. She was sporting her customary wiseass grin. "Are the two of you are going to let one measly little hole in the head ruin your beautiful relationship? *Morons*," she barked. "Wake up and smell the coffee."

I smirked. Ma was right, of course. Still, I foresaw a huge period of adjustment ahead of us. "All of this pampering is driving me nuts. I can't stand it—the two of you are watching me like hawks, worrying that I might go to pieces at any minute. I haven't had a seizure since I was in the hospital. Let's assume that the worst is behind us."

"That's what I keep telling you," Gus said.

"But you don't treat me as if you mean it. I'm not fragile. I'm not going to break."

"I'll testify to that," Ma said, raising her hand as if she were being sworn in to offer testimony. "I always said that my daughter had a hard head." She giggled. "And now we know that your noodle is practically bulletproof."

"Ha, ha, ha," I cackled sarcastically. "So can we all agree to ease the doting-loved-ones vigil?"

Ma nodded.

I could see that Gus was wrestling with my request. "I suppose, but you still have to follow the doctor's orders. For the time being, you have to stop thinking like a cop. Play with Max and do whatever you have to do to get completely better, but hitting the department database has got to be completely off-limits." He gave me a steely-eyed stare. "Is that understood?"

There was merit in everything my loving husband said, but did he really expect me to stop thinking like a cop? *I don't think so. Ain't gonna happen.* He might as well have asked me not to breathe. My law-enforcement gene was strong, dominant in fact. It had been passed down from my father to me and had dictated the way I lived my life ever since joining the force. I knew I'd never be able to go along with what Gus was asking me to do. There are good lies and there are hurtful ones. Some lies can be forgiven and others not. For the sake of our marriage, I nodded and said, "Okay," but my hand was behind my back and my fingers were crossed.

Chapter Eleven

I heard the sound of someone hustling down the street and turned to see Gus trotting down the block. Ma and I had gone out for a walk with Max in the stroller. Gus caught up with us and gave me a pat on the fanny. "There you are." He smiled and gave me a kiss before sticking his head into the stroller and making Max squeal hysterically. "Nice day for some fresh air."

"You betcha. Ma loves pushing the stroller because she can fit a gallon of jug wine in the storage compartment."

She waved her hand dismissively. "*Bah.* Stop it. You make it sound like I'm an old souse."

"Well, if the stroller fits ..." I chuckled.

Ma sneered at me, insinuating that I was a pain in the ass and, of course, I was, but the truth be told, we were just a few doors down from the neighborhood liquor store and, well ... the woman really does love her Chianti. I pulled a twenty from the pocket of my jeans and ran it under my nose. "Smells like a jug of Carlo Rossi to me."

She snatched it out of my hand. "Okay, wiseass. *I* was going to pay for the wine, but just for that, the vino is on you. I might even throw care to the wind and buy the Mondavi."

"Knock yourself out, Ma. You're not going to put me in the poorhouse buying wine by the box."

Gus lifted Max out of the stroller and hoisted him high up on his shoulder. Our little one smiled as he looked around from higher elevation, taking in the pedestrians and engaging some of the passersby in a game of peekaboo as we continued down the street.

Gus had returned to work. He had somewhat capitulated to my demands and was once again taking normal tours of duty. That's not to say he wasn't a nudge altogether, but at least he was out of the apartment most of the day. "You're home early from work today."

"Just came from an interview not too far away. I figured I'd stop home and have lunch with everyone."

"Cool. Pizza it is. I'm dying for a Sicilian slice."

"Not so fast," Ma warned and slinked toward the liquor store with a silly grin on her face.

"Well, it's a nice surprise." I reached up to give him a kiss but he pulled away. "Hey. What the?"

"You've been cheating on me," he said in an unhappy tone.

The doctor hadn't yet cleared me for sex, worrying that the spike in blood pressure could still do some harm to my gray matter. Had he known how worked up I get during the act, he would've insisted on a heavy-duty chastity belt. "Cheating on you? With whom? It's been months since my coochie has seen any action. I'm thinking about taking a vow of chastity."

"I stopped home and checked your laptop. You were back on the department website."

Crap. I'd forgotten to clear the browsing history. "Guilty as charged. Let's not make a thing out of this, okay? I can't just bury my head in the sand. I was checking for updates."

"I thought we had an agreement."

I grimaced in a silly manner. "Every deal has a little wiggle room."

"Come on, Stephanie. Don't bullshit me."

I was doing my best to comply with the terms of my house arrest, but it had gotten to be too much, and for some ill-timed reason, I chose that moment to let him know in no uncertain terms, "Gus, *leave it alone.*"

"*Fine,*" he replied heatedly. He looked around, quickly scanning the street. "I'll have lunch with Max at the deli. I'll drop him off before I head back over to the station."

"That's just great," I said sarcastically. "Okay, be like that."

"Like what?" he scoffed. "A concerned husband?"

"Gus, I'm *okay*. I'm a ten percenter. I took a bullet to the head and survived. You don't have to watch over me like a hawk. God's not ready to take me. I think that should be abundantly clear by now."

Gus was a pretty mellow guy until he was pushed too far, and I had just pushed him past his breaking point. He could've come back at me with any number of retaliatory comments, but he didn't. He'd had enough. "Enjoy the pizza," he said begrudgingly and, with Max still on his shoulders, turned away.

Chapter Twelve

"Where's Gus going?" Ma had returned from wine shopping and had a large jug cradled in her arms, cleverly camouflaged in a brown paper bag.

"He wasn't in the mood for pizza."

"Or was it you that he wasn't in the mood for?" Ma asked with a cutting stare. "Did he catch you doing police work again? I thought I spotted you on the department website."

I shrugged.

"Do you want to screw up your marriage? In case you haven't heard, single parenting isn't exactly a walk in the park."

I sighed with exasperation. "Jesus, Ma. You too? Someone used my noggin for target practice and murdered my partner. Am I supposed to let that slide?"

"NYPD can't track down the shooter while you heal up? God knows, Stephanie, they're not all bumbling incompetents. Don't you think they're capable of apprehending one solitary criminal without your assistance?"

"It's been over a month already," I said as I took the wine from her and stowed it in Max's stroller. "The case is growing cold."

"You don't know that. You're out of touch. For all you know, they're following up on several valuable leads right now."

"*Thank you,*" I said, concurring begrudgingly. "All I've been doing is logging on to stay current on developments. Is that such a big goddamn deal? Who knows how much longer I'll have system access. My CO could call at any minute and tell me I've been declared permanently disabled."

Ma gazed at me with concern. "Would that be so bad?"

My mouth gaped in horror. "*What?* Tell me you're kidding."

"You almost lost your life, Stephanie. Isn't that enough? Maybe the good Lord is telling you that it's time to cash in your chips."

I threw up my hands in exasperation. "I'm going to grab a slice," I said with venom and began pushing the stroller down the block. "Gus is across the street in the deli. You can eat with me or with him. I really don't care."

"Stephanie, don't walk away from me like that. We're all—"

"I know. I know. You're all very concerned about me, but it's your incessant worrying that's killing me." I rapped on the side of my head as I had before. "See that? I'm still hardheaded. The bullet didn't hurt me one bit."

Chapter Thirteen

Gus Lido believed in holistic healing and was about to self-medicate.

His new partner, Detective Silas Coltrane, was an ox of a man, six-four, two-forty with a neck as thick as a sewer main. Gus spotted him at the far end of the gym, where he was working his anvil-sized hands on a heavy bag, pounding it lifeless.

Most men would've been intimidated by the spectacle, but Gus Lido was thankful the good Lord had provided him with a worthy opponent. He tapped his hulking partner on the shoulder. "Want to go a few rounds?"

Coltrane slammed the bag one last time. Had the training apparatus been human, its internal organs would've liquefied from the force of the blow. "Okay. Sure. Why not?"

"Got a mouthpiece?"

Coltrane grimaced. "Get real, you scrawny little piss ant." He grinned, exposing his pearly white teeth. "I'll give you a hundred bucks for every tooth you knock out of my mouth."

Lido was smaller but not by much. He was six-two, two-twenty with cat-like reflexes and speed. He smiled at his massive opponent. "Suit yourself, but don't come crying to me if you need a mouthful of caps. Ya big baby—I know you're afraid of the dentist."

"Like you're not."

Gus shook his head. "Never heard of laughing gas, chucklehead?"

He pounded his boxing gloves together and sneered at Gus with a cocky expression. "Lido, you *do* have a death wish. No hard feelings if I mess up that pretty smile of yours?"

"Go for it." He grinned and tugged on the training gloves. Each of them pulled on their protective headgear and stepped into the ring.

Coltrane was an old-school boxer, like Jake LaMotta on steroids. If LaMotta was the "Raging Bull", Coltrane was the "Runaway Freight Train". He raised his fists and took his position in the center of the ring, unyielding and menacing.

By contrast, Lido liked to move and jab.

"Stand still," Coltrane griped. "Take your beating like a—"

Lido fired off two quick jabs, rattling the behemoth before he could finish his sentence.

"Now you made me mad."

Coltrane lowered his head and advanced, coming for his prey, determined to do substantial damage. He took a wild swing, which Gus easily sidestepped. He moved to his left and slipped a jab into Coltrane's ribs. It was a solid punch, but the big gloves absorbed most of the blow. Coltrane cleared his nostrils and closed in. His technique was crude, a series of hard punches that Gus was able to block and counter.

"Is that all you've got?" Gus said. They were sparring for exercise, and neither wanted to hurt his opponent, but the comment sparked something in Coltrane. He unleashed a wild haymaker that caught Gus on the side of the neck, triggering a sharp pain in his throat.

"You okay?" Coltrane asked.

Gus nodded and coughed into his glove. His eyes snapped wide open as he began backpedalling around the ring.

"Stand still, Mohammad Ali," Coltrane quipped. "I promise I'll be merciful."

"Fine. Let's do this." Gus stopped circling and met Coltrane in the center of the ring, his head buried behind his gloves, patiently waiting for an opening. When it came, the result wasn't pretty. His rage over Stephanie's pigheadedness rose within him and manifested itself in the form of a lightning-fast jab. He was hot and out of control. His fists shot forward in alternating succession like guns firing from the turret of an aircraft carrier, pummeling Coltrane's chest and stomach, and driving him back against the ropes, helpless to defend himself.

"Getting a little worked up?" Coltrane asked as he attempted to push Gus away.

Gus should've stopped, backed off, and shut down, but he didn't. He was lost in the moment, his mind filled with white noise and his arteries surging with venom. He didn't even notice that his partner was submitting.

"I give," Coltrane said. "I've had enough." He pushed Gus away. "A little frustrated, buddy boy?"

It took Gus a moment to clear his mind, to come back to the here and now and calm down. "Huh?"

"I know you and the missus haven't been coitus-cleared by the doc, but man, someone's got some pent-up anxiety issues. I've never seen you like this. You all right?"

Gus was spent. He was out of breath and exhausted. He shook his head. "Sorry, man. I don't know what got into me."

"It's okay. We've all been there. The missus okay? I mean, she's getting better, isn't she?"

Gus closed his eyes and nodded unconvincingly.

"Want to talk about it? A couple of cold beers maybe?"

He looked at Coltrane but didn't answer. His cell phone was lying atop his towel. He could see the display illuminate: Ma.

He'd been living in terror every moment since Stephanie had been shot, in the days before she had emerged from the coma, and now ... he worried every time the phone rang. "I've got to get this," he said and climbed out of the ring. He was still panting when he answered. "Hi, Ma. Is everything all right?" he asked cautiously.

There was panic in Ma's voice. "No," she bellowed. "Stephanie's gone."

Chapter Fourteen

Gus was still in his sweats from the gym when he flung open the door and charged into the apartment. Max was standing up in his playpen and began bouncing up and down excitedly when he saw his father. Gus hurried over to scoop him up, but had his eyes trained on Ma the whole time.

Ma's face was puffy and her eyes were red. She held a tissue to her nose while she spoke. "The note is on the kitchen table."

He kissed Max's cheek as he continued into the kitchen, where a handwritten note lay on the table.

> "I'm sorry. I have to do this.
> I hope you'll both forgive me.
> Love,
> Stephanie"

He gasped and covered his mouth in horror.

"I checked. Her go-bag is gone," Ma said.

"But how?"

"Max was napping. I was in the shower." She shrugged helplessly and sniffled.

"I don't understand," he blurted, frustrated and incredulous. "How could she do something like this? How could she be so goddamn irresponsible?"

"She's—"

Gus was hot. "Save it," he said, cutting Ma off with a raised hand. "I get it. She's a cop. She thinks like a cop, and no one gets off, especially a cop killer, but that's no excuse for a stunt like this."

Ma lowered her head. "I'm sorry. I don't know what to say."

"I'm fuming. I'm absolutely fuming. So she's out on the streets alone and we don't know if she's dead or alive. Is that about the size of it? If she were here, I swear I'd kill her myself. I'd freakin' kill her."

"Try to calm down, Gus."

"Yeah, *right*."

"Is there anything we can do?"

"Oh! You bet your ass there is. She thinks she's calling the shots, does she? Well, she's sadly mistaken."

Max sensed his father's anger and started to whine. "Give him to me," Ma said and forced a warm grin. "Want some juice, little one?"

"This is a joke, a goddamn joke," he grumbled. "Well, two can play at this game."

Ma rubbed his arm. "Calm down, honey. I know you're angry, but it won't help anything to—"

"You're goddamn right I'm angry."

"Take a deep breath—in and out, in and out."

Gus dropped into a kitchen chair and buried his face in his hands.

Ma rubbed his back. "It'll be okay, honey," she said for his benefit alone.

"All I want is a day without all this f-ing drama," he complained. "Are things ever going to be normal around here?"

"I wish I had an answer for you, son, but the truth is that I just flat out don't know."

Chapter Fifteen

The Pod Hotel wasn't exactly lavish, but it was clean and cheerful, and wouldn't cost me a million dollars a night. I was paying for all of my transactions in cash so that Gus wouldn't be able to track me from my credit card purchases, as I knew he would. Most of our monies, Gus' and mine, were in joint accounts, but I still maintained a small stash under my own name at JP Morgan Chase and cleaned out most of it to cover my interim expenses.

The room was kind of basic and utilitarian—white, white, and more white with black and red accents. It was the only room they had available, and joy of all joys, it had bunk beds instead of traditional side-by-side twins. I tested the lower berth and it seemed comfy enough—sleeping has never been a problem for me.

I'd made some purchases along the way, an inexpensive laptop computer, burner phones, and some cosmetic supplies. Staring at the unopened packages, I took a moment to collect my thoughts and consider how badly my actions would hurt Gus and Ma. A tear drizzled down my cheek as I thought about Max, giggling and smiling, while he did his best to amble around the child-proofed apartment, yattering away, "Ma-ma-ma-ma," without receiving a reply from his mother. There'd be hell to pay when it was all over. Serious wounds would need healing. I wasn't sure if I was doing the right thing. Scratch that—I was completely sure that I was doing something wrong and inexcusable, but in my heart I felt that it had to be done. Neither Ma nor Gus was going to cut me an inch of slack nor was I going to lie down and die, so I said a quick prayer, crossed myself, and went to work.

~~~

The first snip took real courage. The rest was a breeze. Armed with sharp scissors, handheld mirror, and a current photo of Jennifer Lawrence I began cutting my hair and watched as locks of sable hair fell into the sink one after another until the small sink was completely full. I hadn't had a lot of experience with hair dye, but all girls know their way around a bottle of peroxide, and with a YouTube tutorial to guide me ... I set the supplies out on the sink ledge: bleach powder, crème developer, red-gold corrector, purple shampoo, blonde dye, plastic gloves, aluminum foil, crumbled bacon, gorgonzola cheese, and ... well, it was just a lot of crap to put on one's hair.

The process seemed to take forever. I examined my new appearance in the mirror after it was finally done and scarcely recognized myself. I looked so different, so completely different. I wondered what Gus would say the next time he saw me, probably that he didn't know who I was anymore. Guilt rose in my gut—no one could blame him because he'd be right. Who was this person, this someone who placed the value of justice before family? Studying my eyes in the mirror, I wondered if the brain surgery had somehow changed me. Would the old Stephanie have gone so far out on a limb? Were the two of us one and the same? Was I the law enforcement zealot who just couldn't let a case go, or were we two completely different people? It really wasn't important, because all that mattered to me at that moment was nailing our shooter as quickly as possible and going back home to my family.

Everything I'd packed was black so as to make me appear as nondescript as possible. I changed my clothes and looked in the mirror again. For a brief instant I wasn't sure whose reflection I was seeing. Was it the pre-shooting Stephanie? Was it Stephanie Chalice who'd survived head trauma and surgery, or was it someone else entirely, some new entity I had just created, a combination of the other two. *Whatever it takes to get the job done.*

Someone knocked on the door while I was in the process of cleaning up. I checked my watch. Harry was right on time.

Chapter Sixteen

Yana's brother, Haruki, scrutinized me carefully before entering the hotel room. He set a duffle bag and his backpack down on the floor and entered slowly. He was just a little taller than I was and moved like one hundred fifty pounds of purposefulness and precision. "I remember you as a brunette."

"I was a brunette—up until two hours ago, anyway."

"It may take some time to get used to your new look. The short blond hair, it's quite striking. Many young girls in Japan dye their hair these days because they're all born with the same dark hair. They dye their hair to stand out in the crowd, but you do it so that you can remain hidden."

"You understand, then. I had to change my appearance. My husband will be looking for me out on the streets, and he's pretty damn good at what he does."

He nodded.

"How was your flight?"

"I slept."

"Twelve hours from Tokyo to New York. You must be well rested."

He didn't address my statement. Instead he examined my head. "I can no longer see where the bullet struck you."

"I've been practicing the fine art of the comb-over." I lifted a tuft of hair, exposing the suture marks. "Thank God I have thick hair—I'd hate to have to walk around looking like the bride of Frankenstein."

He seemed puzzled by my comment. Perhaps my gothic horror reference was ill chosen. *I bet he'd catch a Godzilla reference no problem.* "I'd hate to have to walk around with everyone staring at my surgical scars."

He said, "Oh," but I wasn't convinced that he understood what I was talking about. "Did they give you a metal plate?"

"No. They used resorbable polylactic. I was kind of disappointed. I figured I could've magnetized the metal plate and used it as a place to keep paperclips—you can never find one when you need it."

"You're Chalice all right. Yana used to talk about your sense of humor." His head dropped. "I hadn't seen Yana in so long and now ..."

"There's only one thing we can do about that, Harry."

"It won't bring him back," he lamented.

"There's no next-best thing—justice is all we have. I understand you're a law enforcement officer in Japan?"

He eyed me warily. "Something like that—*Keishichō*, Criminal Investigations Bureau. Yana and I, we both wanted to carry guns ever since we were kids. He came to New York to become a police officer because he objected to the Japanese system of justice."

"And you?"

"I was always the rebellious one, the one who was always truant from school." He shrugged. "I was lucky the police academy accepted me at all. I didn't exactly finish at the top of my class."

"Nonsense. I'll bet there's a thing or two you can teach me."

"I doubt that, Chalice. Yana told me you were the lead detective. He told me how much you taught him." He began circling me within the small room. "He also told me that you were a risk taker, and I wonder if you're not going through this self-imposed trial by fire in order to ease your own conscience. I mean going AWOL from your family and going underground to hunt a killer when you're not well … Putting your life at risk … Do you feel responsible for my brother's death?"

His question stung but only for a moment. "Did Yana die because of me? No. You know I don't believe that, but it doesn't mean I don't feel guilty about what happened, and it doesn't mean I don't wish that he were the one who had lived." Yana was just a couple of years my junior and I thought of him as my younger brother. "We were just a few feet apart when the shots were fired. Had he been hit first, he may have been the one to survive, but he wasn't." I squeezed my eyes shut for a moment. "The wound burns, Harry. It burns like hell and I only know one way to extinguish a fire that burns with that kind of intensity."

"Are you talking about justice or vengeance?"

"Does it matter to you?"

"No, Chalice, it doesn't, because in this case justice and vengeance are one and the same."

Chapter Seventeen

My new roommate showered and changed into fresh clothes. He'd skipped all the meal services on the long flight over from Tokyo and was ravenous. I was wondering what my partner in crime and I were going to eat—not that I couldn't survive a couple meal of sushi and udon noodles.

"I had a Shake Shack burger the last time I visited New York, and that taste has lingered in my mouth ever since."

Really? Do you floss? Maybe there's a chunk of chop meat caught between your teeth. "You're a man after my own heart."

We walked down to the Shake Shack location on Third and ordered lots of grub.

"You can't get food like this in Tokyo," he said as he chomped down on his burger. "I mean you can get a hamburger, but it's not the same." He made an I'm-in-ecstasy face. "I can't remember the last time I had bacon."

"How about a great slice of chocolate cake?"

He rolled his eyes. "You've *got* to be kidding. Eating Japanese-made chocolate cake is like eating kosher sushi." His English had a mechanical chop to it. It almost sounded like a slow Internet connection that could only buffer small parcels of data at a time. He broke his sentences into small segments, which I guess was not unusual for someone translating from Japanese to English as he went along. Somehow I didn't find him overly difficult to understand.

I handed him an envelope.

"What's this?"

"A thousand dollars."

He frowned. "For what?"

"You understand why I can't rent a car under my own name. My husband and others are out looking for me and they'd be able to trace my credit card usage."

He pushed the envelope back across the table. "This is a personal matter for me as well. Don't insult me with your money."

"Sorry. I didn't think—"

He waved his hand dismissively. "Forget it. I don't expect you to understand Japanese culture."

"All right. Look, I picked up a couple of burner phones for us. They're untraceable."

"Good thinking. I'd like to visit the scene of the shooting as soon as we're done."

"Just as soon as you've had your fill of bacon and cow parts."

Harry grimaced. I think he was having difficulty swallowing my zany euphemism for a hamburger. "You have a strange way of speaking, Chalice. Did my brother have trouble understanding you?"

"I don't think so." Yana had moved to New York after graduating from university in Japan. He was a naturalized citizen and, after years as an upper Eastside resident, had somewhat assimilated to local culture. "Didn't he say that he enjoyed my sense of humor?"

"You assume too much," he said with a wicked twinkle in his eyes. "Yana said you had a prolific sense of humor. He never said he enjoyed it."

"What?"

Harry grinned. "Gotcha."

"You were on shaky ground there for a minute, Harry. I've killed for less. Speaking of which, you'll need a weapon."

"Unnecessary."

"We're pursuing an armed murderer."

"I'll take care of it."

"How?"

"Even here, I am not without resources."

"Oh?" I mouthed. "I brought an extra bulletproof vest."

"Okay," he said, casually acknowledging my comment.

He didn't seem all that concerned for his own personal safety, and I wondered if he possessed some mad Bruce Lee-martial-arts skills. I envisioned him flying through the air, leg extended, hands poised to strike. "I don't plan to put you in harm's way. I know that you were the one who reached out to me from Japan, but you're just a citizen here with no official standing, so I'd planned on using your mind more so than your body."

He was finished with his burger. He wiped his mouth with a napkin and balled it up in his hand. "I'm a big boy, Chalice. Let me worry about it." He stood and glanced around the restaurant. "*Keshooshitsu*?"

Shit zoo, huh? That can only mean one thing in any language. "The restroom? I think it's downstairs."

He winked at me and took off.

~~~

Haruki took the metal stairs two at a time. Following the international men's room symbols and arrows, he walked down a short corridor and past a service technician, who was working within a double-door electrical closet. He glanced into the closet as he walked by. It looked exactly like most commercial service panels he had ever seen, with warning symbols and parallel rows of heavy-duty electrical conduits feeding into master electrical boxes, except ... He froze in his tracks. Three small metal conduit boxes were positioned in a row. They were identical to one another, with large black buttons and round green lights beneath them.

"Hey, you all right?" the electrician asked.

Harry felt lightheaded and it took a moment for him to come around. He finally responded, "Sure, sure," but continued to stare at the three metal boxes. "Uh, *rest-a-room*," he said, making it obvious that he was foreign and needed assistance.

"Down the hall and to the right, buddy."

"Thank you." He hurried into the restroom, locked himself in a stall, and slumped against the door with his full weight. He rubbed his eyes, but the image of the three conduit boxes refused to disappear. And why should they? The three conduit boxes were familiar in the very worst way imaginable and their image had been permanently burned into his mind. They looked exactly like the trapdoor actuating buttons at the Kyoto Detention House execution chamber.

Chapter Eighteen

I needed a moment to mentally prepare myself before exiting the car and viewing the crime scene. Gus and the doctors had repeatedly warned me about getting anxious and were worried that extreme agitation might trigger additional seizures, so I closed my eyes, clasped my hands together, and whispered, "Namaste," because I figured it would help to calm the inner me even though I'd only taken one yoga class in my entire life.

"Are you ready?" Harry waited patiently for me to gather myself before getting out of the rented SUV.

"Have you been back here since the shooting?"

"No."

"I think this must be quite difficult for you."

I sighed, "Yes, it is," and took a deep breath. "Okay. I'm ready."

It was a bright sunny day and I had an unobstructed view of the rooftop. The building was eight stories high with a fence around the roof, which served as a sundeck for residents. I pointed to it so that Harry could see from where the shots had been fired. "The sniper used a thirty-caliber rifle. I could hit a squirrel from this distance let alone hit a human target."

He appeared to be studying the rooftop. I saw his Adam's apple catch when he swallowed, and I wondered if he were imagining the shooter with his rifle poised on the rooftop railing, his sight trained on Yana.

The crime scene tape was long gone and our blood washed off the pavement, but the concrete still bore the stains of our blood. There were two large and distinct tinted areas. I studied the perimeters of the stained areas and cringed when I saw where the two pools of blood had run together. There was also a narrow gouge in the concrete not far from where we'd been hit.

That's mine, I assumed, *that's where the bullet must've hit the ground and ricocheted.* It's often impossible to determine the angle of ricochet. It depends on a multitude of variables, but right-angle ricochet is somewhat common. I tried to judge the angle at which the bullet hit the sidewalk and a right-angle ricochet. I positioned myself exactly where I thought the bullet had hit me, and my layman's theory appeared to hold up. From there it was just a hop, skip, and a jump to an abrupt freak-out. I felt my pulse quicken and the blood drain from my face. *Namaste. Namaste. Calm down. You can handle this.* It didn't help.

"You look pale, Chalice. Are you sure that you can do this?"

"I'll be all right, but let's get off the street. I don't want to be spotted out here." Translation: Get me the hell out of here.

"Yes. Okay," Harry said. "I can come back later and look around on my own if I need to. I don't think your husband is looking for *me.*"

~~~

The building elevator smelled from pine disinfectant. The elevator itself was clean polished metal, and the finish looked to me like something that was designed to resist graffiti. The elevator ceiling was made of common Celotex ceiling panels.

Harry seemed pensive on our ride up to the roof and I wondered what was going through his mind. He had flown into New York to bury his brother and had returned to Japan soon afterward. It was during his short stay here that he had come to visit me in the hospital, and then after, the unexpected phone call in which he expressed his strong desire to assist in the murderer's apprehension. "I'm thinking," he said as if somehow knowing what I was wondering about. "I'm thinking about how it will feel to stand where the assassin stood when he pulled the trigger and killed Yana."

I rubbed his arm. "Think about how it will feel when he's captured. Think about the look on his face when he knows we've got him dead to rights. Block out everything else."

"I will try," he said solemnly. "I will try."

~~~

A rooftop deck is a nice feature, but the building was predominately occupied by blue-collar tenants who likely had little or no time for sunbathing. I walked to the railing and looked out from the point where it was most likely the shooter stood. I saw that there was a clear and unobstructed line of sight to where Yana and I had been shot.

"Not a difficult shot," I said, "Especially on that night. Don't ask me how I know, but I have the feeling that the wind was very still." I certainly wasn't recalling from memory. Perhaps it was just my mind injecting what it thought I wanted to believe.

"As you said, 'you could hit a squirrel from this distance.' I understand that the thirty caliber is often used for small-game hunting."

"Yes. It can be, but snipers also commonly use it."

"Yet the bullet was just small enough to slip between my brother's ribs and rupture his heart. Had the bullet been of a larger caliber, it might've hit one of his ribs, been deflected by it, and missed his heart completely." He turned to me. "This is the essence of paradox, is it not?"

"Sadly, yes."

"Have you ever shot and killed a man, Chalice?"

"I've pulled my gun three times and killed two men."

"How does it feel to shoot someone?"

"I take it you've never shot anyone?"

"No."

"It was horrible the first time as well as the second, but they were both kill-or-be-killed scenarios. I didn't have a choice."

"I don't understand why my brother was shot. I'm standing here, and I can't understand. What did he do to bring such violence upon himself?"

"I don't know, Harry. I just don't know. We interviewed the parents of a homicide victim in this building, a seventeen-year-old girl. I really doubt that they had any connection to the shooting."

"Is your memory coming back, or is this what you read in your notes and official police commentary?"

"From the notes, unfortunately. My memory of that day is still a blank. It's been so long now—I wonder if I'll ever remember what really happened that day." As I looked out at where Yana and I had been shot, the shadow of a nearby tree moved as the sun changed its position in the sky. I clutched my heart. The shadow now stretched across the pavement, and the image it cast looked like that of a body sprawled out across the ground.

Chapter Nineteen

Lido clocked in and made straight for the watch commander's desk.

Ridon had the phone in one hand and a breakfast burrito in the other. His eyes were glazed over but then did an oh-brother roll of his eyes when he saw Lido poke his head into his office. He covered the mouthpiece. "Estoban is on the rag again." He shook his head with his eyes pointed upward. "Why me, God? Why me? She's been bouncing around from command to command like a friggin' pinball. *Geez.*" He uncovered the mouthpiece. "Estoban, hold on a minute ... I said hold on a minute." He placed the call on hold. "Bet you dollars to donuts she doesn't even break stride. Guaranteed she'll still be blowing gale-force winds when I pick up the call. Anyway, what's up?"

"Who's working the Ramirez case?"

"Be specific, Lido. There are at least three Ramirez files out on the floor."

"The one Stephanie was working on, Serafina Ramirez. With all that's happened over the last month, I've lost track of who was working it."

"McIntyre and Kelleher. Why?"

"Are they making any progress on it?"

"I did say McIntyre and Kelleher, didn't I?"

"So no, then?"

"Read between the lines, Detective."

"Any chance I could pick it up?"

"Why would you want it? It's a high-jingo nightmare. A pretty little high school girl gets raped and murdered and the department is still tripping on its dick a month and half later. Sure you want to wade through a murky stream like that?"

"What can I say, man? I'm a glutton for punishment."

Ridon's expression read *schmuck*. "Talk to Egan. There's a task force assigned to the case now and the captain is up to his ass in hot water. Like I said, it's all high jingo now. The principal of the school the Ramirez girl attended is an at-large member of CPAC."

"Meaning?"

"The Citizen's Police Advisory Committee, Lido, and they have coffee and donuts with the executive brass once a month. Believe me when I tell you this group has lots of sway and they want this child killer found and punished pronto." Ridon reached for the phone console. "Why are you still standing here? Vamoose—I told you Egan needs all the help he can get." He finally hit the blinking light on his phone console. Once again, Margarita Estoban's incensed voice bled over the earpiece, squealing like a stuck pig. He mouthed, "Someone shoot me."

Captain James Egan was on the phone. He waved Lido into the office. Cupping the receiver, "I'll just be a minute," he said in his customary reserved voice.

Lido sank into a chair and waited until Egan was finished with his call. "Sorry to barge in," he began.

"Forget it, Lido. Spending five minutes with a hardworking cop is a hell of a lot more important than the hour I just spent on the dumb compliance conference call that just wrapped up."

"More red tape?"

"Miles of it, Lido, procedural initiatives, new chain of evidence protocol ..." He puffed out his lips. "Pretty soon the squad will have to spend the bulk of its time in a classroom instead of being out on the street. Anyway, how's Stephanie? Coming along?"

Lido sensed that he was taking too much time to respond and threw out a quick, innocuous answer, "You know Stephanie, she's like a force of nature."

Egan snorted. "I'll bet that woman keeps you on your toes."

He smirked. "You've got no idea, Captain, no idea whatsoever."

"So what can I do you for, Lido?"

"The case Stephanie was working on before the shooting, Serafina Ramirez—can I get in on it?"

"You're just stepping back into the ring, Gus. You're not even up to speed on your own current caseload. Why the sudden interest in the Ramirez case?" He glanced at Lido over the top of his glasses. "You wouldn't possibly be interested because you think it'll help you find your wife's shooter, would you? Not that I would blame you for trying."

"I hear you're forming a task force. I also hear the brass are chewing their way down the ranks."

"Down the ranks and up my ass," Egan flatly embellished. He closed his day planner and pushed back in his chair. "You know, I could give you an earful of shit about conflict of interest, correct protocol, and the rest of that mindless mumbo jumbo, but you're a good cop and I can use all the help I can get. You want in? You're in. I'll add you to the task force, but I'm not pulling you off any of your current assignments, and I'm not giving you carte blanche to carry out a vendetta. Is that clear?"

"Completely clear, Captain."

"Good! Find the Ramirez rapist and the cop killer and find them fast. People are watching us. Important people. I've got the brass so far up my rectum I could shit bullets."

Lido didn't respond verbally. Instead he smirked and gave Egan an enthusiastic thumbs-up.

"Okay then. Get out of here, Lido, and don't make me regret my decision."

"Not a chance," he said, and blew out the door.

Chapter Twenty

It took Lido about two hours to read through the Serafina Ramirez file and schedule an appointment to visit her parents.

He had visited the crime scene before, yet the spot where his wife had been shot still filled him with dread. He couldn't prevent the imagined scene from replaying in his mind, Stephanie and Yana walking toward their car, the crack of two rifle shots, and the two detectives lying on the ground. A shiver raced through him as the scenario tortured him yet again. Just ahead of him was the apartment house they had visited on that fated night and the rooftop upon which the sniper had stood. It took a moment for him to pull himself together, after which he walked determinedly toward the building.

Wearing a flannel shirt and a vinyl trooper's cap with the earflaps pinned at the top, Jack Burns opened the door without questioning who had rung the doorbell. "Can I help you?" he asked in a trusting tone.

Lido flashed his detective's shield. "Detective Gus Lido. We have an appointment."

Burns nodded. "Oh yeah. Come on in." He walked toward the kitchen, leaving Lido to close the door. "Sofia's not home yet, but she should be back soon." A package of bread was open on the kitchen table along with sealed Ziplocs filled with cold cuts and sliced cheeses.

Lido followed him into the kitchen, passing through the small living room along the way. The local news was on and the meteorologist was announcing a storm. It was an old-world TV, an RCA portable built in the days before flat screens replaced antiquated cathode ray technology.

"They say it's going to snow," Burns said. "About time."

He glanced at the heavy winter hat atop Burns' head. *Guess you're all set for the storm,* he mused. Although Lido thought of snow in the city as nothing more than an inconvenience, the announcement was a relief for him as well. He pictured the sidewalk covered with early spring snow masking the bloodstained concrete where his wife had been shot. "Hasn't been much of a year for skiing."

"I imagine not. Say, have you had lunch? I make a mean sandwich."

Lido shook his head. "No. I'm good. Thanks."

"I grew up on bologna," Burns said as he pulled slices off the stack of meat. "I'm a man of simple tastes." He spread mustard on the bread and closed the sandwich. "Mind if I eat while we talk?"

"No. Go right ahead," Lido said, despite finding that the aroma had in fact aroused his appetite.

"Sure you don't want coffee or something?"

Lido shook his head. "No. I'm good."

"What do you want to know? The police haven't sent anyone around in weeks. You some kind of mastermind detective they haul out when the case has gone to shit?"

"No. I'm just a fresh set of eyes the department has recently assigned to the task force. I know this may be redundant, but if you don't mind answering a few questions ..."

"I guess that would be all right." He glanced past Lido to the TV. "Anything to help bring my daughter's murderer to justice. Not that it will bring her back," he lamented.

Lido sat down at the kitchen table and opened his notebook. "You're her adopted father. Is that correct?"

"I adopted Serafina right after I married Sofia. It'll be five years this coming June."

"What happened to her natural father?"

"Ernesto?" he huffed. "What a jerk. The poor guy was a hopeless alcoholic—drank himself to death before he was forty."

"Did you know him?"

"Yeah. He was from the neighborhood. Lived in this apartment, as a matter of fact."

"How's that?"

"I started seeing Sofia about a year after he died. She asked me to move in, and the rest ... well, I guess you can figure it out."

"I see. Well, look, I went over her file in detail and there's no point asking you the same questions you've already answered. It seemed as if Serafina didn't have any obvious enemies. Robbery certainly wasn't a motive. Looking at the file objectively, it appears she was purely a victim of a sexual assault and murder."

Burns was chewing on his sandwich when Lido's final sentence hit him. He closed his eyes and arched his neck until he was facing the ceiling. Several moments passed before he finished chewing the food in his mouth. "I loved that child, Detective Lido. Shit, but your words just ripped the scab off the wound. Please. Please don't say anything like that when Sofia comes home. She's hanging on by a thread and you'll put her over the edge with a comment like that."

"Sorry."

"It's all right. I understand. You're just doing your job. It's just that we're both pretty fragile these days."

"So she left home just after the Super Bowl started to go to her friend Ginger's house, and never made it there."

"It makes me sick to think about it. She'd made that walk a hundred times, so often that you never stop to think ..." He pushed away his plate and took a drink from a bottle of beer. "It's just heart wrenching—she was such a good kid." He shook his head woefully. "Sofia just started going back to work. We figured it would be better for her to keep busy."

"What does she do?"

"Housecleaning. Babysitting. Shopping. Whatever she has to do to make a buck."

"And you?"

"I'm a handyman. I do plumbing, electrical, and a little woodworking. Same kind of thing—anything to make a buck."

"Are you in debt to anybody?"

"I'm in debt to everybody—twenty here, fifty there. No one killed Serafina over a few bucks, Detective."

"No. It sounds unlikely. Just looking at every angle. What about you and your wife?"

Burns wrinkled his brow. "What about us?"

"The revenge angle—piss anyone off lately? Anyone who'd want to hurt Serafina to get back at either of you?"

He cocked his head to the side and squinted at Lido. *"What? You're kidding, right?"*

"Revenge is a common motive for—"

Burns looked strained. "No. I get that, but do you really think ..." He stood and began pacing around the kitchen."

Lido could see that he'd touched a nerve. "Something come to mind?"

"Come to mind? Uh. No."

"The question seems to have gotten you pretty upset. Tell me what's bothering you."

"Nothing. Nothing. I've just never been asked that question before."

"Really? I'm surprised none of the other detectives explored the revenge motive with you. Someone wants to lash out at you or your wife and figures the best way to do it is to go after your daughter. Some people are real SOBs. It's coldhearted, but it happens all the time."

"Oh shit. Really?"

"I can see by your reaction that you're upset. What's on your mind?"

"Nothing. You just made me think. That's all. You've got me thinking about every argument I've gotten into in the last five years. Do you know how I'd feel if ... Jesus, you've got me feeling guilty over nothing. Maybe you ought to go before Sofia gets home. A question like that might kill her."

"I don't understand why. Anything either of you thinks of might help me apprehend Serafina's murderer." Lido placed a pair of business cards on the table. "Well, if anything comes to mind."

"I think you should go."

"You look jumpy, Mr. Burns. Are you sure you don't have something to share with me?"

"No, but thanks for stopping by," he snapped and ushered Lido out of the kitchen. "I'll kick it around with Sofia and we'll call you if anything comes to mind."

"I hope you will. We only want to see justice served and take a monster off the street. You wouldn't want something like that to happen to someone else's daughter."

"Of course not." Burns was practically pushing Lido out the front door. He closed the door, leaving Lido standing alone in the hallway.

Lido knew that he had touched on a sensitive subject and wondered what Burns was hiding. At the same time he felt guilt of his own. Not only had he struck out with Burns, but he had failed to learn anything valuable about his wife's disappearance. He had a long list of questions that would have to go unanswered for the time being. He was too frustrated and impatient to wait for the elevator. The burden of those two disappointments weighed heavily upon him as he gripped the bannister and hustled down the stairs.

Chapter Twenty-One

The lettuce in Lido's salad had wilted. It hadn't been sitting in front of him very long, but all that had been left at the corner deli salad bar was the dregs, the leftovers from lunch, the crap that had been picked through and pushed to the side. He'd picked the grilled chicken out of the salad, leaving the soggy greens behind. For all intents and purposes, he was done with it, yet he continued to pick condiments out of the plastic tray, nibbling on them, trying to fill a void that could not be filled.

He was pecking at the computer keyboard when a dust-covered evidence box was placed on his desk. "Lido?" the delivery officer asked.

He nodded and reached for a pen.

"This box was buried so deep I found it next to evidence recovered from the *Titanic*."

Lido grinned. "Glad I could spice up your day."

"Sign here ... Thanks. It's all yours. Call me if you're looking for the Declaration of Independence. I think I spotted it nearby." The delivery officer smirked and turned away.

Lido shoved the keyboard aside and placed the dusty box dead center on his desk, noticing that the dust had recently been disturbed. *Interesting,* he thought. *Who's been looking at this?* After reading the label, he removed the lid, careful not to get dust all over himself or his desk. The box he had retrieved from archives contained records from before the days when all case documents were digitized and stored on computer mainframes. He opened the top folder and began scanning the documents that had long since yellowed with age. It didn't take long for him to get drawn in by the particulars of the case, the lurid details, interviews, and notes chronicling a child's abduction and abuse. The victim was Jack Burns.

He was still reading when light fell outside the precinct. As he worked his way down to the bottom of the box, colleagues sitting at desks nearby went home for the evening and the office clamor he was so accustomed to diminished and became an inconspicuous undercurrent.

He'd found the case shocking, but it wasn't until he reached the last folder that a notation stole his breath. It was a late addition to the documentation, information contributed long after the case was initially declared cold. A detective's signature at the bottom of a request form stunned him and set the wheels in his head into motion. *No. It can't be.* He scrutinized the signature a second time and then a third, until he was absolutely sure that the form had been signed by his deceased father-in-law, Frank Chalice.

Chapter Twenty-Two

Lido tiptoed out of Max's bedroom and shut the door. "Sorry I got home so late."

"I didn't hear from you all day," Ma complained politely. "Any leads? Any idea where my crazy daughter is?"

He shook his head and let go a pent-up sigh. "I'm afraid not. The thing is ... I know she's okay. Despite the head wound and despite everything she's done to make us nuts, I know that Stephanie can more than take care of herself. It's not the worry that has me bent out of shape. It's—"

Ma interrupted him. "I know. I'm disgusted with her too. She can't be thinking straight and that's what troubles me the most. Being committed to the job is one thing, but this ... it's just too much," she huffed. "I'd like to put her over my knee and spank the daylights out of her."

"Yeah? Well, get in line."

"Yeah, *right*. I've got dinner on the table for you. Take a load off and we'll bellyache about my darling daughter while you eat."

"Best offer I've had all day." Gus plopped into a kitchen chair and twisted the top off a cold one. "So listen, this is going to sound completely weird, but ..."

"But what?" she asked anxiously as she set a skillet on the table.

"I interviewed Serafina Ramirez's father today."

"The family Stephanie was investigating just before she was shot?"

"Correct, the girl who was raped and murdered on Super Bowl Sunday. I asked to be added to the taskforce investigating the case."

"Hoping it would help you find Stephanie," she deduced.

"Well, yeah, I guess that's obvious. I mean I hope to contribute to the murder case as well, but my main motivation is finding your whacky daughter."

"You mean your whacky wife, don't you?"

"Forget about it. I've only been married to her a short period of time. This one's on you, Lisa Chalice. You're the one who made her the nut job she is today."

"*Bah.* Whatever. So what's this weird question you have for me? You've got a strange expression on your face."

Lido sucked down another swig of suds. "So this guy, the girl's father, he weirded out on me during the interview, got real tense and basically kicked me out of his apartment. I was exploring the premise of the crime being a revenge killing and—"

"Sounds like someone has a troubled conscience. Is that why you were so late, because you checked him out?"

Lido nodded and then pushed out his lips. "He was a victim in a really old case. Child abuse. I had the case file retrieved from archives."

"Jesus. What happened to the poor man?"

"Nothing good. The thing is that the case went cold and was reopened more than a dozen years later."

"I'm not following you, Gus. What does this have to do with the girl's murder or finding Stephanie?"

Lido placed his beer bottle on the table and looked at her directly. "The case was reopened by Frank."

Her mouth opened wide. "*My* Frank?"

Lido nodded. "I thought maybe you might know something about—"

"Wait a minute. This guy you interviewed. You said that his last name is Ramirez, didn't you?"

"No, actually. It's Burns. Jack Burns. He's the girl's adoptive father."

Ma gasped and covered her open mouth before pulling out a kitchen chair and dropping into it. "Jack Burns?" She rubbed her forehead. "My God."

"Ring a bell?"

"Oh my Lord, yes. Frank and Jack were childhood friends. Frank felt responsible for what happened to Jack, but ... I never knew that he reopened the case."

"So what can you tell me about it?"

She thought for a moment before ladling pasta into his dish. "You'd better start eating. It'll get cold before I get through the whole story."

"Long story, is it?"

"Oh yes. Frank and I had just started to date when it happened, and let me tell you, it rocked the whole neighborhood."

Gus looked down at the large bowl and smiled as she filled it to the brim with mounds of steaming macaroni. "Looks like I've got my work cut out for me anyway. Take your time."

Chapter Twenty-Three

Manhattan 1973

"That's-that's-that's a do over," Reggie protested in his accustomed stutter as he watched his bottle cap sail past the number twelve square at the far end of the scully board. The white chalk scully board had been marked in the street alongside the johnny pump between two parked cars. Reggie would've won the game and a quarter from each of his friends had his bottle cap landed on the number twelve square. "Hey. Why-why-why'd you d-do that, Jack-O?"

Jack-O was short for jackoff, and Jack Burns was going out of his way to show that he had earned his reputation. He'd pounded the end of his baseball bat on the street just as Reggie was about to take his shot, causing him to miss. "Duh-do-do-do over," he said, teasing his friend. "You sound like a baby with a wet diaper."

"Well, it is a do-do-do over." Reggie stood to retrieve his rare Pepsi flat top bottle cap, a one in a thousand find, one that had miraculously left the bottling plant without getting crimped on top of a soda bottle. He was just reaching for it when Jack crushed it with his bat, permanently deforming it. "Hey!" Reggie's eyes flashed hotly as he looked down on his now mangled treasure. "You're-you're a real jerk. That's the-the only one I've got like that." He pushed Jack with two hands, not hard enough to start a fight, just hard enough to register his displeasure.

Jack pounded the bat into his open palm. "Try that again, dipshit. I dare you."

"Cut it out, Jack." Frank Chalice wasn't as tall as Jack, but he was the oldest by a year and had been working out with some of the older high school boys over the summer. He already had thick sideburns and a girlfriend of sorts, which clearly established his position as the group's leader.

"Why do you have to always butt in, Frank?" Jack griped. "Let buh-buh-brainless fight his own battles."

"Because you've got a bat, nimrod. Maybe you ought to put it down and we'll see how tough you are without it."

Bobby Cohen was the fourth member of the pack. He bent with the wind and was loyal to no one. He took sides with whomever could do him the most good at the moment. "He's right, Jack. Lay off Reggie."

"Butt out, bootlick," Jack warned. "You always side with Frank because you want to go over to his place and feel up his sister. Only reason you don't is because you're afraid Frank will kick your ass."

Bobby gave Jack the finger. He tried to show that he had been offended by the accusation, but his expression gave him away. Every one of them knew how he felt about Frank's sister and regularly caught him ogling her. The neighborhood was tightly knit and held few secrets.

Frank reached into his pocket and handed Reggie a quarter. Bobby followed suit and did the same.

"Pay up, Jack," Frank said.

"Why?"

"Because he would've won on that shot," Frank explained. "He hasn't missed in his last seven turns."

Bobby chimed in. "Yeah. He's like the pinball wizard of scully," *he snickered, likening his friend to Tommy, the idiot savant in The Who song "Christmas." "You know you weren't gonna beat him, man." He mockingly paraphrased the lyrics, "'And Reggie doesn't* know what day it is. He doesn't know who Jesus was or what praying is.'"

"Hey! Cut-cut-cut that out," Reggie complained.

Frank's eyes grew hot. "That's enough!" His command silenced Bobbie. He huffed angrily before turning back to Jack. "So, what's it going to be?"

"It doesn't matter," Jack said. "Let him go again. I'm not paying unless he gets it in the box."

"With the messed-up bottle cap you smashed?"

"It doesn't look so bad. He can still use it."

"Don't be a jerk. Give him a quarter so we can all go home."

Jack lived in a basement apartment a block from the Hudson, three avenue blocks west of where the other boys lived, on a street overrun with junkies, pimps, and hookers, a block where no one felt safe at night. He always carried his bat with him for protection. "Walk me home."

"Now who sounds like a baby?" Bobby said, then leaned over and hawked his spit into the middle of the street.

"Are you gonna pay up?" Frank asked.

"No."

"No?" He was frustrated with Jack and began counting to ten as his father had recommended he do when he felt himself growing angry. He wanted to swear but didn't. "Well then, I guess you'll have to walk home by yourself."

"I can't pay him," Jack said, part explaining and part pleading. He reached into the pockets of his jeans and turned them inside out. "I don't have any money on me."

Bobby wrinkled his nose. "You were playing for money with empty pockets?" He spit on the sidewalk again. "That's a dick move."

"I'm good for it," Jack insisted.

"Take a walk," Bobby said with distaste. *"It's not the first time you've tried to welch on a bet."*

"No, really. I'm good for it."

Reggie and Bobby ignored him and started for home.

Frank watched the other two walk away. "You gonna be all right?" he asked. He could see that Jack was reluctant to walk home alone and clearly understood the reason why. Only a few days had passed since the boys had come to pick him up after dinner to find him cornered in his apartment house lobby by Ray MacAteer, a nasty drunk he'd had run-ins with before. MacAteer was almost thirty but picked on Jack because he was almost a man in size. It didn't matter to him that Jack was all skin and bones. It was only because MacAteer was outnumbered that Jack escaped without a beating.

Jack pounded the bat into his palm again. "Yeah." He pumped himself up to demonstrate his street-worthiness. "No worries."

"You're sure?"

"You think I'm like that wimp Reggie? I'm not afraid. I can stick up for myself."

Frank checked his watch. He felt guilty about letting his friend walk home alone but had plans to meet his girlfriend, Lisa, and didn't want to be late. "All right then. See ya."

"You going over to Lisa's house?"

Frank nodded.

"You think she's gonna let you get some?"

He rolled his eyes. "You really are a jerk," he said, then turned and walked off.

The four boys hung out every day during the summer except for Sundays, which was family day, so Frank knew he wouldn't see Jack the next day, but when Jack didn't meet up with them to play stickball on Monday, he and the rest of the boys began to worry.

Chapter Twenty-Four

"Hey, did you-you hear? The-the cops found Juh-Juh-Jack-O?" Reggie said, his face animated as he turned away from the old tub-style soda cooler. He'd been digging in the cap slot in search of a new flat top bottle cap to replace the one that Jack had crushed days earlier.

"No shit! Is he all right?" Frank asked with concern. He folded his grocery list and slipped it into his back pocket.

Reggie's fingers were sticky with dried soda as he pulled them from the cap slot. "Uh-uh. Don't think so. I heard he's in the hospital."

Frank squeezed his eyes shut. The guilt of not walking Jack home had been eating at him all week long, keeping him awake at night. He could still picture the look on his friend's face the last time he'd seen him, the unwilling cast that announced that he was afraid to walk home alone despite stating that he wasn't. The story had surfaced on Monday afternoon—Jack never made it home on Saturday night. "Shit. Do you know what happened to him?"

Reggie shook his head. "No, b-but my father's mad as h-hell because we didn't wuh-wuh-walk him home. I t-told him about Jack being a jerk and all, b-but he didn't care. He says we're-we're re-responsible for what happened. Told me I'm g-g-grounded—j-just chores and m-my speech lessons."

"Your father's right. We should've walked him home. Remember last week? He almost got his ass kicked by MacAteer. He lives on a shitty block. Besides, we always walk him home."

"O-o-only at night."

"We screwed up," Frank lamented.

Smitty, the grocery store owner, followed his mother out from behind the counter. He was wearing his standard uniform, a white tee that smelled as if it had never been washed and a white apron over stained black pants. His mother, who the regulars referred to as Mrs. Smitty, wore her gray hair in a bun and had long chin whiskers.

"How's your friend Jack?" she asked. Her voice had a muddled tone because it was painful for her to wear her dentures and was often toothless. "We heard some hooligans beat him senseless."

Frank's face turned ashen white. Oh shit! "We don't know. We just heard about it."

"Cops found him passed out under the Westside Highway," she said. "All black and blue. Broken ribs. Filthy dirty. Some of his teeth knocked out too."

Frank stared at her toothless mouth and allowed a haunting image to creep into his mind. He began to feel light-headed and woozy. He leaned against the tub soda cooler to prevent his knees from buckling. "But he's gonna be okay, isn't he?"

Smitty shrugged. "I don't think anyone knows for sure. It's too soon."

"How come you two didn't walk him home?" she asked. "You know that area is bad news. Why, the cops don't even want to patrol over there. Crack houses and whores—why, it ain't safe to walk there at night. Goddamn it. I don't know how his parents think they can bring up a young boy on that block. Why they haven't moved the hell out of there is beyond me."

"Maybe they would if they could afford to," Smitty said derisively.

Frank grimaced and doubled over with a stomach cramp.

"You all right, dear?" she asked.

"I think I'm gonna be sick."

"Not in my store," Smitty warned resolutely. He led Frank toward the door. "Puke in the street if you have to."

Frank had barely cleared the doorway when he hurled.

Chapter Twenty-Five

"I can't believe the other boys aren't here," Maria Chalice **snapped as she fished in her purse for a stick of gum.** *"No respect. No respect whatsoever."*

"Reggie had his speech lesson, Mom," Frank said.

"Okay, so Reggie has a valid excuse, but what about Bobby Cohen? What's his excuse this time? Someone ought to teach that boy the meaning of the word responsibility."

Frank shrugged and lowered his head. "Don't know." He cast his gaze at the highly polished hospital linoleum floor as he listened to the clatter of the staff's footsteps hurrying back and forth.

"Has anyone else been to see him?"

Frank shrugged again.

She shook her head rapidly, almost shuddering. "Disgraceful."

"When's he supposed to get out, Mom?"

"They're not sure, Frank. I spoke to his mother yesterday and she said that he's still in pretty bad shape."

He looked down the corridor toward Jack's room. "You think they'll let us in to see him soon?"

She shook her head once more, slowly this time, conveying an entirely different message as she studied her son's worried face. She patted his leg. "It's not your fault, honey. You're a good boy."

His throat tightened. "I knew better," he fretted. "I knew better than to let him walk home by himself."

"I know you did, Frank. So why did you let him walk home alone? I know you try to look after all of your friends. It was so unlike you."

He glanced at his mother with a reluctant expression. "Because."

"Because why?"

He shrugged yet again. "Because I wanted to go over to Lisa's place."

"Ah," she said with motherly understanding in her voice. "I see." She stroked his hair. "I know how hard this is for you, but you're going to have to let it go, Frank. You see ..." She sighed and remained silent.

"See what, Mom?" he asked but could see that she had something difficult to say. She had been talking to Jack's mother on the phone every day but hadn't revealed much about their conversations.

She finally offered, "Jack's not going to be the same."

"What?" he said with a grimace. "I don't understand. Why not?"

"Those men, the ones who beat him up, they ..." She paused again. A few tears drizzled down her cheek. "They ..." She sniffled and opened her purse. "Now where are my stupid tissues?"

"They what, Mom? Why are you crying?" He'd suspected she'd been crying after speaking with Jack's mother the other day, but wasn't sure. Her eyes were red and she had a tissue in her hand after hanging up.

Her throat tightened. She finally found a pack of Kleenex and used one to dab at her tears. "This is so difficult. Someone your age or Jack's shouldn't even be aware that things like this happen."

Frank was on the verge of tears himself. "Why won't you tell me what they did?"

"Because it's terrible and it's awful and it shouldn't happen to anyone, let alone a young boy, but it did."

"Tell me," he insisted.

She stared at Frank and sighed. Tears were now streaming down her face. "I'm sorry," she said as her voice grew hoarse. "I just can't."

Chapter Twenty-Six

The rest of the summer seemed to drag on and on, so much so that Frank was not disappointed when his mother reminded him that he'd be back at school in just a few days. But Jack wouldn't be headed back with the rest of the boys. He was still healing. His physical wounds were coming along nicely, and the doctors felt that he'd eventually be able to overcome the limp that had developed as a result of the beatings.

He was wearing temporary caps over his two cracked incisors until the permanent ones were ready. The temporaries were crudely fashioned and off-color, which made him look bucktoothed.

He scarcely looked at Frank when he came over to visit. He was watching Captain Nice on the family's portable TV, a show about a police department chemist who discovered a liquid that would transform him into a superhero.

"Hey, Jack," Frank said, greeting his friend in a voice that was still tenuous and laden with guilt.

Jack raised his hand like a welcome flag without taking his eyes from the screen.

"Okay if I watch with you?"

"Uh-huh," he replied without looking at his visitor.

Jack's mother watched her son greet Frank. Her lips were tightly clenched and her forehead was wrinkled with worry. Frank *glanced at her and she forced a smile, encouraging him to sit down.* "Can I get you boys anything?"

Jack shook his head without looking at her.

"No, thanks, Mrs. Burns," Frank replied. Sitting down next to Jack on the old sofa, he noticed a tear on her cheek as she left the room. He sighed before turning away. He'd visited five times since Jack had gotten home from the hospital but still didn't know what to say to his friend. It was as if he didn't know him anymore.

They watched in silence for a few minutes until the commercial break aired. Jack was still facing away when Frank put his hand on Jack's shoulder.

Jack jumped as a breathy gasp left his mouth.

"Hey, you okay?"

Jack nodded after a moment but was still facing away.

"Hey, why won't you look at me, Jack?"

Jack pressed his lips together to hide his oversized temporary teeth and reluctantly faced his friend. He shrugged, then quickly turned back to the TV just as the program returned. The chemist was in his lab, mixing liquids of various colors. "You think that stuff is real?" he asked, talking without looking at his friend.

"What, that potion stuff?"

"Uh-huh."

"Nah. I don't think so. It's just a hokey TV show."

"I wish it were real."

"I wish I could dunk a basketball," Frank said, "but that isn't going to make it happen."

The chemist mixed the final ingredients together and smiled as he drank down the contents of the large test tube. Within a moment he had transformed into Captain Nice.

"Wish I had that stuff," Jack said in a disheartened voice.

"How come?"

He finally turned to Frank. "Haven't you ever wanted to be someone else, someone better than the person you are? You know what I mean, someone bigger than life."

"I guess." Frank smiled, happy that Jack was finally opening up. "I used to want to be Superman, but ... you know that's only kid stuff."

"Wish I could've turned into Superman when those two guys ..." Jack closed his eyes and shuddered. He pressed a hand against his stomach and came close to dry heaving.

"Hey, you all right? Settle down. Want some water or something?" He could see pinpoints of sweat break out across Jack's upper lip. "Should I call your mom?"

Jack shook his head violently. "No," he whispered. "Don't call her—you'll only make her upset. I'll be okay."

"You sure?"

"Yeah."

"Hey, what's going on with you, anyway?"

"You fucking dope!" Jack's whisper came at Frank with the impact of a clenched fist. "You don't have any idea what they did to me, do you? No idea."

"No," Frank replied repentantly. "No one will tell me."

Jack was trembling as he spoke. "They did stuff to me, real bad stuff. They-they hurt me real bad." He started to cry, then wiped away his tears and glanced frantically toward the kitchen to make sure that his mother was out of earshot. His voice trembled. "Real bad."

Frank studied Jack's face and finally felt the full impact of the emotional pain he was suffering. "But you're healing."

"No. I'm not."

"But the doctors said ..."

"Not the regular docs—the shrinks. They say I'm broken."

Frank Chalice was maturing quickly, but there was still much that he didn't understand about life and wickedness. "Broken? What does that even mean?"

"I overheard the shrink telling my mom. He said I might never get completely better. He said I may have to go to some special kind of school for slow kids."

"What kind of school?" *Frank asked, skeptical of what he'd heard.*

"Fucking retard school, Frank. That's how screwed up they say I am."

Frank was enraged. "What the hell did those bastards do to you, Jack?"

Jack turned away. "Like I said. They hurt me. They hurt me really bad."

"You know they'll catch those two douchebags."

"I hope they do. I hope they lock their asses up for good so that what happened to me doesn't happen to anyone else." *He buried his head in his hands momentarily.* "But what's been done to me has been done and there ain't no changing it. I want to go back to that day and start it all over again, but there isn't going to be a do-over."

"No, but you'll get over it. You're Jack-O. You're one of us."

"Was, Frank. Was. I'm not the same guy anymore."

There was such despair and finality in Jack's voice that Frank felt as if a weight was pressing against his chest, and he suddenly found it difficult to breathe. He had just gotten there and didn't want to leave abruptly, but he urgently needed a moment and didn't know what to do. Feeling trapped, he looked around the small apartment in desperation. "I've got to use the john," *he announced, then stood up.* "Be right back."

Taking big steps, he quickly but unobtrusively reached the bathroom and shut the door. Switching on the light, he pressed the stopper into the drain and filled the sink with cold water. He splashed it on his face, getting his hair and tee shirt wet in the process. Looking at his dripping face in the mirror, he said, "Jesus. What am I going to do? I just don't know what to say to him anymore."

Taking a deep breath, he turned to the towel rack, and that's when he saw it, a package of adult diapers. He stared at it and read some of the printed matter on the package: Size Small: Waist Sizes 28-32. "What the?" He was in uncharted waters, confused and befuddled by the discovery. It took a moment for him to understand. He did so by piecing together fragments of stories he'd heard from some of the older boys, stories he viewed as adolescent banter, stories kids made up to appear more experienced and sophisticated than they really were. Nonetheless the pieces slowly fell into place.

"Oh my God." The blood drained from his face and his skin turned to ice. He steadied himself by using his two hands to brace himself against the tiled bathroom wall. "Oh my God," he repeated, taking deep breaths to calm himself down. He began to feel lightheaded and quickly flipped down the toilet seat. He sat down and put his head between his legs so that he wouldn't pass out.

Chapter Twenty-Seven

Lido's dish was empty.

Ma's eyes went wide when she realized that he had finished the huge portion she had served him. "I can't believe that story didn't kill your appetite."

"No, it didn't, and actually, I can't think of much that does. I'm embarrassed to ask, but is there any more?"

"God bless you, Gus Lido, you've got a real man's appetite." She walked to the stove and lit one of the burners. "I'll heat some more up for you. Some story, huh?"

He rubbed his eyes. "I don't know if it's the story that has me rattled or if I'm just brain-dead from exhaustion."

"You're brain-dead from stress. Are you sorry you didn't marry a nice demure girl, someone who's into macramé and crocheting?"

He rolled his eyes. "Bad time to ask, because at this moment ..."

"Having second thoughts, are you?"

"I'm trying to figure out how this information might help the case, but there's just so much I don't know. I mean, how could a case this old have a bearing on a current sexual assault?"

Ma shrugged. "That's your job, not mine. My job is keeping you mentally and physically healthy until my lunatic daughter comes home."

"You know, come to think of it ..." He paused, then looked at her with a guilty expression. "I shouldn't be sharing this information with you."

"Get real," Ma barked. "This is my daughter's life we're talking about. So forget the bullshit privacy protocol and tell me what you're thinking."

He replied reluctantly, "Yeah. I guess. I mean, under the circumstances."

"So what were you going to say?"

"Burns is sort of damaged goods. He has a history of being in and out of psychiatric facilities. Works as a handyman because he can't or won't take steady employment ..."

"So you're thinking he might be a suspect?"

Lido shrugged. "I don't know. I don't peg him as a murderer. Besides, what's his motive? I just don't see it."

"But you're going to look a little deeper?"

"Yeah. I'm going to look a little deeper. Just to be sure."

Chapter Twenty-Eight

A man was lying on his side with a teal snake wrapped around his arm, a tattoo nearing completion.

The tattoo artist looked up and grinned when Haruki entered his shop in lower Manhattan. *"Ah. Haruki-san,"* he cheered. The buzzing of the tattoo pen stopped as he jumped to his feet and threw his arm around the visitor. "How long has it been?"

"Too long, Tiru-san. Much too long." Haruki patted his friend on the back before taking a moment to admire his handiwork. "I see reptiles and dragons are still keeping you busy."

Tiru clasped his hands together. "Yes. Thank the gods." He turned to his customer. "Ryo-san, this is my friend Haruki. He's an old customer of mine from back in Kyoto."

Sitting up, Ryo said, "Let me see Tiru's work."

Haruki obediently unzipped his jacket and unbuttoned his shirt. He had three-quarter-sleeve tattoos on both arms that began on his chest and ran to each forearm, a bright orange tiger on his right arm and a carp tattoo on his left. He turned to reveal an onyx and jade fire-breathing dragon that filled the entire expanse of his back.

"I'm envious," Ryo said. "The tiger is far more powerful than the snake."

"But less cunning," Haruki rebutted. "And women ... they like the snake," he added with a sly grin.

"But the work on your back ... it's so impressive." He picked up his smart phone. "May I take a picture for my reference?"

Haruki nodded and faced away so that Ryo could take a picture of the tattoo on his back.

"Thank you." Ryo put the phone down and turned to Tiru. "Finish. Please. I'm eager to see my tattoo completed."

Tiru signaled to the young woman behind the front counter, who smiled and bowed dutifully. "Ryo, I know you're in a hurry to see the work completed but please enjoy a cold beer. My compliments. My assistant will bring you can of Asahi Super Dry. Enjoy, please, while I take a short break to catch up with an old friend."

Ryo nodded as Haruki and Tiru headed off. Tiru pushed aside a curtain of slender bamboo stalks that led to a back room. "You look well, Haruki-san. It's good to see that you're thriving in Kyoto town. What brings you back to New York?"

"Tadashi's killer still roams free. I can't live with that hanging over me. It's been more than a month and the police haven't arrested anyone."

"I see. Still, it was not a good idea for you to come to my shop in person. Many of my customers are *ninkyō dantai*. You could be recognized, and you know there is no honor among thieves."

"The yakuza is everywhere. I've learned to live with that."

"But here, Haruki-san, here you may not be safe."

"I accept this risk." He opened a sketchbook and looked at some of Tiru's drawings. "Can you help me put out the word? The New York police are not even close to an arrest, and the longer it takes, the colder the trail grows."

"Of course I will help, but I am an old man and I do my utmost to stay on the outside of *ninkyō dantai* matters. Your family name is still a trigger for the yakuza. Asking questions about your brother might raise suspicions that you are back in New York, and once the word is out ..."

"I'd rather run that risk than die with the dishonor of knowing I did nothing to avenge my brother's death. Please, Tiru. Please do what you can."

Tiru bowed his head. "As you wish, Haruki-san. It shall be done."

~~~

Not twenty feet away, Ryo studied the photo he'd taken of the tattoo on Haruki's back and attached it to a message that he sent to his partner.

Chapter Twenty-Nine

"Where were you?"

Harry had just returned to the hotel room. He dropped his backpack on the floor and shut the door. "Visiting an old friend. You said you needed to spend time doing research on the computer."

"I just finished. I made a list of all the cases Yana and I worked together over the last year. I'm going through them one by one to see who might have wanted to take a shot at us."

"And what did you find?"

"A couple of cases might be worth digging into—one in particular."

He pulled up a chair. "Show me," he said with keen interest.

"Eduardo Sanchez. We collared him for the murder of a rival New York street gang member. Three time loser—he was tried and sentenced to life imprisonment."

"How does he hurt you from behind bars?"

"I remember both Eduardo and his brother, Rodrigo, being pretty menacing characters. They did their best to frighten the jury with intimidating expressions and terrifying outbursts ... you get the picture. They showed no great love for either your brother or me."

"They're both gang members?"

"Trinitarios."

He shrugged.

"Fastest growing street gang in New York. Mostly Dominican—their trademark is the machete-style execution. The Trinitarios started in the prison system, so even if Rodrigo wasn't acting on his own and carrying out a revenge killing, it's conceivable that Eduardo could have reached out from prison to take his pound of flesh."

"You have pictures? Addresses?"

"Sure." A few taps on the keyboard brought up pictures of the menacing duo. They looked like a pair of mangy flea-ridden dogs. "Imagine running into these two in a dark alley."

Harry grimaced, the euphemism apparently lost on him. "Alley?"

"It's just an expression. It's a way of saying they're pretty nasty-looking characters."

"Yeah. I agree. I'll try to avoid alleys," he said with a chuckle. "Forward their pictures to my phone along with Rodrigo's address. I'll take them."

"*You'll* take them?" I said with surprise.

"Yes. I have friends on the street."

"You're a cop from Japan."

"Correct. A cop from Japan with friends on the streets of New York City."

"Explain."

"Sorry, Chalice, I'd like to tell you everything, but I can't reveal the names of my contacts."

"Like hell you can't. You're not going anywhere alone. What if you run into trouble?"

"I'll be fine. Look, it's smarter for you to stay off the streets, and I'm free to move around any way I wish. Let me do the legwork."

"Um. Let's see. Give me a minute to think about it ... No. Not a chance, Harry. Where you go, I go. I'm not sending you out in a strange city to interrogate murder suspects. I understand that you're a competent law officer, but—"

He cut me off uttering assertively, "I'm a professional police officer."

I'd obviously insulted him and it was beginning to surface in the tone of his voice.

"I assure you I know how to handle myself, Chalice. Yana was your partner, but he was my brother. As you Americans like to say, we're both off the reservation. So I will ask some discreet questions while you work the computer." He offered his hand in a spirit of cooperation. "Do we have a deal?"

I considered his offer. "For today, Harry, but I'm not committing beyond that. Let's take it a day at a time and see how it goes."

Chapter Thirty

"I'm going to bed," Ma said, her eyelids heavy and hanging low.

Gus was on the couch with a computer on his lap.

"Any luck?" she asked.

"I'm going to kill her," he swore. "I'm absolutely going to kill her."

"Oh Jesus, what did my crazy daughter do now?"

"We have each other's passwords. I just tried to log into the department intranet with her credentials and was denied access. She changed her goddamn password."

"Why would she do that?"

"So that I can't check the system log and see her last inquiries. The system administrator would know if she's been logging on, but I certainly can't march into the IT department and ask if an officer on leave is accessing the system."

"I guess she's covering her tracks."

"Yeah. Stephanie's sharp all right, too sharp." He shook his head heatedly. "I just can't believe she'd go to such great lengths to keep me from finding her. It just really makes me angry."

She plopped down next to him on the sofa and patted his leg. "Look on the bright side. At least we know she's okay. She's the old Stephanie again, bullheaded and blind to everything but justice."

"I suppose. Hey, before you go to bed, would you mind looking at something?"

"Of course, Gus. What?"

Lido picked up a folder and pulled out some pictures. The first was of her husband as a teenager.

She gasped and snatched the photo out of his hand. "Oh my goodness. That's Frank. Look how handsome he was. Is it any wonder I fell head over heels for that man?"

"There's no denying that the man was a stud, but that's not what I wanted to show you." He handed her three additional photos. "These were his friends at the time. This one is Jack Burns, the boy who was assaulted. Do you recognize him and the others?"

She looked at each of the three pictures in turn and then spread them across her lap. "Oh my God. This brings back such memories." She tapped the picture on her left leg. "Yes. This is Jack. It must've been taken after the incident because ..." She sniffled and had difficulty swallowing. "He was always so full of himself despite the fact that he was all skin and bones. But after ... Well, he just wasn't the same. You can see it in his eyes. He always looked tense, as if the sky might fall on him at any moment, and his mouth is closed because he's hiding the awful caps the dentist made for him. It's really so sad. It's no wonder he never bounced back—a real tragedy."

"He's still got a little bit of that look in his eyes even today, like he's always processing that painful memory." Lido pointed to the center photo. "This one was marked Robert Cohen."

She grinned sadly. "Bobby was a wise guy before the term became popular. He always had a smartass answer for everything—always working an angle. You just knew he'd amount to no good. Do you know what became of him?"

"Died of a heart attack two years ago," Lido replied regretfully.

"Ah, he's gone too? That's terrible." She peaked her eyebrows and grinned. "Well, I guess *he's* not a suspect."

"Unlikely, Madame Detective."

"What about Reggie?" she asked as she lifted and examined the third photo. "The neighborhood kids used to make fun of him all the time. The poor thing stuttered terribly, and as if that wasn't bad enough, he was so terribly underdeveloped. My uncle Mickey used to say that he looked like he was raised in a veal box."

Lido snorted. "Shit. I shouldn't laugh. That's terrible."

"He definitely went through the school of hard knocks. I hope *he's* still around."

"He's still around," Lido confirmed. "He's a building manager."

"Oh, I'm glad—that sounds like a nice safe job. I do hope he outgrew his awful stuttering." She handed the photos back to him, picked up a throw pillow, and pressed it to her lap. "So much water under the bridge," she said sadly. "Frank and Bobby gone … and now here you are questioning Jack Burns—why it's as if two separate worlds have collided with one another." She slapped the pillow with both hands. "I'll check on Max and then I'm going to turn in. You should do the same."

"Are you all right in the guest bedroom?"

"Am I all right?" she snapped. "I'm so tired I could sleep standing up."

"You don't miss your own bed?"

"Honey, it's okay. I'll be back in my own place soon enough. Give yourself a break and get some rest."

"I don't think I can sleep."

"*Bah!* Have a glass of wine. It'll put you right out."

"Maybe in a bit. I'm going to go through this file until I get tired."

"Okay, honey, but don't stay up too late." She kissed him on the forehead. "You need your sleep."

"No promises, Ma." He looked into the empty evidence box and noticed the corner of a slip of paper peeking out from under the bottom box flap. Pulling it out for examination, he saw that it was an evidence receipt. "Holy shit!" His blood pressure spiked as he stared at it. The receipt was only a few days old, and his wife had signed it.

Chapter Thirty-One

Haruki studied the stores along the street as he headed crosstown. The area seemed mundane in comparison to the shopping districts of Kyoto. Sure, Times Square was billboard central, but beyond Broadway the lights gradually faded with each pace taken away from Manhattan's epicenter. By contrast, Kyoto was a neon city, an homage to fluorescent lighting and bright colors, where the sizzle of electricity was so intense it felt as if it would sear your skin off the bone.

Chef Aguri Maeda's hands moved like precision machinery, slicing yellowtail into identical slivers of sashimi and placing them in staggered rows upon a porcelain platter decorated with lotus blossoms. He claimed that his personal takobiki knife was the finest sashimi knife in the world and sharp enough to split a hair standing on end. He glanced up as Haruki entered the small restaurant, splitting his vision between him and the fresh fish fillet so that the slicing continued unabated. Finished, he handed the porcelain dish to a customer sitting in front of him at the sushi bar, bowed, and motioned for Haruki to join him at the end of the bar where they'd have some privacy. He bowed to Haruki, then wiped his takobiki knife clean and laid it on the cutting surface in front of him. He stepped away momentarily, ladled miso soup into a small bowl, and offered it to his guest. "To what do I owe this honor?" Maeda asked.

"Anata no oishī tabemono."

Maeda bowed again. "You're hungry? You flatter me with your praise, Haruki-san. I'm glad you came here for dinner."

Haruki had made copies of Eduardo and Rodrigo Sanchez's photos. He placed them atop the refrigerated glass case for Maeda to see.

"So," he began with eyebrows raised high. "I see that you have a special dinner request." He examined the pictures and flipped them over, where Haruki had scribbled the names and last known addresses of each of the two men depicted, noting that Eduardo's current address was the federal penitentiary in Lewisburg, Pennsylvania.

Haruki tapped Rodrigo's picture. "This one. The address is an old one. I checked. He's not there any longer, but I need to find this man right away."

Maeda nodded and slipped the two photos into the pocket of his chef's jacket. "How are your parents?" he asked, intentionally changing the conversation.

Haruki shook his head sadly.

"That's too bad. I was so sorry to hear about your brother. This is why you are here?"

"*Hai.*"

"These men?"

"Possibly. It's just a lead I'm running down."

Maeda unwrapped a slab of bright red tuna. "*Kaiseki ryori?*"

"Yes. Sure. That sounds great." He tasted the soup and offered a compliment, "*Sore wa subarashī kotodesu.*"

Maeda smiled. "Anything to start?"

"You have *natto?*"

"I think there may be a little left." He measured the tuna by eye and began preparing identical chunks of the raw fish. "The information you need may take a couple of days. I'll do my best."

Haruki spoke in an appreciative tone. "Whatever you can do is appreciated, my brother."

Maeda served Haruki a bowl of *natto* before returning to the task of preparing his sashimi.

Haruki ate his meal in silence while he concentrated on the case he'd traveled across the Pacific to solve. He was so self-absorbed that he failed to notice the man sitting at the bar close to the entrance. It was Ryo, the man he'd seen in Tiru's tattoo shop the other day, the one who was having a snake freshly tattooed on his arm, and had photographed the jade fire-breathing dragon on his back.

Chapter Thirty-Two

Haruki had taken the bait. I hadn't so much baited him, but I had successfully gotten him out of the hotel room without making it obvious that I wanted him out of the way. I did indeed want him to follow up on the Sanchez brothers even though, in truth, they were not at the top of my list of suspects.

I'd been watching the building Jack Burns had entered almost two hours earlier. Fragments of my memory were returning, kernel by kernel, each popping in my mind and dominating my conscious thought for an instant. The image of Jack Burns had come to me in a dream. I'd pictured him sitting next to his wife on the sofa while Yana and I interviewed the two of them about their daughter's murder. A solitary frame from that dream had repeatedly summoned my attention. I remembered thinking, *There's something wrong with this guy.* He seemed simple and yet troubled at the same time, at ease but nonetheless hiding something. I used the word *simple* because I had interviewed mentally challenged kids with poor coping skills who were easily riled. There was something about Burns that reminded me of them, as if he were struggling emotionally, enough to prompt me to check his history and subsequently pull his old file.

I'd been correct. Burns had been abducted and abused. I'd read and copied some of the case files before returning them to the evidence room. The evidence clerk recognized me and didn't bother to check my shield before asking me to sign the official register and chain of evidence receipt. He never checked the computer to verify that I was authorized to sign out evidence.

Burns, the poor man, had every right to act the way he had. He'd been abducted and sexually molested as a child, and no amount of time could heal the wounds he had suffered. Yet as much as I wanted to be sympathetic, I knew that the kind of abuse he'd suffered often gave rise to aberrant behavior. As I said, his image kept coming back to me. Call it a sixth sense if you will, but there was something about the man I needed to understand better.

Burns was a very basic kind of guy, a neighborhood handyman. He had been wearing a tool belt and carrying his toolbox when he entered the building. Whose apartment he was in and what he was repairing was unknown, but my gut told me to stick with him and so I had.

Another forty-five minutes passed before he emerged from the apartment house. Sometimes you can just sense when something is off with a person and this was definitely one of those times. I could see his face clearly enough to perceive that he looked upset. I sensed it in his expression and his posture as he hurried down the block.

What happened in there, Jack? What's gotten you so upset? As I'd said, he seemed like someone who could be gotten to easily. He could have had an argument with his customer over the work he did or the price he had charged, but either way, the man looked to be clearly agitated.

I started the engine and rolled slowly from the curb. Burns was moving quickly despite the weight of the large toolbox he carried with him. I didn't have to follow him far. He turned at the corner and entered a bar. It looked like one of those old eclectic neighborhood watering holes, one Burns was probably very familiar with—it looked like it was a hundred years old, replete with old neon Miller and Budweiser signs so worn that the lights were dull and darkened in selected spots. The Miller sign no longer read Miller High Life. It simply read Miller High, which probably drew in a great many customers.

I could see Burns through the window as he took a seat at the hardwood bar, ordered a shot, and quickly threw it back, no doubt to settle his nerves. A second shot followed, and yes, even a third.

He's good and rattled. That's for sure. Were I officially on the job, I could've sent in an undercover DT to chat him up and get a handle on what was eating at him, but the situation being what it was ... I'd have to go it alone. I took a couple of minutes to get my story together before getting out of the car and joining him at the bar.

"Mr. Burns."

He practically jumped off the barstool, then turned to me with an angry scowl on his face before recognition kicked in. "My God. Detective ..." His expression resolved into one of puzzlement when he remembered my name. "Chalice?"

"That's right."

"But I thought you'd been shot."

I was hoping that Burns wouldn't ask how long an injured cop needed to lie low before returning to active duty because I didn't want to make up some cock-and-bull story to explain why I was there. *Play it loose and cool,* I thought. "Yeah. It was lights out for a while, but I'm back. Okay if I sit down?"

"Yeah. Sure. I was really sorry to hear about what happened to you."

"Thanks."

"Damn scary thing—first my daughter and then you and your partner. That was right after you came from our apartment, right?"

I nodded.

"Sofia and I just couldn't believe it. It was about ten minutes after you and the other detective left—we heard sirens and ... we came downstairs to have a look and when we heard what happened ... it made us both physically ill. I can't believe the shooter hasn't been caught yet. The news used to cover the story all the time, but I haven't heard anything about it in a while."

"It's yesterday's news, I suppose. Serafina and us ... I guess there's always a new catastrophe du jour to fill the headlines, but we'll get them. We'll get them both and when we do ..."

"That why you're here?"

I couldn't confirm so I shrugged and looked away. There was now a glass of beer in front of Burns to go along with the three empty shot glasses. "Someone's thirsty. You okay?"

He seemed surprised by the question. "All right? Yeah, I'm all right. Why do you ask?"

"You're sucking up a lot of alcohol. Do you normally drink this much?"

"Um, no. I'm not an alcoholic or anything like that. I just feel like drinking is all. Been doing more of that ever since ..."

I shrugged. "I understand. How are you and Sofia dealing?" I placed my hand on his. "I know it can't be easy."

He looked into his glass. "Terrible thing, losing a kid like that. I don't think you can ever be the same afterwards. Do you, Detective?"

"I don't know, Jack. I really don't know how families get through something as difficult as this. I can't imagine anything worse."

"Sofia still cries herself to sleep every night."

I sighed. "I'm so sorry for you and Sofia." I called the bartender and ordered a ginger ale.

"No alcohol. I guess you're officially on duty?"

Redirect. Redirect. "It's not about that. I can't have any alcohol for a while on account of the Swiss-cheese treatment the bullet did to my head. I'm not even supposed to have caffeine and I'm a coffee-loving fanatic."

"Sorry. Does it still hurt?"

"Only when I think."

He grinned at the joke. "I should've come to visit you in the hospital," he said with regret. "You being Frank's kid and all. I still can't believe it. I'm sorry I never made it over there to see how you were doing."

"That's all right. I was asleep most of the time."

"Yeah. I heard on the news that you were in a coma for days. My wife, Sofia, and I said a prayer for you in church."

"And see? It worked. Thank you."

He took a sip of beer. "I think about your dad all the time. Frank Chalice was a good man and a dear friend." He paused momentarily. "I'm not sure if you know this, but I was attacked when I was a kid—got messed up real bad. After I came home from the hospital, your dad would stop by almost every day to see how I was. Not like my other fair-weather friends ..." He shook his head sadly. "What are you going to do? It's all water under the bridge now, I suppose. I still can't believe you're his kid. Small world, right?"

Three shots of hooch and a conversation chaser had settled Burns considerably, making it difficult to ask why he'd been so worked up. I eyed his toolbox next to him on the floor and shifted the conversation. "Just come from doing a job?"

"Yeah. Bathroom leak."

"Get it squared away?"

"Yeah, I got lucky. The leak was from the cold-water pipe, but I was able to get to it by taking out the medicine cabinet and didn't have to chop up the wall. Saved me a lot of wear and tear, but the place will still need fresh sheetrock and new tile under the sink. It was leaking for a long time and you know how it gets—everything got yellowed and rotted—stunk like hell. I should've been called much sooner."

The bartender poured a glass of soda from one of those mini bottles that didn't contain enough fluid to quench a hamster's thirst. I held the paltry glass at eyelevel. "What's *this* gonna do?" I complained lightheartedly.

"That's the only size we've got, but you're on the job, right?" the bartender asked.

"It's that obvious, is it?"

"You might as well be in uniform," he chuckled. "Don't worry, the ginger ale's on the house."

"In that case, thanks. Keep 'em coming."

He winked at me and moseyed off down the bar.

"How's the handyman business treating you, Jack?"

"Good. I've been getting a lot of calls since ..." He sighed. "I guess the neighbors feel sorry for us since everything happened. I suppose they figure we could use the money. Friends in the community took up a collection to pay for Serafina's funeral. That was really nice of them."

"So this was a neighbor's house you did the plumbing job for?" *Shoot.* I realized it was a cop question as soon as it came out of my mouth. I sounded as if I was probing him, and I could see him shutting down before my eyes.

"Yes," he said in a sober voice as he chugged down the rest of his beer. "Anything else I can help you with, Detective? I've got to be heading home. Sofia will be wondering what's keeping me so long, and she's afraid of being alone at night these days. You understand, don't you?"

"No. That's it. I'll let you know if I hear anything. Get home safe."

"You too, Detective." He threw some bills on the bar and picked up his toolbox. "You know, I was surprised you came around tonight. I mean, especially since Detective Lido stopped by to see me earlier in the day. The two of you don't speak to each other?" he asked suspiciously.

Shit! Reach down deep and think of something clever. "It's a big taskforce, Mr. Burns. I'm sorry if it feels like we're smothering you. I'll chat with the detective and we'll make sure we give you enough space."

"That's all right—I know you've got important work to do. I was just asking." He grinned uncomfortably, then turned and left immediately.

You're rusty, I told myself. I'd failed to learn why he'd been so upset, but made a mental note to keep an eye on him, because something about the man just wasn't sitting right.

Chapter Thirty-Three

Tiru's shop had closed hours earlier, yet Tiru was still there, leaning against the counter with an artist's pencil in his hand, dutifully creating a fresh design. His intricate tattoo designs required several hours of precision, painstaking sketch work, and he had never been one to rush the process. A book of seventeenth and eighteenth century art was open on the counter to lend inspiration. The image he studied was a *moku hanga*, a woodblock print, and the *ukiyo-e* subject matter was typical of the period and referred to as pictures of the floating world.

He was deep in concentration when the delicate clatter of the wind chime from the back room filtered through his ears. The sound was so subtle that he absorbed it without becoming alarmed. By the time he felt another presence in the room, it was too late for him to react save for the gasp of air that caught in his lungs.

He froze when he felt the cold razor-edged blade against his throat. He'd practiced the martial arts for years, but now at the age of sixty-eight, he lacked the confidence to strike. His unknown assailant stood behind him. He could feel the slightest trickle of blood run down his neck. He cursed himself for being caught off guard and for the years of inactivity that had most certainly taken their toll.

"Where do I find him?" he demanded. "Where do I find the man with the jade dragon on his back?"

Tiru immediately understood that he was being asked about his friend Haruki and knew his attacker was most certainly Ryo Goda, the customer he'd introduced to Haruki. He felt the blade cut slightly deeper, his assailant's response to the slow reply. "All I have is a phone number," he offered, knowing better than to play dumb with someone who was likely a yakuza assassin. He added, "I have it written on my pad near the register." His assailant was silent while another tense moment passed. All the while the sharp blade was held fast against his throat.

Tiru's gambit worked. As he anticipated, the blade was removed from his throat, and he was shoved in the direction of the cash register. It was the moment he'd been waiting for, and in that instant he garnered the courage to strike. He dropped down low and spun, his leg sweeping his assailant's legs out from beneath him. The assassin fell backwards. Tiru was on him before he could spring back to his feet, one hand on his throat, steadying it, while in the other the artist's pencil was clutched firmly in his grasp. His eyes widened when he confirmed that his attacker was, in fact, Ryo Goda, the customer whose arm he had recently tattooed with a snake and who had been in his shop when his old friend Haruki had come to visit.

Tiru possessed detailed knowledge of the human body, thus his blow was deadly accurate. He jabbed the pencil into the soft tissue of Ryo's neck just to the side of the trachea, puncturing the carotid artery. Blood surged forcefully from the wound. With fire burning in his eyes, Tiru watched the life drain from his enemy's body. He kept his hand in place around the man's throat, shackling Goda to the floor long after his life had fled. He finally felt the pounding in his chest begin to subside and rolled off his enemy into a pool of blood, panting, and trying to grasp what had just occurred.

Moments passed as thoughts raced through his mind and he worked to formulate a survival plan. He wondered if his enemy had come on his own, foolishly hoping to be a hero, or had he come on orders from another. His training had taught him to embrace the worst possible conclusion whether it was warranted or not. He had likely murdered a yakuza assassin and had imperiled himself and everyone he knew. Before collecting everything that was of value to him, he made a mental list of all the people he needed to warn, and left his shop for good.

Chapter Thirty-Four

Sofia stirred and opened her eyes just enough so that she could read the time on the alarm clock: one thirty a.m. She'd been sleeping poorly since her daughter's death and was prone to being awakened by even the slightest disturbance. She wasn't quite sure what had aroused her, but an ensuing thud made her query moot. She jumped up and looked around. In that instant she realized that she was alone in bed. "Jack?" she called out. "Jack." She threw on her robe and tiptoed to the bedroom doorway, where she could see her husband leaning over the kitchen sink, washing his hands. "You okay, papi?"

He looked up, trying to hide his emotions, but his expression divulged his distress. He quickly averted his eyes.

"What's wrong?" she asked.

"It's nothing. You should go back to sleep."

"What's going on, Jack?" She drew closer and saw that blood was swirling in the sink. "*Dios mio.*" She rushed to his side, her eyes widening. "You're bleeding. What happened?"

He had a white kitchen towel pressed against his hand. It was stained crimson. "It's nothing," he insisted.

"Let me see."

He slowly removed the towel, revealing a deep gash on his arm near the wrist.

"Oh my God—that's a deep cut. You have to go to the hospital, Jack."

"No. No hospital. It's not so bad. I'll bandage it up and it'll be fine."

She examined the wound and he gasped when she probed the area. "You need a tetanus shot and stitches. How'd this happen?"

"I don't know."

"You don't know?" she asked incredulously.

"I-I mean that I don't know what's happening to this neighborhood. I think maybe we have to move."

She read terror in his eyes and fought to stay strong. "Here, sit down and keep pressure on the wound. I'll get something to bandage it with." She hurried away, more shaken by her husband's apparent dread and confusion than by the injury he'd sustained. *First, Serafina and now this ... what's happening to us?* she wondered. *Will this ever end?* She returned to the kitchen with tears in her eyes, dried the wound, and began wrapping gauze around his wrist. "I want to know what happened," she said firmly. "Did someone do this to you?"

He nodded. "Some kids. They wanted my toolbox, but I pulled the hammer from my belt and they took off."

"But they cut you first? With a knife?"

He nodded again.

"We have to call the police."

"No! No police."

Sofia applied tape over the gauze. "It's still bleeding, Jack. You have to go to the hospital."

He averted his eyes but didn't respond.

"Jack, I'm talking to you. Did you hear me?" Another moment passed in silence. "Why aren't you answering me?" She stood up and dried her eyes. "Gloria. Gloria has a suture kit in her house."

"The nurse? You can't bother her at this hour. It's almost two o'clock in the morning."

"Either I wake her up, or we go to the hospital. That's your choice," she said with defiance. "I'm not going to let you bleed to death."

"All right. I'll go to the hospital, but I don't want anyone to know. You hear me. No one."

"But why, Jack? What's the big secret?"

"I just don't want any more pity is all. The way people look at us since Serafina died. I just can't take it anymore."

"How do you expect them to look at us? Our daughter was murdered. You expect smiling faces? My God, Jack, what's happened to you?"

"Nothing. Look, I'll go to the hospital, but when we get there, I'm saying it was an accident. I'll say I was cutting a piece of wood and the saw slipped. No police. Agreed?"

"Yes, all right, Jack. Give me two minutes to throw on my clothes." She hurried off.

Jack pressed on the bandage with added strength, hoping to stem the bleeding and avoid a trip to the hospital, but it didn't help, and he knew that one way or another, more blood would spill.

Chapter Thirty-Five

Gus looked in the bathroom mirror, trying to determine if he could get away without shaving. He rubbed his chin and felt his whiskers prickle the pads of his fingers. Premature five o'clock shadow would raise questions. "What's with the chin whiskers, Lido? You moonlighting as a porn star?" On and on it would go, one snide comment followed by another and another. His eyes burned from a night of fitful sleep, yet somehow he found the reserve to lather and drag a razor across his face.

Everything he saw reminded him that she was gone: the fragrance that still lingered on her pillow and the conspicuous absence of undergarments he routinely found on the floor in the morning. He saw her in Max's smile when he fed him breakfast and when he tucked him in at night. Even his gun was alone when he retrieved it from the lockbox that morning, where the two firearms normally rested side by side.

Ma had been a rock, caring for Max, cooking, shopping, cleaning, and keeping the family together during a very difficult time. She'd temporarily moved in to help during Stephanie's recovery and then to help keep the family together during her absence. She had breakfast ready for him the moment he sat down, not just breakfast, but a hearty meal, purposefully prepared to imbue the senses and lift the spirit—eggs, bacon, toast, and freshly brewed coffee that filled the apartment with aromatic heaven.

"You don't have to do all this, you know. Taking care of Max is a full-time job on its own."

"The hell I don't," she said as she sat down with a mug of coffee. "You're up all night trying to figure out the case. The least I can do is load the furnace so you've got the energy to make it through the day." She angled her head to examine him more carefully. "You did a hell of a job shaving this morning. Your beard looks like one of those sculpted English labyrinth gardens."

He smirked. "That bad, huh? I'll touch it up before I go."

Max was picking up Cheerios and putting them on his tongue one at a time.

"Your daddy forgot how to sleep," she said. "Your mommy made him crazy."

Max played with his lips before placing the next piece of cereal on the tip of his tongue.

"Who's on your hit list this morning?"

"Reginald Coffer."

A quaint smile overtook her face. "Oh my God, little stuttering Reggie. Why do you think he can help?"

Lido speared a cluster of eggs with his fork. "I'm not sure he can help at all, but I don't know where to focus and I figured additional background on Jack Burns might be helpful."

"I see," she said halfheartedly. The investigation was moving along at a snail's pace, which meant that in all likelihood her daughter wouldn't be coming home anytime soon. "Anything I can do to help?"

"Well, yeah, sure. The bathroom could use a fresh coat of paint and there's an intermittent drip under the kitchen sink," he quipped. "Aren't you doing enough already?" He grinned sadly and got choked up. "I don't know what we'd have done without you." He rose with a piece of toast in his hand and gave her a quick casual hug. "You really are the best, Ma, the absolute best."

"Bah. We're family. This is what family does." Tears began to well in her eyes in the next second. "My wonderful, beautiful daughter—I just don't understand her sometimes. How she could ..." She glanced at Max and quickly wiped away her tears. "I really wonder," she began in a whisper, "if the bullet changed her in some way—you know, affected her wiring. She's always been overzealous, but this ..." She glanced toward heaven. "God, please help me to understand my daughter," she implored.

"We'll get through this," Gus said, giving her a reassuring pat on the arm. "Stephanie's tested us before, hasn't she? It's always works out in the end."

She pulled a tissue out of the box and blew her nose. "I know, but ... don't ask me why, but I started thinking about her father last night, not Frank ... her biological father."

He frowned. "Clovin? Don't do that to yourself, Ma. There's no reason to believe—"

"That mental illness is hereditary? I looked it up on the computer and they say it is ... At least it can be."

"The Internet will make you crazy—you read up on any illness long enough and you'll end up convinced that you have it. Besides, Clovin's psychopathy came about as a result of hallucinogen abuse. Remember?"

"Thank you," she recalled with relief. "Yes."

"He was a guinea pig in an army testing program, for Christ's sake. They experimented on him with LSD, BZ, and God knows what else. He became dependent and ended up substance-abusing the rest of his life."

Ma was still sniffling. "I'm sorry I brought it up, but at least now I can put the worry out of my mind."

He smiled and said, "Anytime," but had to take a couple of deep breaths to calm himself down. *God, I wish she hadn't said that.* They'd been through so much already, and the idea that Stephanie might've inherited a mental illness from her biological father ... He pushed his plate away. "I can't finish."

"Oh, Señor. *What?* When was the last time you didn't have appetite enough to finish your breakfast?"

"I have to get my day started. The idea of sitting around while Stephanie's out there running around vigilante and all ... She's a damn good detective and I shudder to think about what she'll do if she finds the shooter first. I know that *I'd* have trouble with that decision." He stood up, grabbed Max's hand, and kissed it. "Make her smile, Max. Your nonni is under a lot of strain."

Her expression brightened. "I can shovel your breakfast into a sandwich and you can take it with you."

"All right, Ma, anything to make you happy. No doubt my appetite will return."

Chapter Thirty-Six

I sensed movement outside my hotel room door. My first instinct was to grab my gun, but then I thought, *Don't be so jumpy. It's probably some drunk trying to get into the wrong room.* I could see a shadow in the space beneath the door. *Harry?* I thought. The shadow drifted away and then returned. *Screw this. Like they say, 'an ounce of prevention'* ... I grabbed my LDA and made a move toward the door, advancing silently on the carpeted floor.

I took a position to the side of the door and listened attentively, but my visitor was silent. *Are you ready for this, girl?* I hadn't seen any real action in months. Sure, I'd fired a lightweight gun at the range, but there was no danger in shooting at a paper target. I silently unlocked the door, took a deep breath, and pulled it open.

An elderly man jumped when he saw me spring into the corridor and land in a combat stance with my gun pointed at him. For a split second it appeared that he might've entertained the notion of attacking me, but then his hands went straight up, signaling surrender. *Good move,* I thought. *You might be fast, but faster than a speeding bullet? You don't look like Superman to me, fella.*

Instead of saying, "Don't shoot," he blurted, "Haruki. Haruki."

"You're waiting for Haruki?"

He nodded. "Yes. Are you Chalice?"

"What other half-crazed woman would be running around with a gun drawn in the middle of the night?" He seemed to be having difficulty interpreting my rhetorical query. I continued to hold my gun on him. Knowing Haruki's name was one thing, but my training had taught me to be more thorough than that. "Yes. I'm Chalice. Who are you?"

He bowed politely. "I am Tiru, an old friend of Haruki-san."

"You have ID?"

"Yes."

"Show me."

He reached into his pocket.

"Slowly," I warned.

He cautiously removed his wallet and opened it. I viewed his driver's license through the clear plastic window and was able to confirm that he was, in fact, who he said he was. He slid a business card out for me to see. It read: Tiru's Traditional Tattoo and Body Piercing. Tiru Kondo, Proprietor. The card also noted the store address in lower Manhattan.

Harry suddenly appeared in the corridor behind Tiru, saw us, and came running. "He's cool, Chalice. He's a friend."

I lowered my gun. "*You're* out late. I fell asleep waiting for you."

"Unavoidable," Harry quickly offered. "Let's get out of the hallway."

"Yeah. Good idea." I closed the door after they entered the room and flipped on the lights. "All right, boys, what's the deal?"

Harry slung his backpack over the chair. "Tiru is an old friend of the family. Yana and I have known him since we were young. He's volunteered to help us find the shooter."

I didn't want to sound skeptical, but that's the way it came out. "It's two o'clock in the morning—he's one hell of a volunteer." Shrugging, I added, "Does he plan on tattooing the perp into submission?"

The quip was completely lost on Tiru, but Harry knew what I was getting at. "Tiru is far more than a tattoo artist, Chalice. He's very highly trained in the martial arts. We have a lead we want to follow up on immediately."

"That's such a relief," I said sarcastically.

Tiru quickly glanced at Harry. There was something in his gaze that told me Harry wasn't exactly on the up and up. I wasn't sure why Harry felt the need to be dishonest, but probe him, I would. *Okay,* I thought, *I'll help you dig your own hole.* "Great! What did you find out?" I picked up on another of Tiru's worried glances. Apparently he was far less comfortable with dishonesty than his old family friend.

"We understand that Rodrigo Sanchez might be leaving the country. It's not out of the question to suppose that he may be trying to flee before he gets pinned for the shooting."

"Do you know where he is?"

"No," Harry replied. "I have someone else running down that lead."

"Well, give me a few minutes to get myself together and I'll go with you."

Harry remained cool, but I could see that Tiru was still sweating it out.

"That may not be a good idea," Harry said. "Our contact ... he's not a very trusting person. I'm afraid that if he sees a gaijin, he might spook and take off."

"What's a gaijin?"

"It's slang for foreigner."

I'm a foreigner? Me? He has got to be kidding?

Harry bowed his head. "I didn't mean to insult you, Chalice. Surely you can understand that you'd be considered an outsider."

Whatever. This is a cock-and-bull story anyway. It was clear that Harry had his own agenda and that it was now them against me. "Stay in touch, Harry," I said in an offhand manner. "I'm going back to bed."

Harry slipped his key card out of his pocket and laid it on the small desk. "Tiru and I will find another place to stay. This room is far too cramped for the three of us."

"Will I hear from you again, Harry?"

"Why, yes, of course. I'll keep you up to speed on everything, Chalice." He held up the burner phone I'd given him as a symbol of open communication.

There was no hiding the sarcasm in my voice. "Marvelous." I locked the door after they were gone, and got back into bed, but didn't sleep. All of Harry's cagey ninja shit was really starting to get to me.

Chapter Thirty-Seven

Prior to being wounded, I had searched the NCAVC database for murders with similar MOs to that of Serafina Ramirez. I had gotten two hits and was just now ready to revisit those cases. One of the two hits was a student at Rutgers University in New Jersey. The second was a housewife from Jamaica, New York. Serafina had been raped and murdered, which is a somewhat common MO, but what made her case unique was the way in which she had been posed and strangled.

She'd been found in an unoccupied loft with her wrists tied to the foot posts of a standard double bed. The medical examiner had assessed that Serafina had been raped repeatedly over the course of a few days. Her stomach was empty at the time of autopsy, demonstrating that she hadn't eaten for at least forty-eight hours prior to expiring. She was found naked, on her knees, and bent over an unfinished four-foot-long blanket trunk firmly secured to the foot posts of the bed it was contiguous with. A pillow separated her face and tender skin from the raw wood panels.

Five-millimeter-wide woven straps, like the ones used by movers to hoist heavy appliances, were used to tightly bind her wrists to the bedposts, and a long length of strap was looped around her neck and knotted. A broomstick had been broken in half. The broken broomstick had been passed through the strapping material and tightened like a tourniquet. Variations in the ligature patterns indicated that the tourniquet had been tightened and released multiple times during the period of her captivity. The ME's had postulated that the tightening of the tourniquet coincided with the multiple rapes that had taken place until a merciful end finally ended the torture.

And the standard-size bed?

Serafina's DNA was not found anywhere on the bed sheets or pillowcases. She'd spent days on her knees, repeatedly raped and suffocated, and at night she was forced to watch while her assailant slept peacefully.

The analogous crimes had not been solved. The attack in New Jersey had taken place a year back and the Queens assault happened the year prior. I decided to start with the fresher case. These were interviews I had planned to carry out when I first began investigating Serafina's murder and certainly would've done so at that time had a bullet not embedded itself in my gray matter.

The Eldridges were broken people. They looked like two adoring parents torn to pieces by the murder of their daughter, who'd been not just murdered, but raped and abused. I could see distress in their postures as they got out of the car, a Volvo Cross Country that was still caked with winter salt and probably hadn't seen the inside of a carwash tunnel in over a year—funny how simple little things like that cease to matter after the spirit is destroyed. I watched them trudge along the path to their front door with their heads hanging like branches on a weeping willow. It looked like the weight of the entire world was literally bearing down on their shoulders.

I'd picked a bad day to visit, the anniversary of their daughter Lara's murder. I gave them fifteen minutes to cool their heels before ringing the doorbell.

They were quite vocal as they approached the door.

"Richard, you can't blame your cousin for not coming to the cemetery. He has the flu."

"He has the flu? This year it's the flu. Last year it was an important prior commitment. I mean, Christ, he missed the goddamn funeral because ... Ah shit, I can't even remember the bullshit excuse he made up."

"He sent beautiful flowers to the chapel."

"He can take the flowers and shove them right up his goddamn ass. Let him get off his fat keister and pay his respects like a loving family member is supposed to."

The door flew open suddenly.

"Yes?" Richard Eldridge asked impatiently.

"Sorry to disturb you, Mr. Eldridge. I'm Detective Chalice. I phoned for an appointment."

"Right," he huffed. "All right, come on in. I completely forgot. You picked a hell of a day to pay us a visit. This is the anniversary of—" His head dropped and then he ushered me into the house without completing the sentence.

"Won't you please come in?" Elaine Eldridge said, making a concerted effort to remain pleasant. "We're only home a few minutes."

"Yes. I understand today marks the one-year anniversary of your daughter's death. I'm so terribly sorry for your loss."

"I'm surprised to see you here, Detective," she said. "We read that you were shot by a sniper and that you were in a coma."

I rapped lightly on the side of my head. "Thankfully we Chalices have hard heads. I received some truly excellent care from great doctors and bounced right back."

"Thank God," she concurred.

The parlor was beautifully decorated and it was evident that one or both of them had a flair for interior design. Somehow, though, the atmosphere seemed gloomy. With the lights off and only gray daylight filtering through the windows, shadows darkened the color of the painted walls, transforming them from an eye-pleasing cedar green to a drab olive. We sat across from each other on opposite sides of a coffee table.

"Did he attack someone else?" he asked.

I closed my eyes and nodded. "I believe so. It wasn't shared with the press, but the MO was virtually identical to your daughter's murder and the murder of Nina Stoffer in Queens."

"Son of a bitch. So what now, they're going to let him get away with this forever? Every television station has a dozen programs on CSI and true crime. With all that accumulated knowledge they can't capture the animal who murdered our daughter?"

"We're doing everything we can to put him away, Mr. Eldridge."

"Of course you are," he said in a cynical tone. "Meanwhile the police department is going to waltz into our home once a year asking the same questions they asked when our Lara was killed. How many times are you going to rub salt in the wound, detective? How many times are you going to put us through this misery?"

"I'm sorry. I can't imagine the pain you're living with."

"No. You can't," he stated emphatically. "So let's make this fast."

"No one ever thinks something like this can happen to them," she said. "You read about this kind of thing in the papers and people talk about it, but you just can't imagine a tragedy like this touching you or one of your loved ones, and then after it does ..." She began to sniffle. "It's as if your life has been stolen. You breathe, you eat, and you sleep, but you're not really alive anymore. You just exist. In many ways it's worse than dying." She dabbed at her tears with a tissue. "All right, dear, what would you like to know?"

"Your daughter attended Rutgers University, is that correct?"

"Dean's list five semesters running, until some piece of garbage stole her life," Mr. Eldridge said. "Two years, three dead women, and they still have no idea who's doing this?" He shook his head. "It's a disgrace."

"And it was there that her body was found?"

"Backstage in the auditorium." He pointed to the coffee table. It was a lovely piece made of antique cherrywood with a tinted glass center panel. "See that, Detective? We used to use an antique trunk for a coffee table, but we had to get rid of it because every time we looked at it we were reminded about what happened to Lara."

Lara had been found in the same state that Serafina Ramirez had been found, naked and bound in such a manner that she could not get off her knees. Her assailant had used a vintage actor's trunk to prop her up. She was fixed in place, doggie style, as the *playuhs* call it. In place of woven straps, her wrists were bound with men's loudly striped silk neckties, which, like the trunk, had been used in the school production of *The Wizard of Oz*. The bastard had a macabre sense of humor. He'd tied her up with the wizard's neckties and bound her to the prop trunk that contained the cowardly lion's medal of courage, the tin man's heart-shaped clock, and the scarecrow's university degree. The killer's elaborate tableaus left little doubt that he was severely twisted. I was surprised he hadn't forced her to wear Dorothy's ruby slippers. A third garish necktie had been used to fashion the tourniquet around her neck. A wizard's magic wand replaced the broomstick that had been used to tighten the loop around Serafina's neck.

It appeared that there was a tie-in between the victim and the accoutrements the killer used to bind and murder each of them. Serafina's mother was a cleaning woman and he used a broom and mover's straps on her. The killer exploited Lara's love for theater by using stage props in his murderous montage.

"The assailant is meticulous. He never leaves behind any DNA. In general, serial rapists have grown adept at concealing their identities. They cover their hair and wear gloves. They use condoms and dress in microfiber clothing."

"What galls me is that this never should've happened," Mr. Eldridge said. "They had a year to catch this creep after he attacked the woman in Queens. If the police had done their job, Lara would still be alive and you wouldn't be here reminding us of our loss."

"I understand that you're bitter, Mr. Eldridge, and I'm sorry there's nothing I can do to bring your daughter back, but I'll try my damndest to prevent someone else's daughter from suffering the same grisly fate."

"Fine," he said with anger in his voice. "What do you think we can tell you that will help you crack the case? We've been over this with the authorities dozens of times."

"All right. Settle down," his wife said as she patted his leg. "Try to be helpful, Richard."

"I'm waiting to hear a question," he grumbled.

"I understand that Lara and the others were in the auditorium rehearsing for an upcoming performance. Why didn't they wait for her before leaving for the evening? Why did they leave her alone? I mean, it was late at night, and I understand there are warning signs all over campus for students to avoid situations that might put them in harm's way."

"Because there was no such thing as good enough for Lara. She had to be the best. She had to be perfect. Her friends used to wait for her, but they got tired of doing so rehearsal after rehearsal and after a while ..." She shrugged and I could see that she was trying not to cry. "It was hardly the first time she stayed after everyone else had left the auditorium. She was overzealous ... fanatical." She sniffled and looked into my eyes. "Do you know anyone like that, Detective?"

It was the last question I needed to be asked. I'd been feeling terribly guilty about disappearing on my family. Her question and the sadness in her eyes brought it all crashing down on me. I felt my heart begin to thump. "I see. So there was a history of her being there alone at night. Her attacker likely knew about her habit of working after everyone else was gone and had readied the trunk along with all the props he'd need for his assault."

There are messages that you hear over and over again but don't truly grasp or see vividly until it's offered in a particular way. It seemed that I had painted that vivid picture the Eldridges had not yet been exposed to, and it had evoked all manner of painful memory. Elaine Eldridge began to sob once again and I could see that her husband was seething. He shut his eyes and clenched his fists, no doubt praying for the good Lord to place Lara's attacker in front of him so that he could crush the man's throat with his bare hands. He must've needed to channel his anger in a physical manner because he abruptly slammed his fist on the wooden edge of the coffee table with such force that the leg cracked, the table collapsed, and the center glass shattered.

"*Richard,*" his wife shrieked. "Dear God. What are you doing?"

"Sorry. Sorry. I—" He was ashamed of his actions, but froze when he saw the expression on my face. "Are you all right, Detective? I didn't mean to upset you."

I tried to answer him but couldn't. My throat was frozen and my body was twitching with spasms. It wasn't just the shattered table that had set me off. It was the surge of guilt and ... I suddenly realized that I'd forgotten to take my meds before leaving the hotel in the morning. My back tensed and I slid off the couch. I closed my eyes just before my face made contact with the crippled cherrywood coffee table.

Chapter Thirty-Eight

Thank God. The Eldridges had called 911 and summoned an ambulance. Yes, the police responded to the call as well but only to assist and provide support for the EMS team. I'd been attended to in the ER for minor wounds, put through a battery of tests, sedated, and put to bed. I slept well into the evening only to wake up to find a visitor in my room. "Oh shit!"

"Busted," Gus said with an unpleasant grimace on his face.

"You startled me."

"Do I have to handcuff you to the bed, or are you going to be civil?"

Gus was clearly unhappy so I figured I'd jest in order to diffuse some of the tension. "You can use manacles if you're planning to use a pair of those kinky, leather-laced, *Fifty Shades of Grey* handcuffs, and you've brought along a cat-o'-nine-tails and a bottle of lube. I've been *bad*, really bad."

"Not funny, Stephanie. Not funny in the slightest."

"*I* thought it was humorous."

"It's hardly the time or the place."

Got it. It's not a laughing matter. I nodded, expressing my understanding of our dire predicament, the difficult situation I was responsible for creating.

"What *the hell* did you do to your hair?" he asked hotly.

His question took me by surprise. With all that had recently transpired, I'd forgotten that I now had short blond hair, a look that must've shocked the hell out of my husband. "Oh, this," I replied as I examined a golden lock of hair. "You don't like it?"

"I didn't say that. I'm just trying to understand who the hell you are."

"I'm still me, Gus, same old whacky Stephanie Chalice. I didn't want to be recognized. I figured I'd be visiting crime scenes and conducting interviews and I didn't want to be spotted."

"Spotted by whom?" he asked angrily. "By me?"

"No. By ... Shit! Yes, by you," I confessed. "I needed to see this through, and frankly ... well, I knew you wouldn't let me do it."

"Wait until Max sees you," he grumbled. "Christ, wait until Ma sees you. She's going to take a fit. When the hell did you become Mata Hari?"

"I thought you'd like it. I thought it would make for some great role-playing sex after this cop-killer business was well behind us."

"Ah, come on—don't patronize me. So what happened, Stephanie?" he asked in a somber voice. "How'd you end up in the emergency room?" I could see that he was emotionally worn and ready to snap. His eyes were red and he looked exhausted.

Christ, I lamented. *What did I put him through?*

I shook my head woefully. "Somehow I missed a dose of medication. There was a bit of commotion during the interview I was on, and I guess the combination set me off."

His face tightened. I think he wanted to cry, but he managed to hold back the tears. "What am I going to do with you?" He sniffled, then bent over and kissed me.

I put my arms around his neck and locked him in. "You can't say I haven't made your life interesting." I kissed him on the cheek and let him go. "How did Ma take the news of me being in the hospital?"

"Your mother is the best, the absolute best. She hasn't let anything come in the way of taking care of Max or me. I honestly don't know where she finds the strength." As much as he was lauding my mother, he was also giving me a dig because I had created the difficult situation. "How did she take it? More relieved than freaked out, I suppose. You do understand that we were both worried you'd turn up dead, either from the brain injury or from charging headfirst into a wolves' den."

"Gus, I really am sorry, but as I said, it was something I had to prove to myself, and I wasn't going to sit idly by while Yana's killer slipped through our fingers and disappeared forever."

He rolled his eyes. "I'm just grateful that we found you in one piece. The doctor is going to release you in the morning. You were lucky as hell that you didn't do additional damage to your brain when your head hit the table."

"I've logged more hours in an MRI tunnel than I care to admit, but my brain is wired pretty tightly. I'll be okay."

"Thank God." He rapped on the end table that wasn't made of real wood, but it was hardly the time to split hairs. "You're lucky the incident took place in New Jersey. If it had happened in one of the five boroughs, executive command would've come down on you like a ton of bricks. I called in a favor to keep a copy of the report from going to NYPD. The last thing you need right now is to be brought up on disciplinary charges."

"You actually know someone in New Jersey?"

He didn't laugh. "Just say thank you."

"Thank you," I said with the utmost sincerity.

"All the thanks in the world won't get you out of the bind you're in with me. What you did was unthinkably reckless and selfish. How could you just up and disappear on your family like that, especially with what you've been through, what we've all been through? Neither Ma nor I have been able to sleep for days, not knowing where you were or what you were doing. We didn't know if you were dead or alive."

"Easy, Gus. I get it, I really do, but you know full well that I'm a big girl and that I can take care of myself."

"Like you did today?" he replied indignantly. "You lost your shit at a piece-of-cake interview while sitting on a comfy sofa. What if you had been in a dangerous situation when the seizure took place? We'd be holding services for you right now. I don't want to be a widower, damn it, and your son deserves to grow up with his mother. Shit, Stephanie. How could you? Do you know what you put us through?"

"I'm so sorry, Gus, but you wouldn't let me do *anything*. You wouldn't let me turn on the goddamn computer, for Christ's sake, and you know damn well that I can't live like that. I had to prove to myself that I'm not an invalid."

"You're certainly not an invalid, Stephanie, far from it, but you're not the same as you were before, and you're going to have to learn to accept the hand life has dealt you. You were shot. Your brain was damaged and you have a seizure disorder. Under the right circumstances, none of that will have any bearing on your future, but as a headstrong, risk-taking cop ... I just don't see how you can expect to go on business as usual. I know that you don't want to die." He looked into my eyes. "You don't, do you?"

"Of course I don't, but I can't live like I'm some kind of porcelain doll that'll crack if you touch it the wrong way. I'd rather live a short life on my own terms than a never-ending one as some kind of inert and fragile woman, and I can't deal with everyone watching me and waiting for me to come apart at the seams."

"Looking back, maybe I was a little too tough on you, but the doctors were insistent that you got lots of peace and quiet, and they expressly said to limit your time watching TV and on the computer. I was determined to keep you calm whether you liked it or not."

"But I wasn't calm. Maybe my activities were limited and you controlled my environment, but I wasn't calm. I was anything *but* calm. I couldn't remember what happened when Yana and I were shot, and I was forbidden to do anything about tracking down the shooter. You think I wanted to go rogue? Of course I didn't, but I would've exploded if I didn't get out from under you and Ma." I looked into his eyes imploringly, fighting back tears. "Don't you understand?"

He sighed and rubbed his eye. "Yeah," he muttered. "Unfortunately I do." He sat down on the bed next to me. "I've had a lot of time to think about what I'd do when I found you and … Look, I want you to live a long life, Steph, but I think it's more important for you to be happy. No one can guarantee longevity or good health or … shit, no one can guarantee anything of real importance. So this is what I've decided. We do this together, me as the cop and you in an unofficial capacity. If anyone asks, you're a department consultant until you're officially reinstated, and if I get run off the force for misconduct, well then, shit … so be it."

Tears were running down my cheeks. "At least you'll be able to get some sleep at night."

"And Ma will get to stuff you with lasagna."

He extended his hand for me to take. "We're partners again," he said, "for better or for worse."

I was senior to Gus on the homicide squad by just over a year. I should've left well enough alone but I just couldn't help myself. "Remember," I reminded him. "I'm lead."

Chapter Thirty-Nine

After entering the Shinto temple, Chef Maeda ritualistically stopped at the fountain to cleanse his hands and rinse his mouth. He bowed twice and clapped his hands twice with the tips of his right fingers just slightly below the fingertips of his left. He bowed once more before approaching the shrine. He'd felt a strong need to pray and to unify himself with Japan's ancient past. He'd felt unsettled for days before coming to the conclusion that he'd been lax and had not visited the shrine in weeks. He hoped that the growing emptiness he felt would shrink after communing with the gods.

His father had always taught him to ask only for what was needed, so all he asked for was continued good health and to restore the emotional balance he felt had been off-kilter. He'd been friends with Haruki since the age of fifteen and still felt a strong connection with him even though he'd not seen or heard from him in many years. More than that, he felt indebted to him for helping his parents settle a dispute, one they wouldn't have been able to overcome without his assistance.

Before leaving the temple he purchased an *omikuji* and took a moment to read the fortune and reflect on the sage wisdom of the poem. "If we falter in resolve ... Just because the task is hard no accomplishment can follow. It is the world's way," Emperor Meiji.

He thought immediately of Haruki and the request he'd made, a request he was honor-bound to complete. He'd been called upon to assist him in finding his brother's killer, thereby restoring harmony and balance to his life.

"*Doki. Doki,*" he whispered, words to emulate the thumping of his heart. He'd been slow to respond to his friend's request and reengage in a life he'd long ago abandoned. There was no question in his mind as to who he had to call upon in order to obtain the information Haruki sought, but he had hesitated in taking action. As he stepped out of the shrine into the sunlight he felt riddled with guilt and dishonor for delaying his friend's act of vengeance. Glancing skyward, he formally apologized to the gods for dishonoring them, "*Makoto ni moushiwake gozaimasen deshita.*"

Before proceeding, he typed the address of the man Haruki sought and quickly sent him a text message. He sighed deeply with relief for completing his assignment and had barely taken a step when a knife sliced through his neck. He clutched his throat in a feeble attempt to preserve his life, then fell to his knees as his life forces ebbed away. As his surroundings narrowed into a narrow band of light, he heard the screams of onlookers and the rapid steps of his assailant, desperate to escape.

Chapter Forty

"Tell me about Reginald Coffer." The rental car company had picked up the car I'd been driving, and we were now on our way back into Manhattan in Gus' cruiser. We just gotten off the George Washington Bridge and were headed southbound.

"So we're getting right into it, are we?"

"No time like the present." It felt good to be back with Gus, but I had to admit that I felt strong tension between us, tension that would probably take a long while to dissipate. In the scope of things, I guess that wasn't too bad. I couldn't blame him for being pissed, and I guess men had considered divorcing their wives for smaller stunts than the one I had pulled. I couldn't ignore the uneasiness—it felt as if I was expecting the other shoe to drop, a big smelly worn-out shoe, and with it some devastating announcement like, "Steph, when this is over, *we're over*. I love you, but living with you is just too hard for me." It wasn't a particularly thrilling prospect to look forward to.

"So what about Coffer?" I asked.

"He recently got a job as a building manager. Never married. Lives alone in a basement apartment."

"So no red flags?"

"Not even a checkered one."

"You mean checkered as in the flags they use to start a road race?"

"*No.* I mean checkered as a metaphor for a checkered past, bulletbrain," he snickered.

Well, wasn't that sweet? Bulletbrain was an apt description of my recent injury as well as a sarcastic allegory for being slow on the uptake and it stung. *My road-race comment had been a quip and he knew it.* It was becoming obvious that he harbored lots of animosity over my disappearing act. *You brought this on yourself, kid. Take your lumps and deal with it.* "So he's clean?"

"He appears to be. He came across as a humble guy. Said he'd been homeless for a while and was thankful he'd recently landed the superintendent's gig because the job came with a rent-free apartment."

"You obviously got to Coffer because of the childhood connection he had with Jack Burns."

"And your dad."

"Yeah," I reflected. "I couldn't believe that one either."

"When did you pull his file?"

"It was one of the first things I did after hitting the streets. I've started to get flashes of memory from the day of the shooting, and one of the things that came back first was the interview Yana and I had with Burns. I just remembered him being very odd. That and his having known my dad ..."

"Can you blame him for being strange, I mean, after all he's been through? He was molested as a child and then his adopted daughter was ..." He shook his head woefully. "Is it any wonder he's strung out?"

"No. Not really. That kind of trauma can damage you for life. I caught up with him the other night. He'd just come from doing a job, and I guess he needed to blow off some steam—knocked down three scotches and was draining a tall beer after I saw him entering the corner bar. He seems like a man with a lot of worries on his mind."

"I don't see Burns as a murderer, though. You?"

"Not in a million years, but he knows something. It's bothering him and I can't help feeling that it's something that might help us with the case."

"Yeah. I'm with you on that one. I paid him a call and he gave me the bum's rush when I asked if revenge could've been the motivation for Serafina's murder."

"Yeah. He's touchy that way. So Coffer didn't have any insights for you?"

"Nothing we didn't already know."

We had the police radio turned down low. Partially because we were too far away to respond to any calls and partially because Gus was afraid that too much loud radio chatter might fry my delicate corpus callosum and send me into apoplexy while we were crossing the Hudson River. However, something came over the radio that caught my attention. A man described as Asian had been attacked in front of a Japanese temple on the Upper East Side and was dead at the scene. "We need to take that," I said with urgency.

Gus frowned. "Why, you don't have enough on your plate? You want to grab someone else's case too? Let the up DT run with it."

"No. You don't understand. We have to go."

"I need a reason," he insisted.

"Harry's in town and he's been helping me track down the shooter."

"I know a lot of Harrys. Which Harry are we talking about?" he asked in a sharp tone.

"Yana's brother. He took leave from his job in Japan and came over to help find his brother's killer."

"Oh fuck. Really, Stephanie? It's not bad enough that you've gone all Rambo on us, do we need a vigilante Japanese cop running outside the law as well? When were you going to tell me?"

"As soon as you calmed down a little," I retorted. "Listen, Gus, can you lay off me long enough for us to do some righteous investigating? I know you're pissed and you have every right to be, but the angry-husband thing just isn't helping us get the job done. You can lay into me as soon as the shooter is behind bars."

He glared at me and then finally acquiesced. "Fine. Read me the address. We'll go have a look."

Chapter Forty-One

"It's not him?" Gus asked.

"No. Thank God. It's not Harry." The victim appeared to be Asian, but looked completely different. The crime scene unit was busily snapping pictures and assessing blood spatter. We'd arrived before the assigned detective had gotten to the scene. The temple was in our jurisdiction and I recognized the cop on duty. "Steigler," I hollered. "You causing trouble?"

"Hey, Chalice," he began with a grin. "How's the noggin?" he replied as he walked over with his arms spread for a hug.

"*Fantastic.* You haven't lived until you've had your head ventilated by a small-caliber slug."

"I didn't realize you were back in action already. I mean, it hasn't been that long. I'd have milked the bejesus out of it if I were you."

"I'm just helping out unofficially. What happened here anyway?"

"I didn't see it go down, Chalice. I was around the corner, paying the rent, when I heard people screaming."

I grimaced. "Paying the rent? You were writing traffic tickets? Shit. Let the meter maids do that."

He shrugged. "What can I tell you? Some white-shirt decision came down from on high and now our unofficial quote has become an official quota—no one get a pass."

"Jesus, what a waste of resources. So anyway, I presume that you heard screams and ran around the corner with your summons book drawn, is that it? Then what?"

He chuckled. "I saw a man down. I checked for vitals and radioed for a bus. I didn't see the perp."

"Witnesses?"

Steigler pointed to a small group of people loitering about in front of the Shinto temple. "They're waiting for someone to take their statements."

"Any of them get a good look at the assailant?"

"One guy saw the perp running straight at him." He pulled out his notepad and read back his notes, "Heavyset Asian male, black leather jacket, crew cut, tattoo on the left side of his neck."

"Sounds like the witness got a pretty good look at the perp. What kind of tattoo was it?"

"He wasn't sure. He said it could've been a red serpent or animal head of some kind sticking out above the guy's shirt collar. He already offered to work with a sketch artist."

"Don't you just love helpful law-abiding citizens?"

"Yeah, Chalice, I love 'em to death, and just to show my heartfelt appreciation, I just issued tickets to about thirty of them. Life's a bitch, ain't it?"

"You know it."

"Another witness said he saw the victim come out of the temple. The perp came up behind the victim and slit his throat."

"ID?"

"I was waiting for a DT to check it."

"Mind if I have a look?"

"You're a DT, aren't you? Guess it's my bad for not asking if the case was assigned to you. Help yourself, Chalice. Just put everything back the way you found it."

I slipped on blue gloves and introduced myself to the lead crime scene tech before checking the victim for a wallet. His business card stated that his name was Aguri Maeda, a sushi chef at Restaurant Kanpeki. I had just made a note of his address when I spotted the CBS News truck coming up the avenue and didn't want to be in a position to be questioned by a nosey reporter. I put his card back into the wallet and the wallet back into his pocket before getting back into the car with Gus.

Gus seemed much calmer than before I'd gotten out to check the scene. *Maybe he's over it,* I thought. *Nah, it's too soon—he's just cutting me a break.*

"How'd it go?"

"I'm not sure."

"What did you hope to find?"

"I really don't know. I just wanted to make sure it wasn't Harry. Guess I have a guilty conscience. He's just trying to help me and I don't want him to become the next victim."

"You know that you really shouldn't be encouraging him, Steph. He could get brought up on charges for vigilantism. Even if the charges don't stick, it could ruin his career in Japan."

"Trust me, he's much more concerned about avenging his brother's death than he is about his career. You know all that stuff they say about the Japanese and their sense of honor?"

"Yeah?"

"Well, it's all true." I took a moment before dropping the next bomb. "Besides, he's in the wind."

"What?"

"He's doing things his own way. He played nice for the first couple of days, but then he went his own merry way. He's got a friend over here and they've become some kind of Batman and Robin team. Actually he alluded to the fact that he's got several associates over here, so I guess he's forming his own Justice League."

"I don't get it, Steph. He thinks he can accomplish more on his own than he can working with you?"

"Yeah. That's the gist of it. I'm yesterday's news, a wounded lady cop who can't take charge of her own vendetta. He told me his friends wouldn't cotton to working with an interloper. Actually the word he used was *gaijin*. It means foreigner."

"You?" He laughed. "You're about as foreign as apple pie."

"Yeah, I get that, but I'm not Japanese. He said that his friends are touchy that way."

"But you can contact him if you need to, correct?"

"Yeah. I gave him a burner phone and I'm hoping he hasn't tossed it." I turned to take in the crime scene in front of the temple. A detective from our squad had just arrived and was getting the lay of the land from Steigler. "I think I'll let Harry know about the stabbing."

"And why do you think he'll give a shit?"

"Just a hunch, but something tells me he will. One of the witnesses said the perp had a tattoo on his neck, rising out from under his shirt collar."

"So?"

"Harry's friend is a tattoo artist. Maybe he'll be able to recognize the handiwork."

"From an artist's sketch? That's a long shot, babe. I don't see it."

It probably meant little to Gus, but he'd called me "babe," which was his go-to designation for addressing me. I was probably making more out of it than I should have, but it did seem as if some of his venom was gone and it made me smile inwardly. "You're probably right, but it can't hurt to keep him in the loop. Besides, it gives me an excuse to check in on him."

He cranked the engine. "Go to it," he said with a shrug. "Next stop, home ... Max, Ma, and a spaghetti Bolognese. It's chow time at the O.K. Corral."

Chapter Forty-Two

Gus was correct. My return home was akin to the gunfight at the O.K. Corral. No actual bullets, of course, but lots of stink-eye how-could-you? glances and petty cheap shots at my expense. Fortunately, Max was not one to hold a grudge. He delighted in playing with me, ate a huge lunch, left an impressive specimen in his diaper, and went down for a nap so that the grown-ups could have at it.

"I'm going to get you an ankle bracelet," Ma swore.

"With charms and lockets?" I snickered.

"No. A goddamn tether like the ones they use for house arrests."

"A ball and chain works just as well and costs a hell of a lot less. Oh wait," I said, turning to Gus. "I've already got one of those."

He grimaced and flipped me a tiny little bird, a semi-polite one.

"She's going to be all right," Ma said. "She's just as feisty and rude as ever."

I sneered at her. "The apple doesn't fall far from the tree."

"Now explain the hair," she snapped. "What the hell were you thinking? Your beautiful long brown hair." She did the biting-the-knuckle-utterly-exasperated thing. "I think you've lost your mind. It's a wonder your son even knows who you are."

"He'd know me if I were bald. Besides, he likes me with flashy blond hair. Kids are like fish—they're attracted to shiny objects."

"*Madonna*, you've never heard of a wig? For God's sake, Stephanie Marie Chalice, I hope you donated your hair to Locks of Love so that some poor sick child benefits from it."

It was a great suggestion, alas one that hadn't occurred to me while I was in the throes of clipping my hair. I bowed my head shamefully. "You're right. That would've been the right thing to do."

"Bah," she blurted with irritation, then walked into the kitchen and returned with a huge bowl of pasta. She placed it next to a dressed salad that was already on the table. "I'm warming garlic bread in the oven. Let's sit down to a good meal and talk like a family ought to."

"I'm all for that," Gus said. "Especially the good meal part."

"Amen!" Salad is always eaten last in an Italian household and my folks had always eaten their courses in that order. Gus had no complaints because it meant he could dive right into the pasta without wasting time on the salad, which for him was tantamount to mealtime foreplay, and Gus was a let's-get-straight-to-it kind of guy. I dished out three heaping servings of spaghetti. "Um, so good," I said with a mouthful of food. In our house, talking with your mouth full wasn't considered rude, not when the meal was so delicious that you couldn't help but offer praise.

"Attitude—check. Appetite—check. My girl's back," Ma said with a brimming smile. She pushed the garlic bread my way. "I want to be mad at you, but I'm just so happy to see you eating with such gusto. *Manga*, my pretty little blond-haired *gavone*."

A strand of spaghetti was hanging over the edge of my dish, which for some reason reminded me of limp wiener. "Hey," I began with exuberance. "Why doesn't the GEICO gecko have a wife or children?"

Ma and Gus looked at one another. They turned to me and shrugged, but they were already smiling.

"He's suffering from *e-reptile* dysfunction."

Gus snorted and wine came out of Ma's mouth. She pounded the table with the palm of her hand. "That's my *girl*."

We ate the rest of our meal with smiles on our faces.

"I've got a present for you," Gus said.

"A puppy?"

"Better. It'll keep you busy all day and it won't pee on the carpet. I brought home the case file on the Nina Stoffer homicide."

"Oh, great. Thanks. Seriously, though ... no puppy?"

He'd finished his pasta and was eyeing the salad dispassionately. "I never asked you. Did you get anything useful out of the Eldridges?"

I shook my head. "No. I hit them on a bad day. It was the anniversary of their daughter's death. I spent the entire visit trying to calm Mr. Eldridge and apologizing for the New Jersey Police Department's lack of efficiency. Then I did my Joe Cocker impression of 'She Came In Through The Bathroom Window' and there went that."

"Don't you mean 'She Conked Her Head On The Coffee Table'?" Gus sniggered after offering his impromptu paraphrase.

Ma cackled.

"Terrific. I'm at the dinner table with Lennon and McCartney."

"Couldn't help myself," Gus said with a grin. He nabbed the last piece of garlic bread. "Anyone want this?"

Ma and I shook our heads.

"I'll requisition the Eldridge file as well, but it might be a couple of days getting here from New Jersey."

"Great. That'll give me plenty to do."

Gus narrowed his eyes playfully. "And keep you out of trouble."

"I miss Joe Cocker," Ma said with reverence. "Although it was so hard to watch him perform, always twitching and gyrating the way he did."

I gnarled up my hands and arched my neck like Cocker used to and sang, "'I get by with a little help from my friends. Gonna try with a little help from my friends.'"

Ma took hold of our hands. "Of course you will, dear. We're way more than friends. We're family."

Chapter Forty-Three

If I was right, Nina Stoffer had been the killer's first victim—correct that, she was the first victim the police were aware of. Many serial killers have been able to take lives for quite some time without them showing up on law enforcement radar, more times than we care to admit.

Poor Nina had been brutally assaulted in the most chic manner imaginable. She'd been found latched to a Louis Vuitton double wardrobe trunk inside a Queens, New York, warehouse near a commercial pier, bound and strangled with exquisite Anne Touraine printed silk scarves. An ornate Alexandra Sojfer parasol had been used to tighten the tourniquet around her neck.

I found a manifest in the file that listed the contents of the wardrobe trunk and was once again surprised to see that the killer hadn't dressed his victim in one of the eight pairs of Jimmy Choo pumps found within the trunk. Apparently, our boy preferred his women barefoot. Judging from what I knew of high-priced luggage and accessories, the cost of that kill was up there at around fifty K. Stoffer had been a clerk for a freight forwarder at the pier and hadn't earned that high an annual salary as a full-time employee.

While I doted on the irony of the killer's first tableau, I again phoned Harry and again left a message for him to call, without leaving any specifics. I had no idea where he was or what he was doing, but I was getting pissed off over his lack of courtesy. Then, of course, I began to feel guilty, wondering if he was in trouble and unable to answer the phone. Guilt and I had become closely acquainted of late and it was not a feeling I enjoyed.

"Can I get you anything?" Ma asked, entering the dining room with Max in her arms.

I was set up at the dining room table with the Stoffer case file, but dropped everything, reached for my son, and held him in my arms. "You haven't heard what's going on in here? The garlic bread is repeating on me—I'm setting consecutive world records for the loudest burps and belches ever recorded."

She quipped, "I'm so very proud of you. You should probably go for a walk or something. You're not getting as much exercise as you're used to."

"Maybe later. I want to get through this evidence box first."

"See anything in common?"

"Only the killers MO. So far he's used an expensive wardrobe trunk, a cheap worn-out actor's trunk, and an unfinished pine blanket trunk. He's neat and efficient, leaves no DNA evidence, and chooses locations without security cameras or disables them in advance."

"So still no idea why you and your partner were shot?"

I shook my head. "Sadly no, and still no clear direction on the Serafina Ramirez homicide either."

"So what now?"

Making a silly face, I said, "It's a good time to tickle Max." I made him giggle like crazy. "Funny how this wipes all the misery out of my mind. This little guy is Mommy's best antidepressant. Aren't you?"

He attempted to tickle me back. I overacted dramatically, but the effect my son had on me was absolutely genuine. For the moment I didn't have a care in the world. Max was getting a little out of breath, so much to his chagrin I stopped and put him down. He was at that stage of holding onto furniture and almost ready to start toddling. I watched him shuffle along, gripping the end of the dinner table like a cat burglar clinging to a rooftop ledge for dear life—one misstep and ... Yup. He fell on his bum, pulled himself up, and went at it again. "My boy's a tenacious little bugger."

"Apple from the tree?" Ma wisecracked.

"Touché. So I'm starting to feel pretty confident that the two cases are unrelated. Is it possible the shooter was the same person who committed the three murders? Sure, but I don't see it. The rapist has such a specific MO ... I don't see him taking a shot at me because I was getting too close to him, because truthfully ... I wasn't. The case was scantly days fresh when the shooting took place."

"Your gut reactions are usually pretty accurate. Are you going to give up on the Ramirez homicide to concentrate on the sniper?"

"Somewhat. Gus is on the Ramirez task force anyway. He'll share anything he thinks I need to know."

"So what now?"

"I asked Harry to check in on a suspect, the brother of someone particularly grisly that Yana and I put away for life. I called him twice already, but he hasn't answered. I'll give him until the end of the day and if I haven't heard back by then, I'll ask Gus to help me out with it."

She patted me on the knee. "Good. The two of you have always made a great team, and ..."

"And what?"

"And I'll kill you if you go off the reservation again." She pointed an intimidating finger at my nose. "We good?"

I showed my palms. "I surrender. I know when I've met my match."

Chapter Forty-Four

The soccer match had just ended. Rodrigo Sanchez flipped through a few stations before dropping the remote on the couch and walking into the kitchen for a cold beer. After grabbing a frosty bottle of Dos Equis, he closed the refrigerator door and was about to turn around when he felt electricity crackle along his spine. His body racked in spasm and his knees hit the floor. "Ah! *Mierda!*" He'd been completely startled. At a loss for what was happening, he didn't even think to defend himself until he felt someone lock his wrists together and the zip tie ratcheting tightly around them. He'd never been Tasered before but understood that it was the only logical explanation for the powerful current frying his nervous system. A black hood was pulled over his head and secured with rope. The jolting electricity finally came to an end. Just before passing out, he felt himself being hoisted off the floor—two strong hands around each of his arms.

~~~

He awoke in the dark. A light breeze on his face told him that he was outdoors. In the next instant he realized that the buzzing in his ears was the sound of cicadas chirping loudly in the trees. He opened his eyes wide and tried to push the grogginess from his head. He was bound in a chair in a rather peculiar way, fastened to it by the ankles, waist, and elbows.

Stacked in front of him were two wooden produce crates. He called out into the night, *"Hola?* Hello?" The ground crunched behind him. "What the hell is going on?" he asked angrily. "Who are you? When I get my hands on you, I'll—" The sight of a handheld Taser in front of his eyes silenced him abruptly. "What do you want from me, man?"

He heard a click and then the hiss of radio noise.

His captor spoke into the radio, "Now," and car headlamps illuminated in the distance, clearly revealing a full-size mannequin some one hundred yards away.

"What the ... what kind of crazy shit is this?"

Without revealing himself, the captor positioned a thirty-caliber rifle with a large telescopic sight in Rodrigo's hands. He'd been bound in such away that he was able to aim the rifle at the mannequin by leaning forward in the chair. His bonds were fashioned in a way so that no other movement was possible.

"Shoot," he was told.

"Fuck you. You shoot. I want to know—" The Taser reappeared before his eyes and this time the current was on and spiking between the two contact electrodes. "Yeah. Hell. Sure. Why not?" He leaned forward with the rifle propped up on the top of the crate to stabilize it and enable a good shot.

His captor raised his binoculars to his eyes and repeated, "Shoot."

Rodrigo pressed his eye socket against the scope, looped his finger around the trigger, and aimed.

His captor studied him briefly before looking back through the binoculars. The first shot rang out. His captor studied the target. "Again," he said. "Try again." A second shot was fired. "Again." The third shot missed the target as badly as the first two. The rifle was suddenly snatched from his hands. His abductor checked the target through the scope and made slight adjustments to account for wind and elevation. "You wear glasses?"

"Glasses? No. I don't wear no stinking glasses."

The rifle was placed back in his hands. "Try again."

Zing.

"One more time."

Zing.

"Come on, cowboy. You can do it. Hit the target. Win a teddy bear for your girlfriend."

"Cowboy, my ass," Rodrigo grumbled. He tried again, and again. "Shit," he swore, knowing that he had missed the target every time. He continued to fire until he heard the telltale *click*. The twenty rounds in the magazine were gone. He grimaced with disappointment. Just then the Taser hit him between the shoulder blades, the current strong and continuous until he once again passed out.

"*Sore wa karede wa arimasen*," the captor said into the radio. "It's not him."

Chapter Forty-Five

"You look really uncomfortable," Sofia said. "Do you need a pill?"

Jack Burns sat in front of the TV, watching a morning talk show and sipping from a mug of coffee. His gaze was fixed on the TV while he answered. "I took one last night and it didn't do a damn thing."

Sofia picked up the prescription bottle and read the label. "It has codeine in it, papi. It should give you some relief."

He redirected his gaze and extended his hand to examine the bandaged portion of his arm. "Yeah. Okay. I'm so tired ... at the very least it might help me to fall asleep."

She opened the vial and shook a pill into his hand. "Is one enough?"

"Yeah. I think so. Anyway I've got a job to do this afternoon. You know what they say about medication and working with tools."

She waited for him to swallow the pill and then sat down on his lap. "I hate seeing you in such a bad way, papi." She stroked his cheek. "Is there anything I can do to cheer you up?" she asked in a seductive voice.

He turned his eyes back toward the TV. "I'm trying to watch the program, Sofia."

"I can think of something that's a lot more fun." She waited for a reaction and grew visibly upset when he didn't respond.

"You know I'm hurting too, baby, and it's been so long since ..."
She kissed him softly on the neck. "I need you, baby. I need you
right now. Come back to bed, Jack. Come on."

"I'm in a lot of pain, Sofia."

She kissed him again and again, her lips warm and moist as
she worked her way along his neck toward his mouth. "I'll make
you forget about everything, papi. You know I can." She ran her
fingers through his hair, then reached for the remote to shut it
off.

He moved it beyond her reach. "I said that I'm trying to
watch the program."

Springing off his lap, her eyes blazed with fury. "Fine. Watch
the stupid show. What's wrong with you, anyway?"

"How can you ask me that?" he snapped.

"Serafina was *my* little girl, Jack. Mine! I know how much you
loved her because you adopted her, but I'm the one who gave
birth to her. You don't think it's killing me that she's gone? Do
you have any idea what it's like for a mother to see her baby's life
taken away? I feel like my soul has been torn out, and when I
come to my husband for a little badly needed affection ... Ah," she
swore in disgust. "I don't know, Jack, you're not even close to
being the man I married. I need someone to hold me. I need
someone to love me. You're all I have in this world, Jack. What's
happened to you?"

"I need more time, Sofia. We're way behind on the bills and
after last night ..." He shrugged. "I'm just not in the mood. I'm
under a lot of pressure right now. Don't you get it?"

"You're never in the mood anymore, and that story you told
me—I mean, *come on*, I didn't believe it for a second. No one
tried to rip off your toolbox. What really happened?"

He responded indignantly, "I told you what happened."

"The kids in this neighborhood aren't interested in your tools, Jack. You think they wanted to build a tree house or some shit and were looking for a hammer and nails? The kind of kids who roam the streets around here are only interested in drugs and money."

"I don't know *what* they wanted. Maybe they thought there was money in the toolbox."

"Sure, because that's what every handyman carries in his toolbox: wrenches, screwdrivers, and a wad of twenty-dollar bills. Give me a little credit. Do you think I'm stupid or something?"

He stood and clicked off the TV. "Damn it. I don't even want to watch this anymore." Glaring at her, he said, "I told you what happened. You don't want to believe me, then don't believe me. A man can only be pushed so far, you know."

A tear rolled down her cheek. "What's happening to us, Jack? I feel like we're falling apart. This tragedy should be pulling us closer together, but instead I feel like it's just driving us farther apart and I don't understand why. I feel like you don't love me anymore," she said, her anger growing hotter. "I feel like you blame me for what happened because I let Serafina walk to her friend's house by herself. I think you're looking at me with the same kind of anger you have against the kids who let you walk home by yourself the night you were attacked. It's not fair, Jack. It's not fair." She burst into tears. "Don't you think I blame myself for what happened to my little girl?"

"Damn it, Sofia, we just need more time. Look at all we've been through."

She looked into his eyes and saw that he was emotionally unavailable. His words were empty, nothing more than a means to quell their argument. Something was wrong with her husband, something far beyond the scars of the assault he had carried with him since his youth. "Whatever you say, Jack." She wiped her tears, picked up her bag, and slung it over her shoulder. "I'm going out."

Chapter Forty-Six

Burns stood by the open door after Sofia had stormed out, deciding whether or not to go after her. He was in slippers and a robe but raced down the hallway after what seemed like just a moment to find that she had already vanished. He took the elevator down to the lobby, but Sofia had already gone out the front door and had disappeared. He shielded his eyes with his hand to look eastward into the glare of the rising sun, then turned in the other direction but still didn't see her. "Shit!" *How could she have disappeared so quickly?*

He tightened the cinch on his robe and sat down on the stone front steps. They were cold and the chill quickly permeated his robe. He jumped when the name "Jack-O" hit his ears. He hadn't been called Jack-O in decades, and the moniker felt much more like an insult than the nickname his childhood friends had always used. His left eye began to twitch even before Reggie came into view. He eyed his old friend apprehensively as he crossed the street and made his way toward him. He'd only been back in the neighborhood a short time, and Jack was still unsure of how much he wanted to do with him.

Burns had been socially awkward for decades, and the argument with Sofia had left him feeling nervous and uneasy. "Reggie," he began in a cautious tone, "what are you doing here?"

"W-what kind of a greeting is that?"

Jack looked down at the ground. "Sorry."

"It's not like w-we haven't known each other s-since we were kids."

"You've only been back in the neighborhood a few months. I guess I'm still not used to you being around again."

"W-what's to get used to? We grew up together."

Burns eyed him suspiciously. "Did we?"

"W-what the hell is that supposed to mean, Jack?"

"I mean, yeah, we hung out, but I was always the kid from the other side of the tracks, right? The kid who had to walk around with a baseball bat for protection."

"Gee, Reggie, is that the way you remember it?"

"I'll tell you what I remember. I remember no one wanting to walk me home the night those two predators beat my ass and threw me in their van. I remember Frank coming to visit me by himself after I got out of the hospital. You and Bobby Cohen dropped me like a bad habit." He met Reggie's gaze head-on. "That's how I remember it. You see things differently?"

"Shit, Jack, I'm just t-trying to be a friend and throw you a little w-work." He reached into his back pocket and handed him an envelope. "This is for the job you did the other day."

Burns reached out to accept the envelope, revealing his heavily bandaged forearm.

Reggie's eyes widened. "Jack, what the hell happened to your arm?"

"Occupational hazard. It'll be all right."

"Jesus, they bandaged you up like a friggin' mummy. You get stitches?"

"Some."

Reggie averted his eyes and remained silent while an uncomfortable moment passed. "Look, did-did I do some stupid things when I was a kid? Do I feel bad that I wasn't around when you needed friends? Yeah, of course, but-but you were acting really weird, Jack and ... what can I say? I was a k-kid. I didn't know how to deal with it. People were saying all kinds of crazy s-shit about you, that you were raped, and the attack left you m-mentally retarded, and ..."

"Hell of a time to abandon a friend."

"Hey, I had problems of my own. I was this dumb stuttering kid everyone used to p-pick on ... including you. You were the one that caused all the trouble that night. That's the reason no one wanted to walk you home. You d-don't want to accept the truth, J-Jack. You're the one responsible for what happened that night. You want to blame me? Fine, but I was in no position to stand up for anyone. If it wasn't for F-Frank Chalice, I would've gotten my ass w-whooped seven days a week. It wasn't exactly a great time for me either."

Jack lowered his head shamefully. "You hardly stutter anymore and I'm still a broken misfit everyone looks at and asks, 'What the hell happened to him?'"

"I'm trying to be a f-friend and you just want to be b-bitter. I'm gonna go now, and I guess I won't be calling you the next time I need a repair done."

"Don't do me any favors, Reggie. Call someone else the next time a toilet gets clogged."

Reggie held up his hands with his fingers spread wide. "Enough!" he shouted, then lowered his head and repeated with finality, "Enough."

~~~

Lido watched the exchange between Burns and Coffer from the comfort of his unmarked car while he munched on a breakfast burrito and drank strong coffee. He snapped a couple of pictures with his iPhone and noted with interest the large bandage on Burns' arm. Though he was unable to hear the details of the conversation, he observed that the exchange had been heated. "Too bad I couldn't hear what they said." He waited until the two had separated and made a notation in his notebook that an envelope had been exchanged. "Something is rotten in Denmark," he muttered, then put the car into gear and drove off.

Chapter Forty-Seven

"I've got to step out for a few."

Ma's eyes flashed angrily. "Without Gus?" she asked apprehensively.

"Yes, without Gus. I'm just going two blocks down to Tony's."

"Tony's Pizza? Why? I've got a refrigerator full of leftovers. I've got ham, *mortadella*, and *soppressata*. How about I stuff a nice hero with cold cuts, roasted peppers, lettuce, and mozzarella?"

I smirked. "Ham, *mortadella*, and *soppressata,* really? Worry about cholesterol much? Why don't you just cut to the chase and make the sandwich with pig's feet and hog jowls?"

"It can't hurt you if you only eat it once in a while."

"Everything in moderation, huh?" I pretended to mull over her offer. "That's okay. I'm not really hungry. Anyway, I finally got a call back from Harry. We're going to meet at Tony's for a quick debriefing—I figure that it's better not to have him up here with the little one running amuck."

"Is that a good place to eat? Does he even eat pizza?"

I couldn't help but grimace. "Why, because he's Japanese?"

"Yeah?"

"He loves pizza. He just substitutes salmon roe for the cheese and wasabi for the tomato sauce."

She gave me a playful swat on the arm. "Wiseass. Get the hell out of here, but remember, I'm watching the clock."

"Anyway, it's not about the food. It's about the conversation." I checked my bag to make sure I had everything I needed: my phone, a pad, and my fully loaded LDA, of course. "Everything's here." I tossed the heavy bag over my shoulder. "Be back soon."

"You're not a flight risk, are you?"

"I don't know. Would you like me to surrender my passport? How about if I put something valuable up as collateral."

She glared at me. "Your word. I want your word as collateral."

I winked at her and placed my hand over my heart. "So help me, *Ma*."

"How about so help me *God*?"

"I survived a bullet to the noggin. I think God has already gone way above and beyond, don't you?"

"It's Max's lunchtime in an hour. I'll expect you back in time to feed him." The woman obviously couldn't help herself. She hugged me with tears in her eyes. "Take care of this already. I need things to get back to normal around here."

"Will do," I said and got going while the getting was still good.

Chapter Forty-Eight

I had lied to my mother, not about the meeting with Harry, but about not being hungry. I mean, I hadn't been hungry, but once the aroma of tomato sauce and baking bread wafted up my nostrils ... Well, I'm only human. I wolfed down a Sicilian slice and a root beer before Harry arrived.

I saw him enter and motioned for him to join me in the back of the pizzeria. He nodded hello to Tony and made straight for our table. Tony and I have been tight since the days when I used to use his bathroom to put on makeup before school because Ma thought I was still too young and didn't want the other kids calling me a *puttana*, which she often explained was Italian slang for whore.

From the way Tony looked at me with the flashy blond hairdo, he might've been thinking that Ma had been right, that I'd lost my way and become a call girl.

"Hungry?" I asked.

"Yes." He dropped his backpack on an empty chair and sat down.

"What would you like?"

He wrinkled his nose. "I'm not a big fan of cheese."

"Lactose intolerant?"

"What is lactose?"

"It means that eating cheese gives you the shits. Anyway, why didn't you tell me? We could've met somewhere else."

"Food is not my first priority." He leaned in closer. "We found Rodrigo."

"We?"

"Tiru and me. Anyway. He's not our man."

"You're sure?"

"Definitely. He's a terrible shot. He couldn't hit Godzilla with a laser-targeted rocket launcher."

Love the regional metaphor. My eyes widened. "And you know this how?"

His head moved back and forth as if deciding whether or not to tell me. "We have our methods," he explained.

"Evidently. But you're sure?"

"Completely."

"How about a salad? Tony makes a nice Italian salad: lettuce, peppers, olives, anchovies ... the works. We'll tell him to hold the mozzarella."

"It's okay, Chalice. I passed a noodle shop on my way over. I'll grab a bowl of udon when we're finished. You left me several messages. What did you want to tell me?"

"Ah, the messages. You know that was more than twenty-four hours ago. You're not so great at returning calls."

"Yes. I'm sorry, but I was very busy."

"What if I had been in danger?"

"Were you?"

"No."

"Then don't be such a drama queen. Why did you call?"

"A man was stabbed yesterday."

"So? It's Manhattan. I'm sure it's an hourly occurrence in this city."

He was wrong, very wrong. New York City was incredibly safe for a cosmopolitan city of such great population and density, and daytime stabbings were relatively obscure. It wasn't, however, germane to our conversation, so I didn't bother to call him on it. A born-and-bred New Yorker has to stick up for the Big Apple, just saying.

I fished in my bag and pulled out some eight-by-ten photos. "The stabbing victim was a Japanese-American. He was stabbed as he was coming out of a Shinto temple." I placed a picture of the victim lying face down on the sidewalk in front of him. "Recognize this guy?"

Harry picked up the photo and studied it intently. He shrugged. "It's difficult to see his face." The next photo took all the guesswork out of it for him. It was an enlargement of the victim's driver's license. "The victim's name was Aguri Maeda. He was a sushi chef at a restaurant called Kanpeki."

I considered Harry's facial expressions and body language while he studied the second photo. His expression remained impassive, but a slight tensing of the shoulders and neck muscles indicated a reaction. He adjusted his seated position, further indicating a response of some nature. "So, do you know him?"

"Honestly, Chalice, did you really expect me to recognize the victim just because he's Japanese? I had no idea you were such a bigot."

Me? Guilty of prejudice? Not a chance, slick. I laid down the third picture, the artist's sketch of the assailant with an enlargement of the neck tattoo, a red and black serpent's head. "How about this beast? Ever seen this guy around?" The sketch depicted a man with a broad nose, round face, and a truly intimidating countenance. It was no wonder the witness had described him so vividly. I know that frightening image would've definitely seared its way into *my* brain.

"What is it with you, Chalice? Do we all look alike to you?" He pushed the artist's sketch back across the table.

I wasn't buying it and the fine pinpoints of sweat on his upper lip told me that he was full of crap.

"Where's the—"

"The *Keshooshitsu?*"

He nodded and I pointed in the direction of the men's room. Ducking out abruptly as he did indicated to me that I was right. He didn't have a terrible and sudden urge. He was merely buying a few minutes to regroup so that he could come back and tell me some more bald-faced lies. That was okay because it gave me a moment to do something important. I fished in my backpack, found what I was looking for, and took care of business before he returned.

Harry was a cool character. He had steadied himself while in the seclusion of the men's room—he looked calm and collected when he returned from the shit zoo.

"So are you going to come clean, or do I have to get heavy-handed with you?"

"At a loss for what to ask, Chalice? What do you want to hear from me?"

"Harry, it's completely obvious that you know these men, so if you continue to lie to me, I'm going to have to cut you off."

His eyes widened. "You're going to cut *me* off? I only agreed to come here as a courtesy to you. I'm more than capable of tracking down my brother's killer on my own."

"All right." I reached across the table and grabbed the pictures. "These are obviously of no use to you." I stuffed them back in my bag. "Have a good day, Harry. Go grab a hearty cup of noodles—you look a little worn out."

He seemed befuddled. "So that's it?"

"That's it. I know that you were expecting the third degree, but I'm not going to waste my time. As far as I'm concerned, you're on your own."

He shrugged. "Third degree?"

"It means I'm not going to sweat the truth out of you. We both know you're lying, so go find the shooter on your own, and I'll do what I have to do on *my* own."

"Okay. If that's the way you want it." He opened his backpack and attempted to hand me the phone.

"Keep it," I said. "Unlike you, I'll answer if you call me, and I'll come to your aid if you need rescuing, even if you don't deserve it."

He shook his head. "I *don't* need your help."

"Just keep it," I insisted.

He jammed it back into his backpack. "Goodbye, Chalice."

"Yup," I said nonchalantly. "See you around."

He shrugged, tossed the backpack over his shoulder, and turned away without seeing that I was smiling. The phone he'd attempted to give back was not the phone I'd originally given him. The phone now in his backpack was a new one. It contained a tracking chip, and since the silly backpack went everywhere that he did …

Chapter Forty-Nine

"Hey, babe," Gus began. "I staked out Burns' apartment this morning and guess what I saw?"

It felt great to hear Gus briefing me without any hostility in his voice. "Don't keep a girl guessing. Spill!"

"There must've been some fireworks in the Burns' hacienda this morning because Sofia blew out the front door in a hurry, wiping tears from her eyes, and Jack hit the streets shortly afterward, dressed in his robe."

"So they had a spat. That doesn't mean he killed someone."

"I'm not finished."

"Of course you weren't. What was I thinking?"

"So Burns is out by the front steps, presumably searching for his wife and looking like something the cat dragged in, when guess who comes along to pay him a visit?"

"I don't know. Who? Lady Gaga? The Prince of Wales? Who? I'm not a seer."

"Not even a guess?"

"No."

"I see, so you want to be spoon-fed all of this vital information, is that it?"

"Yes. That's it. That's exactly it. So who the hell was it?"

"Reggie Coffer."

"So? They're old friends, so what?"

"It didn't look as if they were very close. They argued and it got pretty heated."

I shrugged. *"So?"* I asked, being playfully obstinate.

"Reggie handed him an envelope."

"Maybe his mail was delivered to the wrong address. Or haven't you heard that the postal system can't get its shit together. I shipped something to San Francisco and they attempted delivery in Alaska."

"At least they got it to the west coast."

I shook my head disbelievingly. "You've got to be kidding."

"Anyway, Jack's arm was heavily bandaged."

I was prone to agree with him even though his news was circumstantial—something was going on. "Aha. All right, how do you want to work this?"

Max was having a mac and cheese party. Ma always made it from scratch with fresh cheddar, milk, and Romano, but the poor thing was running on vapors, so I ordered her to take a nap and quickly prepared a box of O Organics Macaroni and Cheese. It wasn't homemade, but it had gotten a GoodGuide health score of 8.5 out of 10. To tell you the truth, Max wasn't all that fussy, and the mac and cheese had nice adhesive properties, which facilitated his face-art effort—the child was clearly a Picasso in the making, an absolute prodigy.

"We *could* just ask him," Gus offered. "Jack seems to be a pretty straight-up kind of guy. Maybe he'll just fess up if we ask him about Reggie."

"Just like that?"

"Stranger things have happened. He doesn't appear to be all that sophisticated. Maybe he'd be happy to unburden himself."

"Jack, the guy who went bonkers when you interviewed him? Jack, the guy who's obviously hiding something? So just ask?"

"Yup. Just ask."

I checked the time. "I want to clean and change Max before Ma gets up. The poor woman is exhausted. We can leave to see him right after."

As if on cue Ma walked out of the bedroom, yawning. "Go. Get out of here and close the damn case while I still have life in this tired old body."

"Couldn't sleep?"

"I catnapped." She smiled at Max. "Someone ate hearty." Turning to me, "I'm not going to find an empty mac and cheese box in the garbage, am I?"

"Run!" I shouted. "Let's get the hell out of here."

"You rotten kid. How hard is it to boil some macaroni and melt some cheese." She threatened me with an open hand. "Bah. I don't know why I bother writing down all of my recipes for you."

"*Hey*, I'm capable of preparing a meal," I said, pretending to be offended.

"All these recipes have been handed down from generation to generation and for what? You say you can cook, then show me."

"I will."

"When?"

"After we've nabbed the shooter."

"Hear that, Gus? You're a witness."

He did the balancing thing with his two open hands. "Let's see if I understand this. On the one hand, if we find the shooter quickly, we'll avenge Yana's death and have closure. On the other hand, if we find the shooter quickly, we'll have to eat a Stephanie-prepared meal. Oh gee, that's a tough one."

I smacked his arm. "I see that dark new alliances were formed in my absence. You do know that the penalty for treason is death."

"Anything to keep you out of the kitchen," he chuckled. "You've got a lot of strengths, but cooking isn't one of them."

Chapter Fifty

"You look a little lonely."

Jack Burns was sitting on the front steps in basically the same spot where Lido said he had seen him earlier. He'd changed out of his robe, but looked like a lost soul, a person torn and conflicted without a clear direction in life.

"You come to keep me company, Detective? Your father used to visit me when I didn't have any friends. He hand you the baton or something?"

Gus was down the block in the car. Burns was an emotional guy, and we thought he'd react badly if the two of us ganged up on him. I had something of a connection with him because he and my dad had been friends, so we decided I'd probably get further with him than Gus would. "Mind if I sit?"

He didn't answer but moved over to give me room. When he did, the gauze bandaging around his wrist was visible. "What happened to you?" I said, peering at his wrist.

"Ah, that's nothing. Work related."

"You better be more careful. Hard to be a handyman without hands."

"Yeah," he chuckled. "Don't worry. I'll live."

It was too soon in the conversation to take him to task, so I transitioned to a more generalized question as covered in the detective's textbook on interrogative strategy: 101—make the subject your friend. Make the subject forget whom he or she is talking to. "So what's going on, Jack?" I casually asked.

He made a face indicating that he questioned everything he knew about the world and felt truly helpless.

"I know that you and your wife must be coming unglued over it, but we *will* catch this creep."

"Pretty soon it's not going to matter," he said dejectedly. "Sofia and me ... we're falling apart, and I ain't exactly the best at patching up relationships."

"Good at carrying a grudge, are you? Me too."

"Sofia's the only woman who ever gave me the time of day."

"Everyone has their shit, Jack, but if you love her, you have to fight to keep your marriage going. I won't tell you that putting Serafina's killer away will solve all of your problems because it won't. I have no idea what it takes to get past a tragedy like this, but people do it. Do they wake up with smiles on their faces every morning? I really doubt it. Time may not heal all wounds, but it will make them fade into the background. I hope the two of you are going to counseling. There are several groups that support loved ones after a devastating loss."

"We were kind of hoping to see the bastard arrested before we did anything like that. You know, first things first—getting your ducks in a row and all that. It's been so long, though, we didn't think we'd still be in this kind of pain almost two months after Serafina was murdered. That's why I'm sitting here like a bump on a log. Sofia got annoyed at me this morning and took off. She's been gone all day. I've been sitting here waiting for her to come home the whole day. Didn't even do the repair job I was supposed to do."

"Sometimes waiting is all you can do. Don't you have any friends you can talk to?"

"Friends?" He shook his head. "The only real friend I ever had was your dad. In case you haven't noticed, I'm not the kind of guy people are attracted to."

I'd been tiptoeing around the question but figured he'd given me a reasonable segue. "What about your old friend Reggie?"

He turned and gave me a hard stare. "Reggie? Why would you ask about him?"

"I didn't do it to pry, but when I went through your old police file I noticed that Reggie was one of the boys you were with the night you were assaulted. I noticed he lives close by, so I just assumed that the two of you were—"

"Tight? You think that we're tight? Well, we're not, far from it. We bumped into each other a few times, but we're not friends. I did some plumbing work in the building he manages, but I'm not going to do it anymore. He only gave me the job because he saw that I was still a basket case. I don't want his sympathy. Shoot, he only moved into the neighborhood a short while ago. Before that I hadn't seen him in almost thirty years." He mumbled something I couldn't hear, something unpleasant. "You know that Reggie's the reason I got attacked, right?"

"No. I didn't know that. I read that you were with my father, Reggie, and a third boy named Robert Cohen just before you were abducted. Why was it Reggie's fault?"

It took him a moment to expound and I could see that it was unpleasant for him to summon up the memory. "We were playing scully, you know, that street game where you shoot bottle tops into boxes on a board you mark in the street."

"Before my time, I'm afraid. But go on."

"Well, we were playing and I was being a jerk, I guess. I pounded my bat on the ground just as Reggie was going to shoot and made him miss. Somehow things got out of hand and that stuttering twerp played on everyone's sympathies. No one would walk me home."

"And that was when you were attacked?"

He nodded sadly. "I lived in a shitty area and used to carry a bat for protection, but those two guys came out of nowhere. They jumped me, took my bat, and threw me into their van. They were men and I ... I was a skinny kid. Guess they figured I was an easy target."

"I'm so sorry, Jack. I didn't mean to stir up old painful memories. I *am* surprised that my dad didn't walk you home even if the other boys wouldn't."

"He wanted to and I think he was going to, but he would've been late to see his girlfriend Lisa."

My eyes widened. *Ma?* It took a moment, but then it all made sense. They had been high school sweethearts. I had a difficult time fighting back tears but somehow managed.

"Hey, you all right?" he asked.

"Yeah. I'm okay. I was just thinking about my dad."

"Those two," he began with reverence. "It was love at first sight. I knew it, but I hated her because she was taking Frank away from us. Your dad contacted me years and years later, and it sounded like he was still trying to find the two animals that attacked me. Can you believe it? He never gave up. Your dad, he was one of the good ones." He got quiet for a moment and I assumed he too was thinking about my dad reverently. "But you didn't tell me, why'd you go to the trouble of looking through my police file?"

"Because I think you know something that you're not telling me, and I thought the information in the file might better help me to understand why you wouldn't tell the police every single thing you knew about your daughter's murder."

"That's ridiculous. Why would I hold back information like that?" he asked angrily. "Do you honestly think I'd protect my daughter's killer?"

"Not for a moment, Jack, but I think you're trying to deal with something that's so big that you don't know what to do about it. That's why I stopped by today—I was hoping I'd get you to tell me what you're struggling with."

He stood. "Detective, I've got a lot on my mind, my daughter, my wife, and the bill collectors too. So don't try to analyze me. I don't like shrinks. I've seen enough of them and they're all full of shit. They feed you pills and talk to you about brain chemistry, and Oedipal complexes, and Sigmund Freud, all the while knowing that some minds just can't be fixed. You'd think they'd have the guts to tell you important stuff like that up front and not waste your time, but I guess everyone has to earn a living. They wasted a lot of my time, Detective, and they never fixed anything, but I get along. I work as much as I can. I try to take care of my family, and I never hurt anyone."

He rubbed his eyes. "And then some monster had to come along and attack my daughter, just like those two animals who attacked me. Shouldn't things balance out? Shouldn't Serafina have had a better life because of all the crap I went through? You'd think so, right? But no, some people have all the luck and others ..." He took a deep breath and wiped his nose. "Look at me pouring my heart out to you. You Chalices, I guess you're magnets for other people's shit."

I was hoping he'd unburden himself but not in the way he had. I was hoping he'd tell me something valuable about Serafina's murder, but he hadn't. He was right about the Chalices—we were all made of the same stock. "It's okay, Jack," I said in a comforting tone. "I'm here to listen."

Chapter Fifty-One

"**Look who came to see you,**" Ma said excitedly as she opened the door for Gus and me to enter.

My eyes opened wide. "Nigel?" I rushed into the room and put my arms around the strapping psychiatrist. He was a gorgeous man in and out, a dark-skinned Adonis with a mind equaled by few.

"Hello, love," he said in his husky British baritone. "How is my dear friend?"

"Living, breathing, and busting balls—same old same old."

He brushed my hair with his fingers. "I'm loving the Posh Spice look. All you need now is a checkered mini and go-go boots."

I winked at him. "Gets your motor running, does it?"

"*Indeed.* I've always wanted to kick Mrs. Beckham's tires."

"Kick her tires or stuff something in her boot?"

He chuckled. "Boundaries, love ... boundaries."

I could see that I'd embarrassed him. "Sorry. Anyway, when did you get back?" Nigel had crossed the pond to look in on his "mum," who'd been ill.

"I landed last night."

"And how's your mum?" I said in my best Paul McCartney cockney.

"The old gal's doing much better, thanks," he offered ebulliently. "They finally found an antibiotic that would kick the snot out of her pneumonia. I'm afraid she'll be hoarse for a while, though. I guess that's not all bad—she sounds exactly like Rod Stewart."

I grimaced. "No wonder you left. That hoarse voice can't be pleasant to listen to."

"She's made 'Maggie May' her own."

Gus was waiting patiently to say hello. He stepped forward and shook Twain's hand. "Welcome home, Nigel. Glad your mom is on the mend."

The boys were close now, but they hadn't always been the best of friends. Gus was my love, but Nigel was most certainly my secret lust, the man who tiptoed through my dreams dressed in little more than a loincloth. Though I'd never cheat, Gus sensed my secret longing and had been jealous of Nigel because of it.

My two gorgeous men bro-hugged, not just because they were seeing each other after a long absence but because ... Well, I could see it in their eyes and from their expressions that they were both deeply relieved that I'd survived the shooting.

"What's with these two wussy men?" I interjected. "Over four hundred pounds of sinewy muscle and there's not a dry eye in the house. What's going on here?"

"Ah, that's so sweet," Ma said. "They both love my little girl." She sighed melodramatically. "Enough of this emotional crap," she blurted. "Who's hungry?"

Leave it to Ma to put a smile on our faces and a pot roast in our bellies. Max was awake for part of the meal, but I put him down before we had coffee—decaf for me on account of my loose screws and faulty wiring. I was dying for a cup of real honest-to-God java, but more so dying to sleep with my husband and was still waiting for the all clear from the doc. Needless to say, if I could go two months without Gus' riveting lovemaking, I could survive a little longer without a jolt of caffeine.

"How's Ricky?"

"So much better, thanks to you, Nigel," Ma replied.

My brother, Ricky, had gone through severe emotional problems and had come a long way under the guidance of my dear friend Nigel.

"He's like a new man," Ma continued. "Living on his own. Working. Thank God Max came along to keep me busy. I used to spend so much time with Ricky—I don't know what I'd do with myself."

"I made sure he had my cell number before I left, but he hasn't called," Nigel explained. "And that's a *very* good sign because independence is a wonderful thing. Still, we have our monthly appointment next week and I'll be calling in advance to remind him of it."

What the? As Nigel sipped his coffee, he glanced at Ma, giving her some kind of signal. I wasn't going to call him on it, but I made a mental note and put it in the vault.

"Let me clear this table," she said.

As if on cue, Gus stood as well. "You've been doing everything—I'll help you."

I gave them both a knowing sneer and waited until they'd left the room before turning on Twain. "Spill," I ordered. "What are the three of you up to?"

"I'm surprised the world's greatest criminal investigator can't figure it out. You disappeared into the night. You left your husband, son, and mother without the slightest clue as to where you were or what you were up to. On top of that you'd just sustained a near-fatal head injury and had memory loss. What's going on? I'm wondering if you haven't lost your mind."

I gritted my teeth. "No one gets it. They made me a prisoner in my own home—don't go on the computer, don't watch TV, no alcohol, no sex ... don't do anything, nothing at all." I huffed. "My partner was killed not ten feet from where I stood, shot through the chest by a sniper. And they expect me to twiddle my thumbs while this assassin runs free? No sir. I don't think so."

"Stop ranting," he insisted. "There aren't many people who understand you as well as I do. Trust me, I know what makes you tick, but you must see how bizarre your behavior was. You could've been lying in an alley, beaten or worse, and twitching like a kipper with a seizure. Do you know how cruel it was to abandon your family under those circumstances?"

"Did you say kipper?"

He glared at me. "Be *serious.*"

"Easy, Nigel. I understand ... *now*, but at the time I was jumping out of my skin. Did I act irrationally? Yeah, I guess I did, but everyone knows that I'm more than capable of taking care of myself. I'm a sturdy little cop."

"Knock it off, Stephanie. You took a crazy risk and you know it." He narrowed his eyes. "Do you have any idea what *they* thought?" he asked with his eyes glancing in the direction of the kitchen.

Oh my God. What could possibly make this any worse?

He took a moment before continuing. "They were worried that Zachary Clovin's genes had kicked in and that a serious mental disorder was emerging."

I recoiled at the comment. "That's just plain stupid. My biological father was a lab rat who willingly participated in hallucinogenic experimentation. Psychopathy isn't hereditary. It's a result of traumatic circumstances."

"That's what the great minds used to believe, but it has recently been demonstrated that there are biological factors at work in the development of the psychotic mind, and some of those factors are strong contributors to many of the more serious character disturbances."

"Really, Nigel, that's what you're telling me? As if I don't have enough shit to worry about, I can now add to the list that I may go as bat-shit crazy as my biological father?"

"Calm down. Calm down." He took my hand in his. "I'm sure you're just fine. I'm just trying to elucidate upon the risk you took and the effect it had on your loved ones."

"Job well done, Nigel." I closed my eyes and took a few deep breaths.

"Are you all right?"

"I'm trying to calm down before I short out my brain wiring," I said sarcastically. "All this tough love is giving me a huge headache. Figuratively that is. I don't want everyone to freak out and rush me back to the hospital."

"Point well taken," he said. "Still, I think the two of us should have a few sessions together."

"I understand now and I *won't* do it again."

"It's healthy therapy, Stephanie, and it just makes good common sense. Promise you'll come see me."

"After I close these cases."

He smiled quaintly. "That's all I can ask."

As I mentioned, in addition to being a caring friend, Nigel was the be-all and end-all of psychological geniuses. He was a vetted and authorized NYPD consultant, so we were able to share our case information with him over dinner in order to gain insights into the murderer's psyche.

Many of the old behavioral analysis axioms once considered unshakable were now widely considered myths. Myth: All serial killers are dysfunctional loners. Myth: All serial killers are white males. Myth: All serial killers are only motivated by sex. Myth: All serial killers are insane or are evil geniuses. Myth: All serial killers want to get caught. I fully understood that there were now holes in the old maxims, but the operative term in these newly listed myths was the word *all*. Granted, there were no absolutes, but the bulk of the psychopaths that had been, are, or will be, did adhere to these five tenants I'd listed and Nigel had been hard-pressed to believe differently.

Gus' cell phone was buzzing as he approached the table with a Trader Joe's Chocolate Brooklyn Babka, which to the chocolate-addicted like me was the baked goods equivalent of crack cocaine. He placed the loaf of chocolaty goodness in front of me and answered his phone. "Really?" He glanced at me with wide eyes and I knew that something really big had just happened. "When? Uh-huh." He yanked out a pen and scribbled on a napkin. "Address? Okay. I'll be right there." He disconnected. "Cut yourself a slice and eat it on the run," he announced. "Reggie Coffer was just found dead."

Chapter Fifty-Two

"**Is that him?**"

"*Was,*" Gus corrected. "As in past tense. Expired. Kaput. Is no more."

"Are you a homicide detective or a friggin' thesaurus?"

"How dare you stifle my creative energy," he chuckled. "What's a matter, don't like the new intellectual me?"

"I prefer the old savage va-jay-jay-pounding you."

"I think that abstinence has made me smarter."

"Easy, Costanza, that was an old Seinfeld episode—word spreads about this and you'll get hit with a theft of intellectual property suit."

"Oh yeah, that's right, the one where George becomes super intelligent and Elaine turns into a blithering dolt."

"Correct. Be that as it may, I can't wait to get the all clear from the doc and bang your brains out."

"Damn it but you're adoringly superficial."

"Deal with it. All right, Stephen Hawking, apply that big brain of yours to the task at hand. Solve something … anything."

Crime scene activity had considerably whittled down by the time we arrived, which was fortuitous because the superintendent's apartment was tiny, a basement hovel buried beneath tons of prewar concrete and bricks, a bunker if you will. There was barely room for the few of us who were still there.

Coffer certainly hadn't been a neat freak. There was stuff piled everywhere. In his defense, he'd only been living there a short time and probably hadn't had time to organize. What's more, it was somewhat obvious that a struggle had taken place. A telltale floor lamp had been knocked over and the glass light bulb had shattered. The sheetrock was fractured where someone had likely slammed into it, and the wall was stained with blood.

It appeared that Reggie had been beaten to a pulp. His face was bloody, but uncharacteristically was not swollen, which meant that his assailant had continued to pound his face after he had expired, or as the ME would put it, beaten postmortem.

"Someone got a good ass kicking," Gus said.

The back of Reggie's head was bloody. I pointed to the broken and bloodstained wall. "It looks like Reggie's head might've slammed into the wall during the scuffle." Wearing gloves, I rapped on the wall in the vicinity of the bloodstain. "Uh-huh, there's a beam behind here. Reggie probably lost consciousness after his head hit the wall, dropped to the floor where he now lies, and was beaten to death by an emotionally-charged assailant." Of course, there could've been other factors contributing to his demise, but they weren't apparent to the naked eye and would have to be determined in the morgue.

The carpeting looked as if hadn't been replaced in decades. It was worn, badly stained, and squished as I approached the bathroom, something that really skeeved me out.

The condition of the bathroom was an assault on the senses. I mean, it was gross: dirty, dusty, and damp, with mold and God knows what else growing on the wall beneath the sink. I thought about taking a pass on Reggie's shitter but persevered. Something gave me the impetus to continue, so I ventured where no health-conscious woman dare to tread.

Like the rest of the apartment, the john was small and utilitarian. I spotted plaster dust and sawdust on the sink ledge. *What happened here?* I opened the medicine cabinet for a quick look-see. It contained banal bathroom articles, an electric razor, Band-Aids, and what have you. The shelves were full except for the space directly in front of the razor-blade slot. *He used an electric razor,* I thought. *Why'd he need easy access to the blade slot?* Modern-day vanities no longer have them, but in the old days, medicine cabinets, as they were called, were all manufactured with a narrow cutout through which worn razor blades could be discarded. The blades would fall through the slot into the wall cavity, where they'd remain forever out of harm's way. My mind flashed back to the night I chatted with Jack Burns at the local bar, and a portion of the conversation we'd had.

"Just come from doing a job?"

"Yeah. Bathroom leak."

"Get it squared away?"

"Yeah, I got lucky. The leak was from the cold water pipe, but I was able to get to it by taking out the medicine cabinet and didn't have to chop up the wall. Saved me a lot of wear and tear, but the place will still need fresh sheetrock and new tile under the sink. It was leaking for a long time, and you know how it gets— everything got yellowed and rotted—stunk like hell. I should've been called much sooner."

"Son of a bitch!" Emerging from the bathroom, I called out to Gus, "I need a Phillips-head screwdriver and two strong arms. STAT!" *I've got this,* I mused. *The bullet may have set me back, but it didn't mess with this detective's nose for crime. I'm still one hot shit investigator.*

Chapter Fifty-Three

I cleared the contents from the medicine cabinet, and then Gus stepped in and put his massive forearms to work.

"You want to explain why we're doing a remodeling project during an active homicide investigation?" Gus quipped as beads of sweat appeared at the edge of his hairline.

The small room was woefully ventilated. I leaned over the tub and past bottles of dandruff shampoo to crack open the window. "The place reeks like a cesspool. I'm guessing old Reggie didn't have many lady callers."

Despite the fact that the screws were old and rusted, he was able to remove them with relative ease, and I was pretty sure I understood the reason why. He pulled on the corners of the cabinet and it came free from the wall without the expected crackle of years of caked-on paint, caulking, and plaster giving way as they should have.

"Now what?" Gus asked.

I almost retched as I leaned forward over the crusty toothpaste and spit-laden sink to look into the wall cavity with my flashlight. I was up on my toes but couldn't rise high enough to look down between the wall beams. I handed the flashlight to Gus. "You've got a good six inches on me. Look down into the wall and tell me if you see anything."

"Got a hunch about something?"

"Yup. Put that six-foot-two-inch frame of yours to work, Detective."

Gus leaned over the sink, braced his forehead on the wall just above the cutout, and peered downward with the flashlight. He studied the wall cavity for a moment, then turned back toward me with a grin. "You're spooky, you know that? You're one hundred percent spooky."

"You see something down there other than discarded razor blades?"

"I do indeed. There's a crossmember just a foot below the opening." He reached in with his glove-clad hand and pulled out a small pile of cards. The card on the top of the pile was Serafina Ramirez's city bus pass.

Chapter Fifty-Four

Gus smiled at me. "Stephanie, you just blow my mind. How in the world did you know there was something hidden behind the medicine cabinet? I wouldn't have thought to look there in a million years."

"It was something Jack said the other night. He told me that he fixed a bathroom leak and that he got lucky because he was able to get to the pipe by taking out the medicine cabinet. I pointed to the copper water pipes running behind the wall. One of them looked as if it had recently been repaired. The old oxidized pipe had been cut and repaired with a shiny copper pressure coupling and solder. "This is the pipe he fixed, Reggie's. That's why you were able to get the old rusty screws out so easily. Jack had removed them just days before."

Gus' eyes flashed with revelation. "He must've seen these cards while he was doing the repair, put two and two together, and realized that Reggie had killed Serafina. He probably left them there so that Reggie wouldn't know that he'd been found out. That's why he was so worked up when you saw him the other night, and why he headed straight for the bar to get drunk."

"Yeah. That pretty well explains it. It also makes Jack the prime suspect in Reggie's murder." I felt sick to my stomach. Jack Burns was barely capable of keeping his own shit together and the ungodly knowledge of knowing the identity of his daughter's killer most certainly had pushed him over the edge. I felt certain of the premise and pitied him for the consequences that would likely befall him. "That poor guy. He just can't seem to catch a break."

I wanted to tell Gus that it was time for me to step back from the case. I was unofficial at best, and my time would be better served tracking down Yana's assassin, a matter that was surely unrelated to Serafina Ramirez's death.

I was about to open my mouth when one of the crime scene investigators filed into the bathroom. He held out a clear plastic evidence bag, which contained a key attached to a paper identification tag. "I found this in a sugar bowl on the top shelf in the kitchen." It looked like a common padlock key, and the tag identified it as the key to unit 611 at Mott Street Storage in lower Manhattan.

"Wonder what we'll find there?" Gus asked.

Might as well see this thing through to the end, I thought, just as my cell phone buzzed. "It's Nigel," I announced. "I'll make it quick," I said and hit the Accept icon. "Dr. Twain, what a pleasant surprise. I'm at an active crime scene and—"

"I don't mean to interrupt, love, but something occurred to me. I was thinking about this killer's MO and how he bound these women to trunks and raped them."

"Yes?"

"Well, his last name, love. It's Coffer. It's not just his name. It's a psychotic play on words. Coffer, love, it's a synonym for a box or, more to the point, a trunk. His name and his MO are one and the same."

"Ah," I gasped. "That's brilliant, Doctor, and the good news is that I have eyes on him as we speak."

"He's under arrest?" Twain queried.

"It goes well beyond that, Nigel. Let me put it this way. He's got just one more box in his future and it's a coffin."

Chapter Fifty-Five

In all, five identification cards had been found in the wall cavity in Reggie Coffer's bathroom. We found Serafina Ramiez's bus pass, Lara Eldridge's student union card, Nina Stoffer's New York State Driver License, and the driver licenses of two other women. The two new names were found in the NMPDD, the FBI National Missing Persons DNA Database. We now knew with reasonable certainty that they too had been Reggie Coffer's victims. One of the women had disappeared a year prior to Nina Stoffer's murder. The other woman disappeared a year before that. It now appeared that Reggie Coffer had taken at least one life a year for the past five years, on dates that roughly coincided with his birthday.

"Hell of a birthday present to give yourself," Gus commented as we pulled up outside Mott Street Storage, a converted six-story building with the windows bricked up and some of the most original graffiti I'd seen in a great while. The graffiti artists had exhibited some wicked imagination. They'd drawn a couple of *sistas* twerking a *brutha* front and rear. To tell you the truth I had no idea a woman's butt could actually be that big.

"What do you think of the art work?" I asked.

Gus smiled and then harmonized, "I like big butts and I cannot lie."

We checked in at the front desk. As stated, we had the key to the storage unit, but ID was required before entering the main storage unit area. Gold badges are accepted anywhere except as all-access passes at Disney World. We took the elevator to the top floor and held our noses as we marched past several units because there weren't a sufficient number of urinals in the facility.

We unlocked unit 611. It could've contained the bodies of the two women who hadn't been found or worse, but it didn't. It contained lumber and a table saw. The boards were pine, like the wood used in the construction of the blanket trunk Serafina Ramirez had been bound to. A blueprint for the construction of the trunk was taped to the wall. It looked familiar—the dimensions and construction were roughly identical to the one found at the crime scene. A partially constructed trunk sat on the floor. It was obviously a multiday project and appeared to be about halfway complete. Fortunately the incomplete trunk was one that Coffer would never have the opportunity to use.

"What would drive someone to do this?" Gus asked.

"A badly messed-up childhood, trauma, abusive parents … who knows what pushes someone this far over the edge. There are a lot of screwed-up people in the world. Fortunately they're not all serial killers."

"Ma said he had a terrible stutter and that the other kids picked on him mercilessly."

"That's a good start, but I'm sure there was more. All the ridicule he must've taken over his stuttering no doubt led to low self-esteem, but something traumatic must've happened to him that made him snap. There must've been a trigger, an incident that launched him into murder mode."

Most serial killers approach their victims in a social situation and talk them into getting in a car or some other type of analogous situation. I wondered if Serafina had known him. I'm sure she'd have been more trusting of someone she was familiar with—it only stood to reason. "Let's look around to see if there's anything here besides tools and lumber, something that will explain Coffer's connection to his victims."

"We'll have to make it fast," Gus said, holding his phone so that I could see the display. A text message indicated that Jack Burns was at the police station and that he was asking for me.

Chapter Fifty-Six

February 1, 2015

The smile on Reggie's face told a lie.
His evil heart held the truth.

It was Super Bowl Sunday and the streets were empty. More than one hundred and eighteen million were watching the-game-to-end-all-games from the comfort and privacy of their homes—at least those who were lucky enough to have a home. Reggie was not so fortunate. He had been homeless more than two months, living in his car and crashing with others when and where he could.

He sat in his car, silently watching a lone teenage girl cutting through the parking lot in great haste. On his lap rested a small empty bag and the syringe he had used to mainline cocaine. He'd felt hopeless only moments before as he faced the reality that his life had hit absolute rock bottom. He'd been caught smoking pot in the school basement where he worked as a custodian and had been let go that Friday afternoon.

A security guard had watched as he cleaned out his employee locker, not knowing that the soft-sided duffle bag he removed contained the IDs of the four women he'd killed, along with woven straps, neckties, and scarves, the choices of bindings he'd used to lash his victims to wooden trunks. He enjoyed picking the appropriate paraphernalia for each of his victims, expensive silk scarves to mock the poorly paid Nina Stoffer and theatrical attire for pretty little Lara, the theater major with the big blue eyes.

It took just scant seconds for the wicked stimulant to reach his brain and tear down the black walls that surrounded him. He could feel his every inhibition being stripped away.

Her friends called her Sara, but he knew the name was short for Serafina. She was one of the more popular girls at school, a long-legged, raven-haired beauty, a sweet girl who was kind to everyone, including stuttering Reggie the custodian, who was often the butt of students' cruel jokes. She had always acknowledged him with a pleasant smile when they passed in the school corridors, and he felt confident that she would do the same when she recognized him sitting in the car.

He assumed that she was still too far away to see his face clearly, but he knew who she was, not because his vision was better than hers, but from the way she moved, the unmistakable rhythm the confident teenage girl projected with her walk. He had watched her stroll down the school corridors many times and had memorized the ebb and flow of her provocative gait.

Happy birthday, Reggie, *he mused. He'd have preferred to have crossed paths with one of the nasty girls from school, who'd belittled him in front of her friends, but Serafina ... she was sweet and unassuming, naïve, and trusting to a fault, and there was more. She was the adopted daughter of his old friend Jack, a kid he had never liked and would enjoy bringing sorrow. He took a moment to envision her in his kill room in the abandoned loft in which he had been squatting. He envisioned her fine young body naked and fixed in position at the foot of his bed. His nerves sizzled with excitement.*

He stashed his drug paraphernalia in the center console and checked his lap to ensure that it was not coated with fine cocaine powder. Taking precaution not to appear obvious, he continued to monitor her forward progress through the darkened parking lot by stealing furtive glances he felt would go unnoticed. She seemed to be in a hurry as she traversed the cold, windswept outdoor parking lot.

She was no more than twenty feet away when he glanced up, his eyes locking on hers with a warm smile and a contrived look of surprise on his face. He waved to her in a casual manner and she waved back. He assessed that she was not alarmed by their chance encounter and found the courage to roll down the window. He'd been let go after recess on Friday and was confident that the students hadn't yet heard of his recent dismissal. "It's freezing out here," he said. "Where are you going, S-Sara?"

Serafina came to a stop outside the driver's door and smiled, her cheeks rosy from the biting cold. Her hands were in the pockets of her short quilted jacket. She pressed her fists together to prevent the wind from rushing up her jacket. "Hi, Reg," she said, greeting him with a smile, addressing him by his commonly known name. She took a moment to examine the badly weathered paint on the beaten-up old Honda, and scanned the backseat, which was strewn with his clothes. A soft-sided bag was next to him on the passenger seat. "Going to my friend Ginger's house."

"Is this a short cut? I mean cutting through the p-parking lot?" She nodded.

"Gonna watch the Super Bowl with G-Ginger and her family?"

"No." She smirked. "Don't think so."

"Not so much a girl's thing, is it?"

She shook her head as a shiver raced up her spine. "Nope, but I'm sure Ginger's father will be watching—he's a big football fan. I want to see Katy Perry at halftime, though—she really rocks. So how come you're not home watching the game?"

He shrugged. "I had to r-run an errand," he said as Ginger's face appeared in his mind. She was one of the uppity girls who treated him like dirt. "Say, doesn't Ginger live a g-good ways from here?"

A more suspicious soul would have given the question more thought, but Serafina simply counted the remaining blocks ahead of her. "I guess so." She didn't think about any hidden agenda he might have had or how he knew where her friend lived.

He knew where all the girls lived, especially Ginger, who slept in her bra and panties and often neglected to pull down the shade before retiring for the night.

She shivered visibly, and he responded to the inadvertent cue, "Christ, you're f-freezing. Jump in and I'll run you over there."

"Ah, that's all right. I'm okay."

"It's on my way," he volunteered "I d-don't mind."

She was naïve but not stupid. She wrinkled her nose. "No. I don't think so. Thanks anyway." She turned and was about to leave when she heard the rumble of muscular car exhaust and glanced up to see a black Malibu lowrider filled with men entering the parking lot, each of them leering at her with intent. She tugged down on the bottom of her jacket to cover her rear end.

"I d-don't think it's safe for you out here," Reggie said. "Maybe you'd better let me ..."

She accepted on impulse, "Okay. Those guys are making me nervous."

He reached over, unlocked the passenger door, and Serafina leapt from the frying pan into the fire.

Chapter Fifty-Seven

Reggie's story had completely unfolded by the time we arrived back at the house. Social Security records showed that he'd been a custodian in Serafina's high school. A few calls helped us fill in the blanks. He'd been fired for using an illegal substance on school property and the department of education had benevolently handled the repeat violation, terminating him without filing a police report so as not to prevent him from finding work outside the education system.

The Lara Eldridge connection had been made clear as well. Prior to working for the NYC Board of Ed, he was a maintenance employee for a vendor who routinely did work for the Rutgers University theatrical department. He repaired stage riggings and had likely met or seen Lara several times and knew that she stayed late at the auditorium on a regular basis.

Nina Stoffer was originally thought to be his first, but the discovery of multiple driver licenses indicated differently. He'd had several jobs, holding onto each for no more than several months at a time. He'd been fired from a job four years ago for stalking some of the female employees after work—Barbara Anne McGuire was one of the women he'd harassed. She'd disappeared just thirty days after Coffer had been let go. He was questioned by the police but not considered a viable suspect. We now knew how large a blunder that had been and that another four women had since died because of the mistake. I still questioned the incident that had pushed him over the edge and transformed him from a disturbed individual to a killer.

Jack Burns had come in on his own, but Gus and I already considered him a primary suspect in Reggie Coffer's homicide. There was little doubt in our minds that he'd found those ID cards and licenses and killed Coffer for murdering Serafina. He had motive up the wazoo, but at the moment there was no forensic evidence or witnesses to connect him with the crime.

I watched Jack Burns through the one-way mirror for some minutes before entering the interrogation room. I wanted to shake his hand and tell him that he was a hero but knew that I could never utter those words. I understood his motivation completely, yet when I sat down across the table from him, the first question I asked was, "Why?"

He looked tortured, more tortured than the last time I'd seen him. His eyes were red and strained, and I sensed that the weight of the world rested upon his shoulders.

"What do you mean, 'Why?'"

I sensed that he was about to unburden himself, come clean as it were, and accept his punishment, but once he did ...

"Just a minute." I got up, pulled the blinds, and made sure that the video camera and microphone were switched off. "You know that you have the right to an attorney, don't you, Jack? Maybe you ought to think about that before saying anything else."

"There's no point, Chalice." He smiled introspectively. "You know, that's what I used to call your dad. Anyway, I'm too tired to play games. You and I both know what happened."

By coming to the station he'd saved us the trouble of picking him up for questioning, but that didn't mean he'd made a smart decision. "I don't think you want to tell me what you're talking about."

"What?"

"Once the words come out of your mouth, they're on record and I can't lie about what you told me. Do you understand what I'm saying?"

"But ..."

"As far as I know you've never been to prison. And I can tell you unequivocally that you wouldn't like it very much, Jack. It's every terrible thing you've ever heard or imagined multiplied by a thousand. Do you hear what I'm telling you?"

His face was a study in puzzlement. "Why are you trying to help me?"

I had my reasons but couldn't say. "Why don't you tell me what happened to your arm first."

"Why?"

"Because I asked."

"But I told you, I—"

"I know what you told me; now tell me the truth."

"I—"

"I said tell me the truth, *Jack*."

"We're getting away from the point."

"Humor me, okay?"

He pressed his lips together and seemed very uncertain. After a moment I could see that he was weakening. "I was on my way home the other night and I saw these two big kids pushing around another boy. I yelled at them, but they wouldn't stop, and when I got closer, I could see that the kid they were pushing around ..." He shook his head woefully. "The third kid was kind of tall and very skinny. He reminded me of ... Damn it, he reminded me of what I looked like when I was a kid."

"They had knives?"

"Yeah. Well, I know at least one of them did because he had it out. I'm not sure about the other. There are a lot of kids in the neighborhood that are hooked on drugs. I'm sure they were after money and figured they'd found an easy mark. I had a hammer in my tool belt, so I pulled it out and threatened them with it, but I was too slow. The one with the knife sliced my arm. I screamed bloody murder and I guess they got shook and took off."

I noticed that his knuckles were swollen and red, no doubt from the pounding he'd given Coffer. "And that, Jack, is why you came into the station house today, to file a complaint. Your bandaged arm and bruised knuckles will corroborate your complaint. Isn't that right?"

He examined his hand, apparently surprised that I had mentioned his knuckles. "Look, Chalice, that's not why I'm here and you know it."

"The only thing I know is that your *dear* old friend Reggie Coffer was beaten to death today, and darn, wouldn't you know it, there was no visible DNA evidence left behind to tie his assailant to the murder … No witnesses either. I tell you it's a goddamn miracle, a one-in-a-hundred scenario." I glared at him in an effort to drive home my point. "So would you like someone to come in to take down your complaint? I can't promise that we'll pick up those kids, but at least the complaint will be on file."

"Chalice, look, I found—"

"You found the courage to come forward? Believe me, I understand—you live in the neighborhood and you don't want any more trouble from these kids than you already have."

"*No.* I—"

"I have one last thing to say before you tell me something that will change your future forever."

"Yeah?"

"We found five ID cards in the space behind Reggie's medicine cabinet, and we found lumber and blueprints for a blanket trunk in a storage facility he rented. Reggie was a serial killer, Jack. We're still doing our due diligence, but it appears that he raped and murdered at least five women, including your daughter Serafina. He was a demented wad of scum, and I'm thrilled that he got what he deserved."

Jack studied my face intently. He was apparently still unsure of what was happening.

"You know, gee, did I mention to you that I'm out on medical leave?"

"But I thought ..."

"I don't know how I forgot to tell you, but I'm a civilian at this moment, no different than you. We're just two friends shooting the breeze ... like you and my dad used to do."

He sniffled and a tear popped out of his eye. "Chalice ..."

"I don't know what prompted the crime scene unit to pull that medicine cabinet from Coffer's bathroom and I guess I never will. Just happenstance, I guess."

"But I told you that—"

"That you fixed a broken pipe? Don't you do that every day?"

"But I told you that I pulled the medicine cabinet to get access to the pipe."

"Did you ever tell me whose bathroom you fixed?"

"No."

"So?" I put my hand on his. "As a friend I will tell you that you'll be questioned about Reggie's murder because it appears that he took Serafina's life and you'll be considered a person of interest because of it, but I don't think they'll press the issue."

"I don't know. That new detective they assigned, Lido ..."

I squeezed his hand. "Oh, you met my husband? It's such a small world. You do know that with me being on leave, he couldn't share any details of the investigation with me."

He grinned. "Or you with him?"

I winked at him. "Or me with him." I stood and walked to the door. "I'll get someone to come in and take your complaint. Sound good?"

He nodded, but looked extremely emotional.

"One last piece of advice—if you are charged, don't make it easy for the DA. The next time you feel like you just have to get something off your chest, talk to a lawyer first. Prison is nothing but a world of hurt, Jack, and I don't think you need or deserve any more pain than you've already had. It's time you turned your life around." I grinned at him, hoping that he'd finally gotten the message. I thought about something he'd said to me, *"And then some monster had to come along and attack my daughter, just like those two animals who attacked me. Shouldn't things balance out? Shouldn't Serafina have had a better life because of all the crap I went through? You'd think so, right? But no, some people have all the luck and others ..."* There was nothing I could do to reverse the tragic events that had befallen him and Serafina but at least I could try to balance right and wrong, right and wrong the way I saw it.

"Oh, by the way, we were able to contact your wife, and she's on her way down here right now. She said that she was looking for you, and was relieved to hear that you were all right. You've got a good woman, Jack. She loves you a lot and I'm sure she'll help you get over whatever it is that has a hold on you. Maybe it's time to let it go ... If not for you, for Sofia's sake. She's been through a lot too."

"No one has ever done anything like this for me before, Chalice. I owe you so much, more than I can ever repay."

"My dad always wanted to find the two assholes who hurt you so badly. As a matter of fact, I think he became a cop because of it, and I became a cop because of him, so if you ask me, Jack, in a manner of speaking it's my dad and I who owe you and not the other way around."

I walked back toward him and grabbed his hand. "So can you suck it up for now so that I can go find the guy who killed my partner and put a bullet in my head, because as much as I like hanging out with you, I just can't shoot the shit forever."

My phone buzzed. It was Tully, the ME. I excused myself and took the call. "Tully?"

"What are you up to, *Cha-lee-see*?" he asked in his heavy Jamaican accent. He was a dear friend, a man I liked and respected.

"Tully, why are you bothering me, *mon*?" I kidded him in a cliché Jamaican accent. "Don't you know I need to be convalescing?"

"You can fool some of the people some of the time, but there ain't no fooling this Jamaican boy. You're about as indisposed as a hungry gator about to wolf down a plump little muskrat."

"Is that the way you see me, Tully, as some manner of fierce reptile?"

He answered with a chuckle in his voice, "Better than being the plump little muskrat."

"I love you too, Doc, but I'm trying to wrap up an interview. What's shakin'?"

"Thought you'd want to know that Coffer's back was covered with scars. Some were fresh, but the bulk of them were mature. Some of them could be decades old."

"Do you think he was abused as a child?"

"No question, Chalice, but like I said, some of the scarring was fresh as well. I think that he used to flog himself."

"Come again?" I asked in disbelief.

"I think it's a type of religious sacrament practiced by some highly devout catholic sects. They call it the practice of corporal mortification."

"Self-mutilation? You're sure about this?"

"Definitely? No. I'm a doctor not an oracle, but I would say most likely. We recovered a thick, knotted rope covered with dried blood from his apartment. It looked like Coffer used to whip the rope over his shoulder, hard enough to draw blood. We also found a cilice belt."

"And that is?"

"It's a coarse fabric belt worn under the clothes and around the thigh. In practice the belt is tightened to the point of extreme discomfort as a sign of repentance and atonement."

"So the creep felt guilty about what he did."

"Yes. Presumably so."

"As things stand now, it looks as if he raped and killed five women. I don't think he atoned quite enough, you?"

"Not hardly," he again answered with a chuckle. "Anyway, that's all I have for now, so get back to it, Chalice. I'll catch you around."

"Thanks, Doc." I disconnected and turned back to Burns. "Hey, Jack, was Reggie the religious type? Was he a churchgoer?"

"I don't know about Reggie, but his mother was a religious fanatic. She had bibles and rosary beads all over their apartment—never missed Sunday mass."

"The ME said his back was scarred. You know anything about that?"

"Yeah, he used to scratch something awful. He always had this ugly rash. His back was covered with red skin and welts—kind of gross looking if you ask me. He never took off his shirt, not even at the beach."

"Oh," I responded casually, but knew the explanation lay elsewhere. Reggie never had a rash—it was merely an excuse he used to cover up his lashed and bloody skin. He had been taught to flog himself for religious repentance, a practice he likely continued the rest of his life. I knew there was a factor well beyond his low self-esteem that had motivated him to become a killer. I knew that there had to be a trigger, and was willing to bet that the start of his murder streak coincided with his mother's death. If I was right, the next question to be asked was, had she died of natural causes, or had she been his first?

Chapter Fifty-Eight

I felt happy and renewed as I left the interrogation room. I didn't know whether the medical review board would allow me to continue on as an NYPD homicide detective, but what had just transpired renewed my faith in the universe. It was nothing short of a miracle that Jack had left no evidence at the crime scene tying him to Coffer's murder. There were no absolutes and nothing said that evidence or a witness wouldn't surface later on down the line, but for the moment at least the man had a chance. Had I taken the law into my own hands? Definitely. Was it wrong to do so? Of course. Did I give a damn? No. Not in the slightest. With any luck, it wouldn't come back to bite me in the ass.

I had to be a law enforcement officer and was determined to do so in any manner I could. It was in my blood and engrained in my DNA. Nothing was going to stop me from being a cop. If I couldn't work the streets for the city, I'd find another way to participate.

I pulled a GPS tracker out of my bag the moment I sat down at my desk, turned it on, and waited for it to pick up a signal. A red dot began to pulse after a few seconds, a red dot that indicated Harry's location.

I caught Gus coming out of the men's room. "You taking a cold shower in there?"

"Three times a day. It's the only way I can keep my testosterone level below the boiling point."

"Dear God, I know what you mean. I'm having a love affair with the handheld shower. I'll call the doc as soon as this is over."

"That's a really good idea," he responded, looking down his nose with a look of entitlement on his face. "This celibacy thing isn't gonna cut it much longer."

"Not what it's cracked up to be? Have you considered hormonal castration? I hear it can turn the stiffest pasta into a wet noodle."

"Yeah. *Right!*" he snapped resentfully. "Like I might ever ... anyway, how'd you make out with Burns?"

"Jack got into a scuffle with a couple of kids. That's how his arm got sliced up and his knuckles bruised."

"What the hell are you talking about?"

I took him by the arm and led him toward the station house front door. "I'll explain it along the way. Right now I've got a craving for sushi."

He wrinkled his nose. Gus was not a fan of raw fish. "For real?"

"Yes, for real. I've got a hunch. You can eat some teriyaki or tempura or anything else that pleases your man-palate."

He shook his head. "How can I argue? Besides, you do your best work with your mouth full."

I flipped him the bird. Just saying.

Chapter Fifty-Nine

Ever the chowhound, Gus was devouring a plate of Beef Negimaki and seemed to be quite pleased with his dinner selection.

"Enjoying that?" I asked.

"Uh-huh," he happily replied.

"Careful inhaling those beef rolls. I don't want to have to give you the Heimlich maneuver."

"I thought you'd be happy to wrap your arms around me after such a long period of abstinence," he said with a shit-eating grin.

"Real funny. Don't even think about coming near me with your tear-gas breath after you've eaten an entire plate of those scallion-stuffed stink bombs."

"Oh really? You think I want to kiss you after you've wrapped your lips around those slimy gelatinous noodles."

"The shirataki noodles? They're yummy."

"Yeah, well, maybe, but from here they look like gelatinous worms."

"Try some."

"No way," he scoffed. "I'm just getting familiar with chopsticks. Don't push your luck."

I sneered at him, then sucked a long one out of the bowl and followed it with a sliver of bright red tuna. "You're not going to try the sashimi?"

He shook his head vigorously.

"You're an embarrassment. You're like the guy who eats gummy bears at the opera. Show some sophistication for the art of sushi, for God's sake."

He flipped me an inconspicuous bird and went back to devouring his beef.

I'd looked up the records on Reggie Coffer's mother while we were on our way to the restaurant, and she had, in fact, passed away roughly five years ago, which furthered my theory that her death had been the catalyst for her son becoming a killer. It was my guess that he was mocking his mother and desecrating her memory with every woman he defiled and killed. I'm not a profiler by any means, but I liked the way the theory rang, and with both mother and son dead, we'd never know for sure anyway. Records indicated that she had died of natural causes, but she was elderly and no autopsy was performed. So the jury was still out on that one, and would stay out indefinitely. The exhumation process is tedious and costly. With Coffer already expired, there was no compelling reason to exhume his mother's body other than to satisfy my own macabre sense of curiosity, and life is way too short to waste time on such a frivolous activity.

I'd briefed Gus on my session with Jack Burns. Lido was going to follow through and interview Burns on Coffer's homicide. How far he'd take it? That was his decision. I couldn't put his career with NYPD at risk for the decision I had consciously made. Only time would tell if I'd become the subject of an internal affairs investigation, but for now my conscience was clean.

"So why the sudden hankering for sushi," Gus asked. "As if I didn't know where this was heading."

"I'll show you." We were in the restaurant where Chef Aguri Maeda had worked, the man who had been stabbed in front of the Shinto temple. I pulled Harry's photo out of my pocket and called for the waitress.

"Everything prepared all right?" she asked politely.

"Everything's delicious." I showed her my badge and Harry's photo. "We're with NYPD. Do you recognize this man?"

Her eyes went wide and she nodded. "Just the other night," she said in a delicate voice. A tear drizzled down her cheek. "He was here talking with Maeda-san." Her throat tightened. "Is he ... is he the killer?"

"No, definitely not. We're just trying to locate this man." I already knew how to locate Harry, but I asked about his whereabouts to make my inquiry sound credible. "Do you know how to reach him?"

"No," she answered nervously. "But I can ask the others."

I slid the photo toward her. "Great. Thank you." It was an unnecessary request, but it would've seemed odd if I hadn't followed through, and I needed a way to engage the other sushi chefs.

I could see in his expression that Gus already knew what I was doing. "So Harry knew the stabbing victim?"

"It appears so. I showed Harry the photos of the victim, but he denied knowing him."

"But you didn't believe him?"

"Not for a second. He broke out in a sweat and had to dash off to the little boys' room as soon as he saw the picture."

"So you think that this chef is somehow tied up in the shooting?"

I spread wasabi over a piece of yellowtail. "I really don't know what his business was with Harry, but he's most likely dead because of it."

I glanced at the sushi bar and saw the waitress conversing with two of the chefs. One of them looked up at us, wiped off his knife and, after conversing with the waitress, made his way toward our table. He placed Harry's photo on our table. "Sugi say you are looking for this man?"

"Yes. Do you know where we can find him?"

He shook his head. "*Iie.* No. He come here and speaks to Maeda-san, not me, but someone else ask who he is."

"Someone else from the police department?" Gus asked.

His eyes were large as he shook his head. "Oh no. This man not police. This man ..." He appeared to be searching for a suitable translation. "Fully tattooed this man. He how you say ... hit man. You know. Enforcer."

"Yakuza?"

He nodded slowly and assuredly. "Al Capone. You understand?"

"Yes. Have you seen him before?"

"Ya. He eats here all the time. His name Ryo, Ryo Goda."

"Was he here tonight?" Gus asked.

"No." He tapped the photo. "He not here since that night he ask about this guy in the picture."

I handed him a business card. "Please call me if you think of anything else that might be useful."

He accepted the card with two hands and bowed. "Thank you," he said and backed away.

"What do you think is going on here?" Gus asked. "Why does a yakuza killer have an interest in Harry?"

"We'll just have to ask him." I pulled the GPS tracker out of my pocket and showed Gus the screen.

"You're a sly dog. I should've known you'd hedge your bet."

"Flattery will get you nowhere, pretty boy. Finish your dinner and let's get his and hers matching tattoos."

"Yeah, *right*. Get a life, would ya?"

"Aw, come on. It'll be fun."

"Did you take your meds today?" he jibed.

"Yeah. Don't worry. I'm in no hurry to get a tramp stamp, but I need to know why everyone involved in this dog and pony show is covered in tats."

Chapter Sixty

"Is this the place?" Gus asked as we pulled up in front of Tiru's Traditional Tattoo and Body Piercing shop. The store sign was hand painted with ornately drawn gold dragons in a Japanese motif on a deep red background. The security shutters were down and locked over the windows and the front door.

"Grab the bolt cutter," I instructed.

"We can't do that. Not without—"

"I hear cries for help. Don't you?"

"Oh. Oh yeah," he acknowledged with revelation. "Sounds like probable cause to me too. Someone must be in trouble. New York's finest to the rescue."

"What a ham you've become. Too bad there's no demand for vaudeville actors anymore." He sneered at me as I stepped from the car. "Lucky for this poor unfortunate soul we just happened to be passing along when we did."

Gus approached with the bolt cutter and popped the padlock as if it were a toy. The door had a wood frame with a glass center panel. "The glass is going to shatter if I kick it."

"Yeah. That's life in the big city, my brave little buckaroo. Make it so."

"Stand back," he warned. "Some glass may go flying." He measured the doorframe with a stride, and backed away like a placekicker measuring a football for a punt. He shielded his eyes, then stepped forward and struck the door solidly on the wooden frame. Somehow, the glass remained intact as the door flew open.

"Remarkable precision, grasshopper. I'll bet you can snatch a fly out of thin air with a pair of chopsticks."

He snickered. "Never mind catching a fly," he said as he covered his nose. "Smells like there's a rotting, maggot-infested carcass in there."

There was no mistaking the smell of a rotting corpse. It's revolting in the most offensive sense of the word. The store was silent and seemed unoccupied, but we pulled our guns for precaution, hit the light switch, and entered guardedly.

The body wasn't hard to find. It was lying behind the counter surrounded by dried blood. The victim was lying face up with a pencil through his throat. I pulled the artist's sketch out of my pocket and compared the likeness to our newest stiff. "It's not our guy." My dear friend Herbert Ambler, the SSA in charge of the FBI New York office criminal investigation division, was running the artist's sketch and tattoo rendering through NGI, the bureau's Next Generation Identification system, which cross-references facial recognition features and photos against an international database of high-risk individuals. The system worked pretty damn quickly, so I was hoping for an update before the end of the night. There was no worry about Ambler going to bed before I did—the man never slept. He was a rerun junkie and watched vintage TV until the wee hours.

"No. No way," Gus commented. "This guy is thin, slight of build, and the perp who stabbed the chef looked to be thick and stocky. There's a dragon tattoo on his neck, but the facial features are completely different."

I clicked off several iPhone pics. "I wonder if this is the notorious Al Capone."

"The guy the sushi chef described?"

"Uh-huh. If we swing back there in a hurry, we can get a visual confirmation before they close for the night."

I tugged on a pair of gloves, palpated the flesh, and then tested the compliance of the arm joints. Signs of rigor mortis had already begun to subside.

"How long?" Lido asked.

"The body is just beginning to soften. I'd say about three days, give or take." There were signs of a brief scuffle. A sketchpad and reference book were open on the counter. "I'm thinking that someone snuck up on Tiru while he was doodling over there, but must've underestimated his fighting skills. Tiru probably had the pencil in his hand and drove it into his attacker's throat. He looked like one of those small wiry types with quiet inner strength and mad ninja skills."

"Harry's accomplice?"

"Right. He's Harry's man on the street, his partner in crime, so to speak. Needless to say, Tiru neglected to tell me that he'd just been attacked and had killed his assailant in self-defense, a purported yakuza enforcer no less."

"You shouldn't be around when the troops arrive," Gus said. "I can handle CSU, but there'll be mucho explaining to do if any white shirts show up."

"We certainly can't have that, now can we?"

"*No es bueno*, babe. Why don't you take the car back to the restaurant and see if the chef can make this guy from the pictures you just snapped. You can swing by afterwards and pick me up."

"I can do that."

He cleared his throat to make a point. "Before you get behind the wheel of the car ..."

"Yes. I swear on all that's holy. I took my meds and I'm okay to drive. Trust me."

"One hundred percent sure? I don't want you going all convulsion-like on me while you're behind the wheel."

"Gus," I responded assertively. "I'm *good.*"

"We'll have to pick up this Tiru guy for questioning. He should be with Harry, correct?"

"Should be. If not, Harry will know how to get a hold of him."

He checked his watch. "Gonna be a late night. No hero shit while you're still on the mend, right?"

"Got it. Besides, I'm only going back to the restaurant—I'm not off to North Korea for covert espionage. So how long before you stop treating me like an invalid?"

He grinned. "When you're declared fit for booty?"

"Don't you mean fit for duty? Oh, I get it." Ignoring the rotting corpse lying at our feet, we kissed long and deep.

"When you have me twitching as if I had been Tasered."

I gave him a bad-girl grin. "Smart money says I can do that right now."

"I'm sure you can, love. I'm quite sure you can."

Chapter Sixty-One

"I don't like this," Tiru said over the phone. "I don't like hiding underground like a rat."

"You have little choice," Haruki explained. "They killed Maeda-san and they would've killed you in your shop if you hadn't been so alert. Somehow the *Inagawa-kaï* have found out that I am here and they're killing everyone I come in contact with. I don't have the resources to protect you."

"Why would they do that? They have been coming to my shop for years. We have history."

Haruki paused before answering, "It's complicated. I have to go it alone from now on."

"And me? There is a yakuza enforcer lying dead in my shop. I can never go back. What will I do?"

Harry had difficulty swallowing. "I understand and I'm terribly sorry, but ... you'll know when it's safe to come out of hiding. That's all I can say."

"How?"

"Trust me, Tiru-san, you will know. I'm sure of it."

"*No,*" Tiru said firmly. "I prefer to take charge of my own destiny. I prefer to—" He went silent.

"Tiru?" Haruki sensed that something was wrong. "Tiru?" he repeated. He listened intently, hoping to detect whether there was a problem with the cellphone reception, but there wasn't. Instead of hearing the silence of a terminated connection he heard something that charged his arteries with adrenaline. It was the sound of labored breathing on the other end of the line, just before it went dead.

Chapter Sixty-Two

I'd called Harry several times without getting an answer, which probably meant he was either refusing to pick up or had dumped the burner phone. I was hoping for the former. I hoped we weren't racing toward a sewer drain or dumpster into which he had tossed the phone. "He knows something we don't."

"What makes you say that?" Gus asked.

"I can sense it. His whole attitude was different the last few times we talked. There's something he doesn't want to tell me— information he doesn't want me to have."

"You think he knows who killed his brother?"

"Possibly."

"So why wouldn't he want NYPD's help in apprehending him?"

"Because, Gus, this isn't about apprehending the guilty. This is about revenge. He's out to kill his brother's murderer, so for obvious reasons, he doesn't want us around when he finds the guy he's looking for. Like I said, he broke out in a cold sweat when I showed him the artist's sketch. He tried to play it cool, but I could see that he was shaken. Whatever he was thinking, that sketch must've confirmed his suspicions as to who murdered Yana. I just hope he still has the phone with him."

I was behind the wheel as we approached the source of the GPS signal, a tenement house in Washington Heights.

"You drive okay for a woman with a few loose screws," Gus quipped. "I was a little nervous about letting you get behind the wheel, but you did okay."

"Don't be a dick. It's not as if I just got my learner's permit."

"Just bustin' your chops. It's not as if you don't have it coming." He glanced at the tenement house. "Let's hang back and surveil for a bit. We're not exactly sure what we're walking into."

"Agreed."

"So what's with the Japanese mob?" he asked. "I'm not real comfortable with all the tattooed bodies piling up, and now that the sushi chef confirmed that our stiff is, in fact, Ryo Goda ..."

"I'm not sure, but you know how all roads lead to Rome, right?"

"Meaning?"

"Everything brings me back to Harry. Someone who was probably a yakuza henchman whacked the chef Harry visited, and they sent an assassin to take out his buddy Tiru. I think it's safe to say there's a hefty bounty on Harry's head. I think it's time we had a talk with my ex-partner's brother."

"Shouldn't be difficult," Gus said, pointing through the windshield. "There he is now."

Chapter Sixty-Three

Harry was hurrying down the block away from us, wearing a black hoodie and carrying the telltale backpack.

"Where do you think he's going?" Gus asked.

"I'm not sure, but there's a subway entrance a couple of blocks up, and if that's where he's headed ... One of us needs to follow him on foot before he ducks into the subway and disappears."

"Why don't we just pick him up now?"

"Because he'll just clam up like he did before, and then we'll never know what's going on."

"So you want to tail him and see who he leads us to?"

"Yeah. Flip a coin—one of us walks and the other rides."

"Not a chance, you slippery little stick of butter," he said while unbuckling his seatbelt. "We do this together."

Stunned by his peculiar metaphor, I gave my head a brain-rattling shake and then got out of the car.

Chapter Sixty-Four

My hunch had been correct. Harry boarded the A train at 168th Street and was headed uptown. We boarded train cars directly in front of and behind the car Harry had entered, an old surveillance ploy we'd been successful with before. He was seated and surrounded by passengers.

I had donned a baseball cap to cover up my blond tresses, and was keeping my face down so as to be as unobtrusive as possible. We were both watching Harry through the glass panels in the sliding end doors. My car was packed and the guy standing behind me looked like a groper, a real fanny-pinching lowlife. I made a note to keep a spare eye on Mr. Wandering Hands as well as Harry.

Harry stood as the subway pulled into the 190th Street station. I kept my eyes on him as long as I could before moving toward the doors. I was shimmying between passengers when I felt someone cup my ass. I wheeled around, sneering at the grabber, but the dirtbag was intentionally looking the other way. *Creep!* The doors were sliding shut as I got to them. Harry and Gus were off the train, but Harry stepped backward, reboarded the train, and was mocking Gus, waving to him from inside the subway car while Gus stood on the platform, fuming over having been duped.

Chapter Sixty-Five

It all happened before I could get out of the subway car. I stood my ground, then hurried back to my previous observation point just in time to see that Harry was still inside the train and facing the closed subway door as it pulled out of the station. He'd obviously made Gus for a cop. I was hoping he hadn't spotted me as well. I texted Gus, "I'm on the train. I still have eyes on Harry." I knew, however, that my husband would be none too happy because we'd been separated, which was the very last thing he wanted. "Catch the next train," I texted. "I'll let you know where he gets off."

There were only two uptown stops left. Harry rode the subway to the end of the line. I texted Gus, "Off at Inwood-207th Street. Will hang back. Won't make a move without you."

He replied, "On my way!"

I waited until the last moment before I moved toward the doors. I let most of the riders exit before me so that there'd be a crowd of disembarking passengers between us. I did, however, manage to stomp on the groper's foot as I got off, sneered at him, and flipped him a very hostile bird. Wouldn't you?

Harry was walking briskly and I was in no hurry to be made, so I hung back just as far as I could without losing him. He hustled down Isham Street and turned right where the road ended and a vast park began. This was no tiny playground. I was staring at Inwood Hill Park, acre upon acre of sprawling fields, forest, hiking trails, and caves, not exactly the easiest place to tail a subject. It covered the entire northwest quadrant of Manhattan Island and was bordered by the Harlem River and the Spuyten Duyvil Creek. I glanced at my phone to see if Gus had left any messages. He hadn't and the signal strength was nil.

I'd been to the park many years before—just a bunch of high school kids blowing off steam and looking for a little adventure. I remembered getting lost near the creek and making out with my then boyfriend from the seclusion of the old Indian caves. Harry, however, wasn't headed in that direction, which was fortuitous because once in that rocky area I knew he'd be almost impossible to follow in the dark. I checked my phone again—no word from Gus. *Now what?*

Clouds were moving briskly across the sky. Harry was bathed in shadow and I could just barely see him as he entered the park. He was almost invisible in his black hoodie.

Duh. Stupid. I suddenly remembered the GPS tracker in my pocket and pulled it out. *Thank God. His phone is still on him.* I hung back a little further to keep from being spotted, knowing that the GPS would allow me to stay with him no matter where he went.

I could see that he had a definite destination in mind because he took a direct path along major walkways that led to the small peninsula that jutted into the creek. From where we were, there was a clear view of the Henry Hudson Bridge, which rose some one hundred and forty-three feet above the Harlem River—though my short-term memory was still somewhat restricted, it seemed that the section of my brain reserved for trivia and all manner of useless knowledge was still intact and functioning superbly.

What are you doing? I wondered.

He walked to the furthest extension of the peninsula and was just scant yards from the creek. I saw him looking out over the water, apparently searching for something.

But for what?

It didn't take long to find out what he was looking for. A pair of headlamps illuminated the center of the bridge. I could see that a van was on the shoulder facing north, and strained to see exactly what was going on. I glanced at Harry, and from his expression, it appeared that he was equally concerned about the development.

The driver opened up the rear doors and dragged someone out of the van. I couldn't see what the captor was holding in his hand, but it appeared he had either a knife or a gun pressed against his captive's back. The pair stepped over the safety railing and came to a stop with just the bridge support structure between them and a long drop into the water. The captor was directly behind his prisoner. Although I tried to recognize the captor's face, it was obscured by his prisoner's shadow.

The clouds must've shifted, because the moonlight suddenly became intense and I was able to get a good look at the prisoner's face. It took a moment for his name to roll off my tongue. "Tiru?" The scenario suddenly made sense, and I could almost predict what was about to happen next.

How do I stop this? There was no time to call for backup, so I pulled a small LED flashlight from my pocket and directed the beam at the men on the bridge, knowing I'd not only get the assailant's attention but Harry's as well. The very last thing I wanted to do was give up my position, but I couldn't stand by and watch Tiru die. The span was too vast for the beam to illuminate the men on the bridge, but I was sure they'd see my flashlight beam in the dark as I hollered, "NYPD. Freeze!"

The captor did not do as ordered. The object he'd been holding was finally revealed. The steel of the blade glistened in the moonlight as he dragged it across Tiru's throat. I could hear his insidious laughter echo across the creek as he pushed Tiru forward, forcing him to tumble off the bridge.

I gasped when Tiru's body slammed into the water.

Harry let out a bloodcurdling scream, *"Iie!"* yelling *no!* in his native tongue.

The color red appears black in dim light. Tiru's blood had stained the assailant's knife, rendering it virtually invisible in his hand as he turned to Harry, the hearty rumble of his laughter mocking him. I could see that he was gloating, and then for an instant he glanced my way with an icy stare that was cold enough to freeze my heart.

Chapter Sixty-Six

Harry took off on foot.

What do I do? Call for backup or chase Harry? Tiru's murderer was already back in the van, and I could hear the wheels chirp as the van sped off. Tiru was undoubtedly dead, and there wasn't a backup responder on earth who'd be able to bring him back to life. There was no urgency to get the salvage operation started.

I quickly glanced at my cell phone—there was still no signal. I tried 911 but couldn't connect to a cell tower.

Harry seemed nimble as he hurried over uneven terrain in the direction of the Indian caves, and I was not the athlete I had been prior to the shooting. I had been out of the gym for months and was struggling to keep up. The fear of falling and reinjuring my brain weighed heavily on my mind and slowed me further. I kept my eyes glued to the ground and was cautious not to misstep, which made my pursuit tenuous and slow. I could see his image fading away as the moon once again retreated behind the clouds. I listened for the sound of his footsteps and pushed forward until I came upon rugged stone topography and the Indian caves.

I slowed to a walk and then came to a stop because I could no longer see Harry and hoped that a crackle of a twig would disclose his location, but all I heard was the low rumble of cars traversing the bridge. Harry was either gone or in hiding, and the area was now pitch black. I lit my flashlight and scanned the caves before me. My surroundings were ominous and I was hardly my usual confident self, so I pulled my LDA for a dose of instant courage. There's nothing quite like a pound of finely machined steel to boost your mettle, even though the chances of me firing my gun at Harry were miniscule.

I heard movement and stepped forward to explore a gap between the caves and in my flashlight beam caught a glimpse of a man running though the image was too dim for me to be sure it was Harry. I was thinking that it could've been a vagrant I'd inadvertently rousted until I noticed a cell phone lying on the ground. "Shit!" It was the trackable burner I'd given to Harry. My unexpected appearance at the park had most certainly tipped him off to the fact that I was keeping tabs on him, and he'd figured out that the phone had GPS-tracking capability. I began to hurry after him.

Careful. The terrain was rocky and terribly uneven. Common sense told me to slow down precipitously and proceed with caution even though I knew I'd probably lose my man by doing so. *Hell, who am I to listen to common sense?* I was hurrying forward at an unwise pace when my foot slipped on an angled stone and I lost my balance. I felt my heart skip a beat as I maneuvered to right myself and avoid going down face-first. I tumbled but managed to take most of the impact with my shoulder. The back of my head made just marginal contact with the rocky ground, just enough to send a sharp pain through my skull. I saw a flash of white light and then my vision disappeared. It returned after what seemed like a few seconds, but when my eyes cleared, I saw a terrifying face staring down at me and once again my heart filled with dread.

Chapter Sixty-Seven

It took a moment or two before I realized that I was alone on the ground and that the face I thought I saw was not actually there but instead being recalled from memory, a memory from minutes after I'd been shot. The fall had unlocked a concealed memory and I could hear the sounds of alarmed citizens rushing over to assist Yana and me as we lay bleeding on the street, their voices filled with panic. I could hear a woman making a 911 call as vividly as if she were on the phone at the present moment, and I could sense onlookers gathering and gawking, helpless to assist as blood puddled on the sidewalk.

"Do something," a woman screamed.

"Do what?" a man replied. "I'm afraid to touch them."

Off in the distance the constant wail of a siren started off low and grew louder in volume.

The onlookers all kept their distance—all save one. I recalled the clap of soles alongside me and managed to open my eyes for a moment, just long enough to make out the daunting image of a stocky man towering over me. He stood watching me for a while, just studying me, but making no effort to assist. I could feel my eyes closing and his image fading away. The snippet of memory had run its course and my mind once again went blank, but I wanted to establish a connection. For an instant I thought that the man who had braved the crowd and the man who had killed Tiru were one and the same, but was I correct or was my mind was just playing tricks on me?

"Oh shit. Stephanie, are you all right?" I heard panic in Gus' voice as he approached.

"Yeah. I'm fine."

"What are you doing on the ground?"

"I stumbled," I admitted sheepishly.

"You didn't—"

"Have another seizure? No. Thank God."

"You're sure?"

"Yeah. Positive. Unless you count clumsiness as a mental anomaly."

Gus helped me to my feet. "It's absolutely desolate out here. Why didn't you call me?"

"I did." I pulled my phone and pointed to the signal-strength indicator. "See? No bars."

"Are you sure that you're all right?"

"God, but you're persistent. Yes. I'm fine, but you arrived about ten minutes late to a shit storm."

"What happened?"

"I followed Harry to the water's edge at the base of the bridge."

"And?"

"A van pulled up and Harry's friend Tiru was marched to the edge of the bridge at knife point. I realized what was going to happen, so I lit my flashlight and called out for the assailant to freeze, but ..."

Gus shook his head unhappily. "Are you saying that we have to dredge the creek?"

I nodded. "The assailant slit Tiru's throat and pushed him off the bridge. What I'm not sure about ... Well, I'm not sure if it was my fault."

"Why would you even think that?"

"I'm thinking that the assailant summoned Harry to the park so that he could see that Tiru was being held prisoner. I'm not sure if he was planning to kill Tiru or if he was merely holding him for leverage." My head dropped. "He may have killed him because I had interfered with his plan."

"And Harry?"

"I lost him when I went ass over teakettle. But ... well, I think a memory came back."

He smiled. "Really? That's great. What did you remember?"

"Yeah. I think the guy who killed Tiru was at the crime scene minutes after the shooting."

"But you were unconscious."

"I thought I was too, but ... I bumped my head when I fell just now and a memory put me back at the scene of the shooting. I was on the sidewalk and I remembered hearing voices, a call to 911, and ... this guy was standing over me, just watching and waiting. Everyone else was too frightened to come near me, but this guy was practically on top of me, just checking me out."

"No shit. Think you can give a description to the department sketch artist?"

"I don't have to," I said as I reached into my pocket and pulled the sketch of the perp who'd killed the chef in front of the temple. "Someone already did."

Chapter Sixty-Eight

Jack Burns yawned as he trudged out of his apartment, toolbox in hand, on his way to fix his neighbor's dripping faucet before she left for work.

His relationship with Sofia was far from good, but she had returned home and was giving their badly strained marriage a second chance. Jack was beginning to find a little emotional quiet and it reflected in his attitude when they were together. She had made coffee and handed him a cup as he went out the door. She gave him a kiss on the cheek and there was an optimistic lilt in her voice as she wished him a good day.

Mike Mara cringed when the elevator chugged to a stop and the doors parted. He nodded to Burns as he entered and then closed his eyes.

"Late night?" Burns asked.

Mara nodded with his eyes still closed. "Wish I had time for a little hair of the dog. My head is killing me." The doors closed and the elevator slammed when it hit the next floor. There was a loud thud on the elevator rooftop. "What the hell is that?" he asked. "This goddamn building is falling apart. I hope the stupid elevator doesn't drop to the basement and kill us both." He pointed to the floor indicators, all of which were illuminated. "Some stupid kid must've pressed every one of these goddamn buttons after getting out on the top floor. Real funny, huh?"

Burns shrugged and sipped his coffee. He'd been through far too much pain to let a juvenile prank get to him.

The car clanked on the next floor. "You hear that?" Mara asked. "You sure the cable isn't about to snap?"

His coffee was hot and satisfying, and he was happy that Sofia had gotten up early just to make it for him. "Let's take a look." He placed his coffee cup on the floor, then stood his large toolbox on end. He put his foot up on the end of the box and boosted himself up. "Just steady me, would you?"

"Sure." Mara grabbed Jack around the hips and watched as he slid the Celotex emergency panel to the side.

"Oh Jesus," Burns cried.

"What's wrong?" Mara hollered with panic in his voice. "Is it the cable? Is it about to snap?"

"No. Relax. It's not the cable," Burns replied, his voice trembling. He retrieved a rag from his back pocket and then reached back up into the space above the elevator. "Holy shit!" he exclaimed. "Holy-goddamn-shit."

Chapter Sixty-Nine

Names and contacts for everyone who had witnessed the shooting were on file. Gus and I had visited three of them by 11:00 a.m. the next morning. They were all shown the sketch of the man who'd killed Chef Maeda and asked if they remembered anyone like that loitering about Yana and me as we lay on the sidewalk after the shooting. The first witness didn't recall seeing him at all, but the second two were reasonably sure that the man in the sketch looked familiar.

"It's a shame this guy's mug hasn't popped out of the bureau NGI system," Lido said. "There must be at least a million rats flying under the radar that we don't know about at all."

"Betcha a box of Krispy Kremes that Harry knows who he is, and if he does, there's a fair chance this guy is known to the Japanese police."

"Think we've got enough juice to get the cooperation of a foreign government in a murder investigation?" Gus asked.

"You're kidding, right? A high-jingo case like this, the murder of an NYPD police officer?"

"Do we have an extradition treaty with Japan?"

"Absolutely—been in place since the seventies. Besides, if this mope is wanted in Japan, I'm sure they'll want him back to stand trial."

"Can we send him back in pieces?" Gus said with a sneer. "I can't wait to get my hands on this son of a bitch."

"Not fond of the guy who shot your wife, I take it?"

He nodded determinedly. "I just hope that I find him first. I'll knock his teeth out for starters."

"Easy, boy, I know you haven't been getting any, but try to contain your aggression. We don't want anything getting in the way of this guy getting a life sentence."

"Yeah. I'd feel better about it if we had some hard evidence, prints or some DNA."

"And *I* wouldn't?"

My cell phone buzzed. I was surprised to see Jack Burns' name on the display. "It's Burns. I wonder what this is about?" I hit the Accept icon. "Hi, Jack." The excitement in his voice immediately drew my interest. My eyes went wide before I covered the phone and turned to Gus. "Ask and ye shall receive," I told him. "You will never believe what he just said."

Chapter Seventy

It appeared that a .30-caliber rifle had been firmly wedged under the elevator pulley bracket until repetitious hard floor stops had finally jarred it loose. It had been banging about for a couple of days before a neighbor complained about it and Burns took the initiative to open the escape hatch and look for the source of the loud and irritating noise.

I was face to face with the weapon that had likely slain my partner and aerated my skull. I knew my way around ordnance but had never seen a weapon quite like the one before me.

"It's got all the bells and whistles," Lloyd Bochner, the department ballistics expert, explained. "Pound for pound, one of the most deadly accurate guns in the world. Hell, with one of these mothers I could plug a pigeon's anus at twelve hundred yards while whistling 'Yankee Doodle Dandy.'" The British-made L115A3 AWM rifle was made expressly for snipers. It had a night-optics scope, an adjustable cheek piece to allow the sniper to align his eye with the scope, and an adjustable bipod to support the rifle in a stable position. "It's fitted with a suppressor to reduce flash and noise signature, and a short five-round clip—not large enough to interfere with alignment, but just big enough to give the shooter a couple of do overs."

Do overs? Bochner's use of the expression made me cringe—what a cavalier way to speak about Yana's death. From all we had learned, my guess was that Yana had been the sniper's intended target. The sniper's first shot had missed and ricocheted off the pavement before striking me, and Yana ... Yana was the do over, the killer's second chance at hitting his mark.

"How does a weapon like this even get into the country?" Gus asked rhetorically. "A weapon made exclusively for war." He shook his head. "Fucking black market," he ranted. "You can get your hands on any goddamn piece of weaponry you want if you've got the money and a scumbag willing to sell it to you."

"These rifles were used in Afghanistan and Iraq, two of the world's biggest shit holes. Drugs, guns, and stolen oil—anything is fair game in the world of jihad." Bochner was a former Marine weaponry expert. He'd been deployed to the Middle East and had come home with a devout hatred for the region. "Those Hezbollah motherfuckers! The entire world reeks from their revolting stench."

I winked at Bochner. "Indeed."

"At least we got prints off of it," Gus said.

"No surprise there," Bochner advised. "No marksman worth his salt covers the tips of his fingers. If it's cold, they cut the fingers off their gloves so that they don't lose any trigger sensation."

"We were lucky. The weapon had been wiped down, but in his haste to escape, the shooter had neglected to wipe down the portion of the magazine that fits into the stock, leaving a full thumb and partial index print."

"Lucky is good," Bochner said with a smile. "I'll take lucky any day of the week. So how close are you to nailing this mofo?"

"We've got prints, an artist's sketch, and a solid theory. We'll get him."

"Ballistics will be back PDQ," Bochner said. "Stick around and you'll know for sure if this gun is a match to the slug they yanked out of your gray matter ... Not that there's much doubt."

"No. Not much doubt at all." The longer I looked at the weapon, the more upset I became. I pictured the projectile exiting the long barrel and reaching through the night to strike me in the back of the head. I shut my eyes. "I need a decaf break."

"Decaf?" Bochner questioned with disbelief. "I don't see you as a low-joe kind of gal. Decaf, Chalice? Really?"

"The docs are concerned that caffeine may short out my mangled brain wiring—an enduring gift from the guy who capped me in the head."

"No bean? Damn, that's harsh. Does the caffeine give you seizures or something?"

"They're afraid it might. That's the theory, anyway."

"Sorry, Chalice, I'd brew you a pot of decaf myself if I had any unleaded lying around. Anyhow, there are about twenty coffee shops within a five-minute walk in any direction."

"Thanks, Lloyd. We'll be back," Gus said as we exited the ballistics lab. "You coming unglued?" he asked.

"I'll be all right. It was just that looking at that gun and knowing it almost ended my life ... it's just a little unnerving is all."

"Maybe it's a good time to go home and kiss your son. You know, remind yourself what's really important in life and how lucky you are to still be alive."

My throat tightened. "I'm dying to do that, but I have to stay with this until the end. I have to ... I have to get the SOB who killed Yana."

"Yeah, but you can't make yourself crazy over it."

"You're funny," I snickered. "We both know *that* ship has sailed."

An official request had been made to the Japanese government to assist in the identification of our UNSUB, but we had yet to hear back from them. I was hoping that with fingerprints to beef up our request, a response would be immediately forthcoming.

We hit a café called The Bean, where I was able to get a tall cup of reasonably good decaf and one of those scrumptious Sweet Dream cakepops. "So Harry is once again in the wind and we're playing the waiting game while some Japanese muckety-muck decides whether it's in the nation's best interest to cooperate in an American manhunt."

"Are you all right, Steph? You seem really unhappy today."

"I didn't sleep well."

"Something on your mind? I mean other than scar tissue from the slug the doctors dragged out of your brain, and an unforgiving need for retribution?"

"I'm just wondering if things are ever going to be the same or if they're going to be messed up forever." I shook my head wearily. "I just want things to go back to the way they were."

Gus took my hand. "You know that's never going to happen, right? That bullet changed our future forever, but it doesn't mean we can't be happy. It's the card you were dealt. You've got to pick it up and play your hand."

"Really sucks," I lamented. "You know that my days with NYPD are numbered."

His mouth tightened. "Your days as a homicide detective might be running out, but that doesn't mean you can't go in another direction. Ever think about a career in command?"

"A bureaucrat? *Puh-lease,* I'd rather chew off my arm than spend day after day in meetings talking about policies that civic groups have come up with to jeopardize the safety of officers on the street."

"Like I said, you've got to play with the cards you've been dealt. I'm sure there's a future for you in LE, one that'll keep you happy." He grimaced. "Look, I know this is upsetting, but it'll all work out. I promise." He kissed my hand. "Jesus, Stephanie, we almost lost you. You've got to see the big picture." His cell phone buzzed. He pulled it from his pocket and read a text. "It's from Bochner," he said. "'Ballistics in. Confirmed, the AWM is our murder weapon.'" He smiled. "See that? We're coming down the home stretch."

I grabbed my empty paper cup and chucked it into the trash pail. "Let's turn up the heat on our diplomatic liaison. It's time to nab this dirtbag and put him away for good."

Chapter Seventy-One

"**Chalice?**" Pam Shearson seemed stunned to see me walking down the corridor at One PP. On second thought, it was probably the blond pixie cut that rocked her socks.

Our former CO had rocketed up the ranks and was now a deputy commissioner. She'd never been the soft and fuzzy type, but I knew she was a hardworking lady. Our relationship had improved after she received her first promotion. She'd even come by to visit while I was laid up in the hospital and had brought me a present, an Eberjay pajama set in which I could recoup in silky-soft style. Shearson was a fashion plate with lots of disposable income. She was wearing an absolutely gorgeous cap-sleeve dress.

"Max Mara?" I asked.

She grinned. "You always did have an eye for fashion, Chalice. How are you, and what the hell did you do with your hair?"

I shrugged. "I don't know. It was time for a change."

"A *change*? Honey, this is a total metamorphosis. My hairstylist clips two inches and I go into shock. This ... this would send most women into apoplexy." She swept a lock of blond hair away from my eyes. "My, but you're a gorgeous woman. You certainly don't look any the worse for wear."

"I guess lead agrees with me."

"Lead agrees with you? Ha! You're like one of those comic book characters who suffers a catastrophic accident and emerges a superhero. You got a cape and tights on under your clothes?" She shook her head. "Seriously though—what are you doing here? I figured you'd be on the DL for months yet."

"I am. I just stopped by to see if I could help Gus out with an unusual request."

"What kind of unusual request?" she asked apprehensively.

"Print ID and an artist's sketch on the suspected shooter."

Her eyes grew large. "Your shooter? The cop killer?"

"Yes."

I could see in her eyes that her interest was peaked. "When did we get prints?"

"The call came in just this morning. Ballistics confirmed the murder weapon not thirty minutes ago. We have a full thumb and a partial, but there was no match through IAFIS. We believe the shooter is an illegal from Japan and we're petitioning the Japanese government to assist."

"Oh, that's wonderful news. Who are you working with on it?"

"Wilkins."

"Wayne Wilkins?" she asked with dismay. "Oh Jesus," she lamented. "He's such a namby-pamby little man. He walks on eggshells with his foreign counterparts. He'll get stonewalled in red tape until we're all in assisted living. No. That'll never do. You come with *me*," she insisted. "I'm not going to let Wilkins pussyfoot around this one."

We'd had our differences in the past, but there was no denying that Shearson was a woman of action. "Where are we going?" I asked excitedly.

"To see my boss. You think I'm going to sit back and let some diplomatic wimp play kiss ass while a cop killer is free on our streets?"

"*Hell* no?"

She grinned and put her arm over my shoulder. "Hell no is right. By the way, how did those pajamas work out? It's not easy shopping for a woman who's built like a chiffonier with the top drawer pulled out."

I blushed.

"Don't blush, honey. If the big-ass bra fits, rock it like a porn star."

Chapter Seventy-Two

"Japan is half a day ahead of us, so it's the middle of the night there right now, but we should have an answer first thing tomorrow morning."

"Hopefully. Are you happy?" Gus asked.

"*Happi-er*. You've got to hand it to Shearson. She may be a pain in the ass at times, but she put so much pressure on the commish that he reached out to the mayor and the state department. An official request for assistance was sent out by the White House."

"That's impressive. And to think, she used to bust your balls incessantly. She's certainly changed."

"I guess I'm not a threat to her any longer."

"Guess not."

"She was actually very nice to me."

"Well, why not. You closed some very high-profile cases while you were under her command. She climbed to the top on your sweat and toil."

"True dat. Let's just hope those prints are on file over in the land of the rising sun. It'll be a real letdown if this turns out to be a dead end. Especially now that Harry has dumped the trackable phone I gave him."

"Lighten up," Gus said with a twinkle in his eye. "He was probably using it to call all of his relatives in the South Pacific. Think of all the long-distance charges you're going to save."

"You're a piece of work."

"I aim to please. Speaking of which, any word from the doc? I mean, are your lady parts going to be off-limits forever?"

"Need a release, do you?"

He nodded eagerly.

"Tell you what, if I don't hear from the doc by the weekend, we'll improvise. There's more than one way to choke a chicken."

"*Harrumph.* Well, when you put it like that, it hardly sounds sexy."

"Not to worry, lover, I'll *make* it sexy. Don't you worry your pretty little head, mama knows how to push daddy's buttons."

"Always nice to have something to look forward to. If you'll excuse me, I think I'll go take yet another cold shower. Just the idea of having sex with a blond ..." He glanced over at the coffee table. "Hey, I think your phone is buzzing." He leaned across the sofa and picked it up. He smirked. "It's your new BFF, Shearson." He handed it to me. "She's awfully friendly. Are you sure she's not a switch-hitter?"

"I wouldn't put it past her."

"Neither would I."

"Deputy Commissioner Shearson, I—"

"Oh, for Christ's sake, Chalice, just call me Pam. Listen, I'm having dinner with His Honor the mayor, but I stepped away for a moment because I just received a call from the state department. The Japanese jumped on our request and came through PDQ."

"Already? It's not even 6:00 a.m. over there."

"Well, apparently we struck a nerve, and those fingerprints were a match to a felon with multiple arrest warrants. Do you or the hunk have access to the department intranet?"

"Absolutely."

"Well, log on. A translated report should be in both of your inboxes, along with photos, arrest records, and background."

"That's unbelievable. Thank you so much, Pam."

"You can thank me after this cop killer is behind bars. Now if there's nothing else, I'm off to go powder my cleavage so that I can continue flirting with the hizzoner. Christ, I wish I had your boobs, Chalice. I'd be in the White House by now. Goodbye."

"You seem excited. What did she say?" Gus asked.

"She said that she wishes she had my boobs."

"Yeah, no surprise there. But seriously ..."

"Fire up the laptop. The Japanese got a hit on our fingerprints."

Chapter Seventy-Three

The report described Daichi Shiroo as a confident and ruthless killer, an emerging force poised to take over as the boss, what they called the *kumichō* of *Inagawa-kaï*, one of the largest yakuza families in Japan.

Gus was behind me, trying to read along as I skimmed the report the Japanese government had forwarded to us through the state department. "Stop looking over my shoulder and sit down. I'll read it to you."

"Yes, teacher," he groused.

"It says, 'The killing of Iori Kuba, a local detective, marked the beginning of a cold-blooded career in which Shiroo took responsibility for some of the yakuza's most vicious killings, and enjoyed a degree of power in the criminal underworld superseded only by his brother, Mirai Shiroo, the reigning *kumichō* of *Inagawa-kaï*.' It goes on to say, 'The fact that he liked to shoot his victims from a great distance, which broke one of the yakuza's rules of good conduct, proved no obstacle to his rise. On one occasion, he shot a policeman lighting a cigarette, putting a bullet through his chest from a six-story apartment house window.'"

"Sounds like a great guy," Gus said. "So he's killed cops before."

"Yes, and like Boris and Natasha, he's a member of the Villains, Thieves, and Scoundrels Union. Now don't interrupt me and let me read." I scanned the next paragraph. "Get this, Gus, it says, 'It is believed he was responsible for a car bomb that killed an anti-yakuza judge, his wife, and three bodyguards on a motorway near Narita Airport. According to testimony, Shiroo personally stood guard with a *British-made L115A3 AWM rifle* while his men stuffed a storm drain beneath the road with more than 500 kilos of gelignite, TNT, and plastic explosive.' Sound familiar?"

"The shithead has a gun of choice. I guess he's not smart enough to know that using the same weapon only helps our case against him."

I peaked my eyebrows. "Or maybe he just doesn't care. It says, 'Daichi's rise to prominence was helped considerably by the slowness of the Japanese justice system and probably collusion with certain sectors of the state.' I'm surprised the Japanese government admitted to that."

"Maybe they're too honorable to employ spin doctors over there—wouldn't that be a refreshing change of pace?"

"Maybe. 'He killed businessmen and politicians who opposed his family or showed preference to rival groups. He spent six years in prison during the 1990s for a rash of relatively minor offences, but had to be released in 2000 because his period of preventive custody for bigger crimes had run out. For much of the 2000s he managed to move around with *virtual impunity*, throwing a lavish party for his wedding to the sister of a fellow gangster at Kyoto's most posh hotel, the Hotel Granvia, in April 2011.' It says, 'Policemen were powerless to intervene because, as in the past, no arrest warrant was forthcoming. When he was finally tracked down, the fact that he was unarmed and alone suggested that he did not feel particularly threatened.' He was released for lack of evidence, and ultimately disappeared when his brother, the reigning *kumichō*, was arrested and convicted on murder charges. His brother was sentenced to death and executed three years later. It says, 'There was evidence suggesting that Daichi's brother had been betrayed by a spy, someone inserted into the family by a rival faction, who undermined Mirai's authority and was planning to assassinate them both.'"

"No wonder he skipped town. His brother was headed for the long goodbye, there was a spy in the ranks, and he had open murder warrants. He was lucky to be able to sneak into the States."

"Yeah. No wonder. But why has he surfaced now, and why did he kill Yana?"

"I don't know. What, do I have to figure out everything for you?" Gus asked with a grin. "What are you, useless? Do some sleuthing, for God's sake. Christ, just what the department needs, another pretty face."

"Easy, Bulldog Drummond. How about a foot massage to help free up some of my problem-solving energy?"

"How about you make me a sandwich?"

"A trademark artery-clogger like my mama makes?"

"Uh-huh."

"All that cholesterol and fat is going to block the blood flow to your private parts."

"My private parts are just fine. They're primed and ready to go, and you'd better take advantage before the warranty runs out."

"Yeah," I giggled. "Well, I'm still waiting on the drilling permit." Gus had really put up with a ton of crap from me. Aside from being an overzealous cop who put work before everything and everyone else, the recent shooting and subsequent disappearance had really taken a toll on him. He certainly deserved an occasional gastronomic indulgence. "All right, one monster sub coming right up. Anything to wash it down?"

"Really?"

"Yes. Really. But while I'm gone, get those brain cells going and figure out how Harry fits into this mess and how we're going to take down the shooter."

"Ah, shoot. There's always a catch."

"That's right, there's always a catch, my love, and it's called life."

Chapter Seventy-Four

We had Daichi Shiroo's photo ID, his prints, his history, and his murder weapon. Hell, we had everything we needed to build an airtight case against him, but finding a man with no official records in New York City was a tall order. There were no bank accounts under his name, nor were there credit cards or a driver license. Daichi Shiroo was a ghost, an entity we knew existed but couldn't prove.

He was placed on the FBI most wanted list. His photo and description were dispatched to the media. Rewards were offered. Hotlines were open and had started to ring. As is normally the case, most of the phone leads were junk, Jesus sightings and the ramblings of callers with fractured minds, but one of them seemed credible, credible enough to warrant checking into immediately.

Melvin DeNiro was a rat, an informant who'd cooperated with the police in exchange for dropped charges on a drug rap. His cooperation had sent a group of Dominican meth dealers to prison. He'd informed on other local dealers as well, and his information had always been reliable. He'd come forward to score some of the reward money and had reached out to the narcotics detective he'd worked with in the past. A meeting was arranged at a bar in the Bronx.

We crossed the length of the establishment to where narcotics detective Josh Lax was seated next to DeNiro in a booth near the back of the bar. Lax was a bull of a man, with shaved sidewalls, broad sloping shoulders, and a neck as thick as a water main. He dwarfed DeNiro, a slight man who looked in dire need of elevator shoes. The men shook hands.

"Who's the hot blond twat?" DeNiro blurted as his eyes rolled over me head to toe.

Lax elbowed him in his side. "Manners, dirtbag. This is Detective Chalice, one of New York's finest."

"She certainly is."

Lax elbowed him again and we slid into the booth opposite them.

DeNiro apologized, "Sorry. Sorry. I couldn't help myself—the lady is quite striking."

"No harm, no foul. I've been called worse." *Not much worse, mind you, but worse.* I glanced at Gus, who was having trouble holding back a snicker. "We understand that you have information on our cop killer."

"Yeah. I know this guy you're looking for ... by reputation mostly. I mean, I've seen him in the flesh but never did any deals with him directly. But before I spill, I want to confirm the reward money."

"Ten K if your information leads to an arrest," Lido said, his expression stoic. "That work for you, *Melvin*?"

"Yeah. Ten K works. It works fine."

"So what do you have?" I asked impatiently.

"They don't call him Shiroo or Daichi or anything like that. I don't know if I'm saying it right, but they call him *Burakkuhāto* or Buckaroo or something like that. I was told it's Japanese for Blackheart."

I knew better than to ask DeNiro to spell the name for me. I asked him to repeat it and spelled it out phonetically in my notebook. "So what's his deal with him, Melvin?"

"He used to work with this guy Ringo, but I heard Ringo bought the farm. They found him in a tattoo shop with a pencil stuck in his neck."

I turned to Gus as that aha moment hit us both.

DeNiro continued. "He goes after midlevel dealers, robs them and resells their drugs. He's killed a few of them, I hear."

"And you didn't think it was worth telling me this before?" Lax spat. "It doesn't matter to you that this 'Blackheart' is running around killing people ... *cops*?"

DeNiro frowned. "You bet your ass—not until the word reward was mentioned. Shit, Lax, it's a dog-eat-dog world. I didn't see anyone coming to my rescue when I got pinched. I had to turn informant just to stay out of the can, and now my name is dirt on the street."

Lax snickered. "Your name is listed as Dirt on your birth certificate."

I snorted.

DeNiro flipped Lax the bird and then it was back to business.

"No address or contact?" Gus asked.

DeNiro smirked. "Hey, Lax, this guy for real? An address? You're kidding, right?"

Lax turned to him, the veins throbbing on his twenty-inch neck. "How about if I roll up the reward money and shove the bills up your ass one by one?"

DeNiro flipped his palms outward, a surrender gesture. "Hey, no reason to get hostile, my friends."

Lax gritted his teeth. "I don't need a reason."

"All right, all right. Geez, take it easy," DeNiro said. "I'm trying to help."

"I don't see any reward money in this for you. No address. No phone number. How the hell is this supposed to be helping us?"

"Relax, Detective. I got it covered." He turned to Lax. "You know Mikey Mike over on the Grand Concourse?"

"Yeah. I've heard of him," Lax replied. "He's a small-time heroin dealer. Why?"

"Because he's in Montefiore Hospital with cracked ribs and internal bleeding, and just yesterday these started hitting the street." He reached into his pocket and laid a gram-sized glassine bag of heroin on the table. It was stamped with a black heart.

Chapter Seventy-Five

Gus turned the wheel and piloted our car away from the curb. "I'm surprised a big-time yakuza boss is shaking down penny-ante dealers and selling smack on the street."

"He's on the down low, Gus. He fled his native country to avoid serious jail time and possibly even execution. He's doing what he has to do to eat without popping up on anyone's radar."

He shrugged. "I guess so. A guy like that must have one hell of an ego. I don't see him holding it in check for very long."

I pulled up the records of the victim we'd found in Tiru's tattoo shop. "His name isn't listed as Ringo on his driver's license. It's listed as Ryo Goda."

"Close enough to support the nickname. Think he can play the drums?"

I smiled.

"Got an address?"

"Yup." I read it out loud to Gus.

I know Valentine, the detective who's investigating Goda's homicide. I'll give him a call so that we don't lose time trying to figure out what he already knows."

"That's an inspired plan. Give him a call and let him know we need a powwow."

Chapter Seventy-Six

Richie Valentine met us at Goda's apartment, which had long since been swept for clues and evidence. "You look good, Chalice, but what's with the blond hair? You and Gus into some serious role-playing shit?"

"Yeah. That's it, Richie. Trying to keep the sparks flying— know what I mean? I was a redhead last month and went jet-black goth the month before that—black makeup, nose ring ... the whole nine yards."

"Ha! You're a lucky man, Lido. My wife has had the same hairstyle for the past twenty years. Maybe I'll bring her home a bottle of Lady Clairol and see if she takes the hint."

"Subtle, Valentine. Subtle. Lets talk shop and then I'll tell you how to con your wife into a makeover."

"Yeah. Okay. So you're saying the guy who killed Goda is the same guy they just fished out of the Harlem River?"

"Yes. Tiru Kondo, the expired owner of the tattoo shop. My guess is that Goda recognized Haruki, Yana's brother, at the sushi restaurant where Chef Maeda, the first victim, worked. Maeda was probably killed because he was seen associating with Haruki. Somehow, Goda must've known that Haruki was tied to Tiru Kondo. The ME noticed some light scabbing on one of Goda's tattoos. With all the ink that man had on his body it's not a stretch to presume he'd recently been in Tiru's tattoo shop."

"Maybe Goda saw this guy Haruki there," Valentine offered.

Why Shiroo killed Tiru in such a dramatic fashion, and why he wanted Harry to watch him do it were still the questions nagging at me. I was still unsure if my appearance at the park had caused him to take Tiru's life.

"So you're saying I can close my investigation?" Valentine asked hopefully.

"Looks that way," Gus replied.

"Great!" Valentine said with a smile. "Good night," he chuckled. "Now tell me how I get the wife to look like a streetwalker."

"Not so fast, *slick*. What do you know that will help us find Daichi Shiroo?"

"Oh, that's right." Valentine sighed. "What the hell was I thinking? I forgot we're still looking for a cop killer." He plopped into a chair. "What would you like to know?"

"The perp we're looking for is a Japanese refugee, a yakuza henchman named Daichi Shiroo who's wanted for murder in his homeland. Our information tells us that he worked with Goda. The two of them boosted drug dealers and sold their product on the street."

"We dumped Goda's phone, but we haven't had the time to check all of his calls yet," Valentine said. "Good chance this guy Shiroo's number will pop up."

"Scum like that—he probably uses a burner," Gus added.

"The crime scene boys didn't find any evidence of drug dealing when they checked the place?"

"No contraband, if that's what you mean. Wait a minute ..." From his expression it looked as if he'd had a revelation. He pulled his notebook and began flipping through the pages. "Let me correct myself on that. We impounded several boxes of printed glassine envelopes."

"With a black heart stamped on them?"

"Yeah. How'd you know?"

"Feminine intuition, Valentine." I showed him the bag we'd taken from Melvin DeNiro. "Like this one?"

"Yeah. *Just* like it, but without the illegal contents."

"Was there an invoice for the bags?" Gus asked. "A manifest or something we can trace to see who ordered the bags?"

"You're kidding, aren't you, Lido, a manifest for illegal drug paraphernalia? I think maybe you need some time off, my friend. We're talking street-level drug dealing—all transactions are cash and carry."

"Guess I'm getting desperate," Gus admitted. "This thing has been a nightmare."

"I still want to look around. You don't mind, do you, Valentine?"

"Mind? Not at all. Knock yourself out, blondie. In the meantime I'll call the house to see if they've made any progress on Goda's phone records. Least I can do since you solved my case and are about to help me spice up my marriage."

I winked at him. "Atta boy, Valentine."

The apartment wasn't large, but it was absolutely crammed with crap. I could see that a respectable attempt had been made by the crime scene investigators to sort through it all, but there were boxes everywhere just chocked full of bits and pieces. It seemed that Goda was a hoarder and had a fascination with electronic junk. Box after box was filled with gizmos and cables and such, most of which appeared to have been fished out of the garbage. One small box sat unopened atop the refrigerator. The label indicated that Staples had shipped it. "Hey, Valentine," I hollered. "No one opened this one?"

I heard footsteps approaching the kitchen. His cell phone was cradled in the crook of his neck. "I'm on hold. What's up?"

I held up the small box. "The crime scene guys didn't think it was worth opening this?"

"Yeah. I saw that. I didn't think it was worth examining a cadaver's posthumous delivery of paperclips."

"Then you won't mind if I open it."

"If you must," he said with an I-don't-give-a-crap expression. He turned and left the kitchen.

I used my pocketknife to cut the tape and opened the box. It contained what appeared to be small tubular pre-inked stampers like the ones used to stamp the back of your hands so that you can reenter a bar or dance club. I pulled the cap off one of them and stamped a scrap of paper lying near the sink. Lo and behold, it imprinted the paper with a jet-black heart. "Check it out," I called to Gus. He walked over and I stamped the back of his hand.

"Cool. So we were correct about Goda being Shiroo's partner. It still doesn't help us find—"

"Uh-hum," I coughed to get his attention and pointed to the address label on the box. It was addressed to D. Shiroo and the address was not the one we were currently searching. "What do you say we blow this pop stand and catch us a cop killer?"

Chapter Seventy-Seven

The address the stampers had been shipped to was a livery garage on Southern Boulevard in the Bronx. We had backup from the FBI and the 41st Precinct, which for years had been known coast to coast as Fort Apache. It was at one time a solitary outpost in a neighborhood of death, decay, and gangs. The neighborhood had improved leaps and bounds from those days but was still defined by one of the lowest per capita incomes in New York County, a place where drug dealing and prostitution were regular jobs, and a life could be lost by simply turning the wrong corner.

Command was taking zero chances with a cop killer. SWAT was going to lead the assault by battering down the garage door in the middle of the night. It was half past two when the team was finally in place and ready to move in. Reconnaissance had reported that two Asian women had entered at roughly eleven p.m. and were still believed to be inside.

Shiroo had not been spotted.

Tactical officers in battle gear surrounded the building and sharpshooters were positioned on surrounding rooftops. There was absolutely no chance of Shiroo escaping the all-encompassing dragnet that encircled the garage if he was, in fact, inside the building.

The only hitch was the two women who had entered. Not knowing who they were, SWAT would not enter shooting. They'd attempt to locate the women and vacate them from the premises if at all possible. Once that had been accomplished, Shiroo would be captured dead or alive.

Had the garage been empty, a tactical vehicle could've been driven through the doors, but a wire cam slipped secretly under the doors revealed that the garage bay was filled with cars and car scrap.

I could feel my heart pounding as the moments ticked away, and then it came, the sign from Pembrook, the SWAT commander, the man on the front line. He'd be first in after the doors were rammed. I was so tense that I grabbed Gus' hand and squeezed it. I looked into his eyes and saw that he was as desperate as I was for all of this to come to an end, and to realize that long-awaited feeling of closure.

The garage doors crashed open as the giant rams smashed into them. Pembrook eased into the garage with his men following closely behind. The scattered cars and scrap formed a maze the men threaded through before approaching the office at the back of the structure.

I raised my binoculars and peered through the glass office observation panel. I could only see the topless upper bodies of two women. They were sitting on opposite sides of a table and were presumably stuffing bags with heroin although I could not make out such small details. They hurried to cover up as soon as the SWAT team came through the door.

Pembrook motioned to the door on the back wall of the office and pointed. One of the women nodded. Pembrook raised his finger to his lips, signaling for the women to be silent. One of his men stepped forward, grabbed them by the arms, and was leading them away when a blast of semiautomatic gunfire tore gaping holes in the wall.

It looked as if Pembrook had been hit before his men were able to return fire. He was dragged out of the way as hundreds of rounds were fired at the spot where the first wave of bullets had pierced the wall. There was a moment of silence after the initial exchange. The SWAT team stood at the ready, waiting to see if their target was down. And then the bullets came flying again, this time unabated. Semiautomatic fire came in torrents down the length of the garage, flying directly at where we were standing. I heard the whiz of a bullet and then a dull thud. Gus was wearing a Kevlar vest, but the impact of the slug knocked him back. I pulled him down behind a cruiser and saw that he was clutching his chest and grimacing in pain. "Dear God, Gus, are you—" My heart was racing like a locomotive.

He gritted his teeth and nodded. "It's okay," he wailed. "It hit the vest."

I wanted to call for an EMT but knew there'd be no response until the immediate siege ended.

The crackle of gunfire back and forth sounded like an armed platoon invasion. The wall at the rear of the structure was collapsing as large-caliber rounds sliced through beams and tore through sheetrock. The shooter continued to return fire. "How is the son of a bitch not dead?" It was the sound of bullets hitting heavy-grade steel that offered an answer to my question. The door at the rear of the office must've led to a bathroom, and Shiroo was presumably crouched behind a bathtub, firing blindly over the top of it. It was likely an old one, hundreds of pounds of iron and porcelain, strong enough to withstand the SWAT team's fire, old-world construction probably capable of withstanding Armageddon.

The shooter's fire finally ended and I wondered whether he'd been hit or was merely out of ammunition. A SWAT officer called repeatedly for Shiroo to come out unarmed, but there was no answer or movement. A minute passed and then flash grenades were thrown through the gaping holes in the wall and the SWAT team rushed the bathroom. I think my heart froze until I saw them emerge moments later, dragging Daichi Shiroo behind them.

Chapter Seventy-Eight

Pembrook was okay. One of Shiroo's rounds had pierced his body armor but missed his vital organs. He was in the ambulance being attended to while Shiroo was being led to the police van.

I saw a car pull up. Shearson got out and hurried over after seeing me. She was beaming radiantly. "Did we get him, Chalice?" I nodded and she let go with an uncharacteristic, "Yay!" accompanied by a dramatic fist pump.

She saw that Gus was in pain and signaled for medical attention.

"Gus was hit by errant fire," I said. "He needs to be looked at."

"I'm all right," he said through clenched teeth. "I want to look this bastard in the eye before they take him away."

"Yeah," I said, my throat tightening. "Me too."

Shearson took me by the arm and led us toward the police van. "Stop," she hollered just as Shiroo was about to be loaded aboard. He was surrounded by SWAT officers and had sustained some superficial wounds—none of which appeared to be life threatening.

Hardly a scratch on him. Jesus, I thought, *this guy must be coated with Teflon.*

"Deputy Commissioner Shearson," she announced to the officers taking Shiroo into custody. "One minute."

Shiroo was turned around so that we were face to face. He looked at me with rage burning in his eyes. "You," he said with disgust. "You make me fail."

I wasn't about to ask what he meant. Facing the man who had killed my partner and had almost ended my life was too much for me to take. I was so shaken that I was unable to take stock of my emotions. I was at the same time both relieved and furious. I wanted to strangle him and cry simultaneously. One word escaped my lips, *"Animal."*

"Yes, you failed," Shearson said indignantly. "And now you'll be punished to the fullest extent of the law."

Members of the press were a few yards away, just behind the police barrier, but not so far away that they could not appreciate the fine performance the deputy commissioner was putting on for their benefit. "No one kills a cop in New York City," she boasted in a tone of superiority. "No one!" She flicked her hand, dismissing him. "Take this piece of garbage into custody."

The SWAT officers were once again attempting to put Shiroo in the van when someone cried out, "No! Stop!" We turned to see Harry trying to push past a police officer.

"Harry?" I announced with surprise.

"Who's that?" Shearson asked.

"Haruki," I answered. "Officer Yanagisawa's brother."

Her mouth fell open. "Oh my dear God." Shearson pointed at him. "Officer, let that man through."

Harry leapt forward, tearing out of the officer's grip before he could release him. He was shaking as he approached. "You killed my brother," he said, seething, finally eye to eye with his brother's murderer.

Shiroo didn't cower or turn away in shame. Instead he snarled at Harry and shouted contemptuously, "No! You killed *my* brother."

I could see Harry's chest heaving. His eyes were large and blazing with fury. "Yakuza scum," he spat indignantly.

"No," Shiroo replied furiously. "You the yakuza scum."

Harry leapt forward, his hands extended, reaching for Shiroo's throat. His momentum knocked Shiroo to the ground and their combined weight pulled the two attending officers down with them. In the half second it took for the two officers to recover, a shot went off. When Harry was pulled off Shiroo, there was blood running from Shiroo's chest.

Harry was subdued and his gun seized as EMT personnel rushed forward. Shiroo was writhing on the ground. Blood was gurgling in his throat. "No!" he screamed, reiterating with his last ounce of rage, "You the yakuza scum."

Chapter Seventy-Nine

Gus refused to go to the hospital. He instead insisted on being with me, side by side, to face Harry and get the truth.

Harry had been handcuffed and placed in an interrogation room at the precinct. It took more than an hour for me to get my head around the situation and calm myself enough to confront him. All I could see was the hatred and indignation in Daichi Shiroo's eyes when he was face to face with Harry. All I could hear was the resentment in his voice in those last few moments before he died.

Harry's hands were on the table. His back was straight and his head was held high. He looked so proud that I had trouble believing the words that had come out of Shiroo's mouth. Had Harry killed Shiroo's brother? Was he himself a yakuza assassin?

Gus and I entered the interrogation room and shut the door. Gus told him that the interview was being recorded and he acknowledged with a nod. I pulled out a chair and sat down, my expression callous, my tone demanding. "You're going to give me the truth, Harry and you're going to give it to me now."

He nodded once again and then after a very long moment finally began to speak.

Chapter Eighty

April 2011

Mirai Shiroo was not a suit-and-tie type of mobster. A black tee, jeans, and engineer boots were the staples of his everyday uniform. Full-sleeve tattoos, his yakuza badges of honor, were visible and proudly on display as he entered the offices of the Kyoto, Japan, Marine Transportation Committee. He stood out like graffiti on the walls of a holy shrine in contrast to the traditional dress attire of the government workers going about their daily routine. A smoldering cigarette hung from his lips as he approached the reception desk.

He didn't have a scheduled appointment nor did he ask to be seen. He simply stared at the receptionist with his cold eyes and said, "Mr. Nomura—where?"

Like her colleagues who were passively monitoring the gangster's presence in their office, the receptionist was intimidated by Shiroo and needed a moment to compose herself.

He repeated more firmly, "Mr. Nomura—where?"

She stammered as she asked, "Y-your name?" All of the offices had inner glass walls with nameplates noting the identity of the current occupant. Shiroo was short on patience. He turned and entered the inner offices, ignoring the receptionist's warning. "So sorry, sir, you can't go in there."

Mr. Nomura had been the committee chairman for more than twenty years and was highly respected for the firm hand with which he managed the shipping port. He was on the phone when

Shiroo barged into his office, grabbed him by the shirt, and dragged him off yelling, "Get your filthy hands off of me, Shiroo." He struggled, but the slender gray-haired chairman was no match for his muscular assailant. "Call the police," he yelled as he was dragged out the door before the watchful eyes of his staff. One brave soul positioned himself between them and the elevator. He trembled as Shiroo approached only to be shoved aside. Fellow office workers rushed to his aid after Shiroo and Nomura had vanished into the elevator.

<div align="center">~~~</div>

A black panel van was parked in the lot. Shiroo opened the back doors and pushed Nomura inside.

His driver, Haruki, started the engine and took off immediately.

"Let's have a meeting," Shiroo said, towering over Nomura, who was sprawled out on the floor.

"You are crazy, Shiroo. What do you think this will accomplish?"

"You know what I want, Nomura, and I'm tired of waiting for it."

"This same old song?" Nomura bravely asked. "How many times have I told you that I cannot give preference to your people? Key jobs at the port are awarded based on seniority and performance alone. I cannot give your people special treatment."

"I believe you can. With all of your tenure ... Who is senior enough to challenge you?"

"This is foolishness, Shiroo. Your words mean nothing to me."

He glared at the old man. "Maybe they'll mean more to your successor."

Nomura stared at Shiroo as the threat sank into his head. "You've lost your mind."

"Have I?" *He pulled a small pistol that had been wedged into the top of his boot, and aimed it at Nomura.* "Last chance, old man. You can put my men into management positions, or you can die a martyr. You can be my puppet, or your death can serve as a message to anyone else who is stupid enough to stand in my way. I run the shipping port now, Nomura, not you," *he ranted.* "Now will you do as I ask?"

"Shiroo, you can't be—"

Haruki was shocked and clutched his chest as the deafening thunder of the discharged bullet reverberated within the van. The noise of the blaring gunshot rang in his ears as he glanced back over his shoulder and saw Nomura motionless on the floor, his short-sleeve oxford shirt bloodstained and charred.

The van was traveling at forty kilometers per hour when Shiroo grabbed the lifeless body and tossed it out the back of the van, a clear message for the police and anyone else that Mirai Shiroo was no one to be trifled with.

There was blood spatter on Shiroo's face as he climbed into the passenger seat. He dropped the gun into the center console compartment. "Take me home," *he ordered.* "I need a bath."

"And the gun?" *Haruki asked.*

"Umi e," *he ordered.* "Into the ocean."

Chapter Eighty-One

Shiroo was in his bath, being sponged clean by two of his concubines, when the sound of a loud altercation filled the air. The women stood and covered their naked bodies with silk robes, but Shiroo remained seated in the tub, enjoying his Cuban cigar. He didn't so much as turn his head when the assault team came through the door.

The assault team commander motioned for the two women to leave the room with his officers. He waited for the room to clear before addressing the egotistical mob boss. "Stand up, you arrogant sack of shit."

Shiroo took his time before rising. He stood and faced the assault team commander, stark naked, proudly flaunting his fully tattooed body, posing with his hands on his hips. He didn't speak, move, or show any signs of being distressed.

The commander sneered at Shiroo and barked an order to his men, "Dare ka kono dōbutsu o kabā shi,-sha no naka de kare o nageru." *Somebody cover up this animal and toss him in the car.*

Chapter Eighty-Two

Shiroo endured a full twenty-three days of continuous interrogation and isolation without contact with his attorneys, without cracking under pressure, and without breaking a sweat. It was hardly his first trip to the rodeo—he'd been arrested and had been in and out of prisons many times. He knew the drill well. By law, the police were given a maximum of twenty-three days to break their suspects. The fact that they'd gone the distance told him that the prosecutor's case was weak and that they needed to force a confession.

He gave them no such satisfaction because he knew that Article 38 of Japan's Constitution categorically stated, "No person shall be convicted or punished in cases where the only proof against the suspect is his/her own confession."

He was self-assured as the first day of trial began, his normal cocky self. He had a battery of highly paid attorneys, attorneys who knew that their lives, more so than their legal fees, were at stake. He also knew that the only witness to Nomura's murder was his driver Haruki, a loyal minion he'd come to rely upon heavily. No one else saw him fire the gun. At the worst, someone saw a body fall out of a panel van, which he had ordered incinerated following the execution. The gun he used to slay Nomura, the committee chairman, was now somewhere at the bottom of Kyoto Bay.

Or so he thought until the public prosecutor presented his case. In evidence was Shiroo's DNA found within the panel van, which had been recovered before it could be incinerated, the murder weapon with his fingerprints on it, and a video tape of the murder, captured from a spy cam within the vehicle. The allegedly stolen panel van was in actuality a nondescript police vehicle.

He was sentenced to death by hanging despite vigorous arguments from his legal team. The fact that he had murdered a prominent prefecture official for the purpose of furthering the influence and reach of his crime syndicate was not of itself enough to warrant capital punishment. It was Shiroo's own words on videotape that had sent him to the gallows, "You can be my puppet, or your death can serve as a message to anyone else who is stupid enough to stand in my way." He had deliberately and brutally murdered Nomura to send a message. In sentencing, the presiding judge had sent a message of his own.

And with the absolute certainty of death by hanging now in his future, only one thought occupied Shiroo's consciousness: taking revenge on the man who had betrayed him, murdering Haruki.

Chapter Eighty-Three

Mirai Shiroo's prison cell always smelled like disinfectant, the institutional variety with a heavy concentration of ammonia. It was the first thing he noticed when he opened his eyes in the morning and the last scent to sting his nostrils before going to sleep. His cell was hidden from sunlight—it was just one in a long row of confined cells painted white and green. It was clean, sterile, monotonous, and maddening.

His day started when the lights were switched on and ended when they went off, and night could either be the blink of an eye or an eternity, depending on whether or not he slept. He'd been sentenced to death by hanging and had been waiting for his life to end every day and night for three years. The Japanese criminal justice system did not provide any upfront information as to when the sentence would be carried out. And so any day might be his last. One day he'd be awakened not by the unnatural prison incandescent light shining on his face but by a guard, and from that moment would have less than two hours to live.

With each passing day, his state of mind weakened. He'd close his eyes each night and pray, "Mō ichi-nichi," which meant, "One more day," knowing that his odds for survival diminished with each passing day. Death row inmates were typically executed within two to four years of beginning their sentence. Although it had been rumored that one prisoner had survived the noose for *eight years, by his thinking, he had less than a year to live. His days were burning down like a burning candlewick. In his mind he pictured the taper growing shorter and shorter—like his life, it would soon vanish.*

The torture of not knowing when the noose would snap his neck gnawed at his sanity. In his final days he was consumed with a single thought, the illusion of revenge. His mind was filled twenty-four hours a day with scenarios of torture and death for the man who'd betrayed him. In all he had devised seven execution scenarios but normally entertained just the best two or three.

The guard on duty greeted him with the same slap-in-the-face insult he offered on most mornings, "Dono yō ni kyōdaina geraku shite iru," *How the mighty have fallen.*

Mirai Shiroo had once been the boss, the kumichō *of* Inagawa-kaï, *one of the most powerful yakuza families in Japan. Now he was no more than a tattooed man in a white box, waiting to die. The mind of a leader had been reduced to the mind of a frightened deviant with the ability to do no more than fixate on revenge. Once considered untouchable, his remaining days now dwindled away, and all because he had violated the cardinal rule of his yakuza family and made family of someone his underlings considered undeserving.*

Chapter Eighty-Four

Haruki's security pass was checked before he was allowed to enter the nondescript room with beige walls made remarkable only by the three identical conduit boxes mounted shoulder level on the wall, on center, sixteen inches apart.

The two guards that accompanied him were filled with resentment but remained stoic and did not allow the outsider to see how they felt. Each of the three took a position in front of one of the conduit boxes, waiting for the signal to proceed. All the while a sound system piped in the calming tones of a Buddhist sutra.

To his right was a floor-to-ceiling royal blue curtain. The room beyond it was paneled in bamboo and the floor covered in carpet. Blindfolded and shackled to the wall, Mirai Shiroo, the condemned man, waited. Less than ninety minutes had elapsed from the time he had been informed that his execution was going to be carried out, and in keeping with strict protocol, neither his family nor legal representatives had been notified.

The Ministry of Justice demanded split-second efficiency, and as such, the Keimusho took his position exactly on time. On his signal, Haruki and the two guards raised their hands into position just inches from the three conduit boxes, paused and ready to depress the three black plunger-type buttons.

~~~

Shiroo's eyes were closed despite the fact that he was blindfolded. He had been unshackled and led to the center of the room where he was positioned with his knees over a red panel on the floor, and the noose fitted around his neck. It was only now with his eyes shielded that he allowed his tears to flow. He had been on death row for more than three years, knowing that at any moment he might be ushered abruptly into the execution chamber. The tears he cried were not because he feared death. They were tears of relief, relief from the mental anguish that was finally coming to an end.

~~~

Before the Keimusho *gave the final signal, Kei Katsui, the guard to Haruki's left, let go an uncharacteristic sneer. Haruki presumed it was because he was an outlier, a cop who had no rightful place in the Kyoto Detention House execution chamber. There were only two or three executions each year, and some of Katsui's colleagues had waited years for their chance to press the* kuroi botan, *the black button, and were now denied their honor because a lousy cop had been accorded a special privilege for catching a very big fish.*

"Nanda yo omae-wa?" *Who the hell do you think you are? Katsui whispered contemptuously, confirming Haruki's suspicions. Still there was something in the subsequent glances Katsui stole that puzzled him.*

Why does he look at me like that? *Haruki wondered, but the command from the* Keimusho *focused him on the mission at hand. His hand moved forward, the palm of his hand depressing the* kuroi botan.

When the three buttons were depressed, the Buddhist sutra was interrupted by the clang of the mechanical latch that had been triggered. The trapdoor beneath Shiroo was released. His neck snapped as he dropped into the cold, clinical cubicle beneath the death chamber, where a doctor waited to pronounce death.

Only one of the kuroi botan actuated the trapdoor and in that way neither Haruki nor the two guards were ever to know which of them had sent Shiroo to his death. But deep in his bones, Haruki sensed that it was his touch on the black plunger that had caused Shiroo's neck to snap, and rewarded him with a long-awaited sense of closure.

Chapter Eighty-Five

Kei Katsui treaded carefully over the debris in the old tire plant while looking at the map Mirai Shiroo had drawn for him on a napkin. With every step he kicked up the ages-settled vulcanized dust that lay on the floor. The plant had been closed for over a decade but still smelled of rubber. Heavy machinery stood frozen and rusted, waiting for the day they'd be disassembled and sold for scrap, recycled and remolded into the chassis of Toyotas and Nissans.

Just past the battery of tire lathes was the staircase to the floor manager's office, with a large glass panel through which the factory workers' activities could be observed. The door was locked as Shiroo had told him it might be, but one firm kick cracked the wooden frame and worked well in place of the key Shiroo no longer had access to.

Katsui put his weight against the heavy wooden desk and moved it without first checking for the removable floor panel it covered, the floor panel Shiroo told him he'd find beneath the leg of the massive desk. The panel had been expertly machined without so much as an eighth inch of play separating its sides. He used a pocket knife to slide the panel to the side so that there was now a quarter inch space on one side and no space on the other, just enough for him to pry the panel from where it lay.

The safe was imbedded beneath the floor, sandwiched between two wooden rafters. He followed the written instructions, *twisting the combination dial left and right in the prescribed sequence. The precision-engineered lock opened with a clanking noise. He knew what he'd find within. It was part of the bargain he'd struck with Shiroo, bundles of cash totaling roughly one hundred and fifty million yen, payment for a favor yet to be performed. Shiroo's days and mental facility were dwindling away so quickly that Katsui wondered whether the prisoner would be sane on the day he'd be escorted to the gallows.*

Shiroo had no way of knowing whether Katsui would honor his end of the obligation, but the former yakuza boss had lost all of his connections and power. Isolated, he had no leverage with anyone on the outside. His only option was to rely on the prison guard who had supervised his internment every day for more than three years.

In turn, Katsui stared at the money, then read the name and phone number on the bottom of the napkin he'd gotten from Mirai Shiroo, and pondered whether the vast sum of money justified the actions he was asked to take and whether he could live with himself after sacrificing his honor. "His brother," he mouthed. "Do I dare?" It was more money than he'd earn in ten lifetimes, and would provide luxuries for his family he could never even contemplate. He whispered, "Kami wa watashi o yurushite," God forgive me. He then unfolded a nylon duffle bag and stuffed it with the cash.

Chapter Eighty-Six

Harry had held his head erect the entire time he told us the story and seemed almost proud to share the details with us. Hearing him impart the elements of the story with passion and accuracy gave me a sense of how fundamental a role it played in the decisions he'd made and the actions he'd taken—to go abroad, track down his brother's murderer, and avenge his death. It was a great story, but was it the truth or merely a cleverly manufactured alibi?

Studying his facial expressions, speech patterns, and body language, it seemed that his deeds had been genuine and had been dictated by his heart, but I wasn't completely satisfied. Something told me to look deeper. "How did you know that Mirai Shiroo cut a deal with Kei Katsui, the prison guard?"

Harry's answer was immediate. "Katsui was investigated on corruption charges."

"What was the tip-off?" Gus asked, presuming the obvious. "Did the asshole buy matching his and hers canary yellow Lamborghinis?"

Harry didn't laugh. The dark humor in Gus' question was lost on him. "No. Katsui only spent money on things of true value. He sent his children off to private boarding school, but his supervisor knew that he couldn't afford such an expensive education for his kids on a civil servant's salary and opened an official query."

"I see." I took a moment before asking my next question. I wanted to phrase it in a way that would play right into his hands. "So this was strictly a matter of revenge. Daichi killed Yana to get revenge. In his eyes you were responsible for his brother's death, so he killed your brother to get even. Is that about right?" I took a deep breath and waited patiently for him to answer.

"Yes. That's exactly right, Chalice."

Son of a bitch. Under any other circumstances I'd have been thoroughly relieved to be done with the whole mess. I had yearned for a conclusion, but there was something about his story that just didn't sit right with me. Yana's murder, my life-changing head wound, and the deaths of an innocent chef and a tattoo artist ... I knew in my heart that he was lying to me. I turned to my husband. "Gus, could you give us a minute alone?"

He seemed surprised by the request but must have assumed that I needed time alone with Harry, a moment of healing and a good cry over the death of the man who was his brother and my partner. "Sure. Okay," he reluctantly replied. He squeezed my shoulder to show support. He whispered, "I'll be right outside if you need me. Don't make this any harder on yourself than it has to be."

I nodded. "Don't worry. I'll be okay." I waited for Gus to leave before switching off the video camera, the mic, and drawing the blinds on the mirror.

"What is going on?" Harry asked. For the briefest moment I detected a chink in his armor. He looked tentative and I could see in his eyes that being alone with me made him feel uncomfortable. "Why did you ask Detective Lido to leave?"

I strode back and forth as I answered. "Because this is personal—just between you and me."

My answer must've satisfied him because he looked to be back on his game, once again confident and self-assured. "I understand. We were both wounded by the loss of my brother." He seemed relieved.

Perfect. This is the way I want you, with your guard down. He must've thought that he was still in control of the situation, but I knew better. "I have one last question for you, Harry."

"Of course," he offered openly. "Anything."

"Why did you kill Daichi Shiroo? He was under arrest and he'd be going to prison. You were surrounded by witnesses—you knew you'd never get away with it, so ..." I shrugged. "Was it something that happened in the heat of the moment? Were you so enraged that you couldn't control yourself? I know you hated him for killing your brother, but you're a cop. You've been trained to maintain control under pressure."

"Control, yes, but this ... this was too personal. He murdered my brother. He was arrogant and he provoked me. I guess it was just too much and I snapped."

"Sure. That makes sense," I said, pretending to go along with his story. "A man takes your brother's life ... I don't know that I wouldn't have done the same thing."

He was trying to control himself, but I saw him blow a subtle sigh of relief.

"How'd you find your way over to the garage?"

"As you know, I was searching for Daichi and I was monitoring the police radio frequency. The airwaves were filled with calls about a raid on a commercial garage and the possibility of apprehending the cop killer."

"I see. And you responded to the scene."

"Yes."

"Knowing you were going to kill Daichi if you had the chance?"

"Ye—" He tried to catch his answer, but it was too late. He'd blundered and I could see in his eyes that he knew it as well. "I meant that I wanted to kill him. I was harboring so much hatred for the man. I think you understand what I mean. My English ... sometimes I'm not sure if I'm communicating well enough."

"No worries," I said with a comforting smile. *You're communicating just fine.* I pulled out a chair and sat down opposite him. "Let me tell you what I think."

"What do you mean?" he asked nervously.

"If I heard your story correctly, you were working undercover. You infiltrated Mirai Shiroo's yakuza family and you set him up. He thought he was safe when he threatened and killed Mr. Nomura in front of you, but you had the van rigged for audio and video, and you used the recorded account to send him to the gallows. He ordered you to burn the van and dispose of the murder weapon, but you did neither."

"Yes. I spent years working the case. Infiltrating the yakuza was very difficult. Winning trust and rising within the organization was an all-consuming task. I had to abandon my friends, my family ... everyone."

"Oh, I get it, Harry. Believe me, I empathize with you. Funny thing about organized crime families, though—whether it's the mafia, the Chinese triads, the Russian mob, or the yakuza—they all seem to know their own and they're pretty darn clever about sniffing out rats. You must've put your very heart and soul into that performance, because those people play for keeps." I had to get to the bottom of it. I was baiting him and was afraid he'd know it, so I chose a new line of questioning. "So when did you realize that it was Mirai's brother who killed Yana? I mean, you didn't hear it from me, so how'd you figure it out?"

I could see the gears turning in his head. He was playing chess and trying to think several moves ahead, offering answers that wouldn't lead him into an ambush. "Daichi abducted Tiru, saying he would kill him unless I met him at the park. He told me that he had killed Yana and would give me a chance to save my honor by exchanging my life for Tiru's."

"But he killed Tiru anyway."

He seared me with his eyes. "That is on you, Chalice," he said heatedly. "You weren't supposed to be there, but you tracked me to the park and spooked Daichi."

Trying to turn the tables on me? I don't think so. "Maybe, but I think he planned to kill Tiru all along. He was sending you a message. 'You betrayed my brother and now he's dead. I'm going to kill you and everyone close to you—first your brother, then your friends ... and you last."

"If that's what you have to believe to help you sleep at night, Chalice, but I believe that you forced his hand."

"And I believe this is all on you, your brother's death, my injury, and the murder of your two close friends. You weren't undercover for the police. You were a dirty cop, a cop who'd been part of the yakuza for years and managed to avoid getting a police record. That's why Mirai Shiroo trusted you. You didn't work your way into the family, you were always a part of it."

"That's crazy talk."

"The hell it is. Daichi didn't kill your brother strictly for revenge. He couldn't go back to Japan because of his outstanding murder warrants. He killed your brother to lure you here. It was you, Harry. You were the intended target all along. Poor Yana, he had a higher purpose in life and would've had a brilliant career in law enforcement, but because of you, he was just a means to an end, just chum thrown in the water to catch a bigger fish. That's why Daichi said that *you* were yakuza scum. You were the traitor all along and you killed him not to avenge your brother so much as to silence him forever. He alone knew that you set up his brother and you figured he'd find a way of getting the information back to your yakuza brethren, so it was kill or be killed. A yakuza member working for the police ... they'd cut you up into fish bait, not all at once, but one agonizing slice at a time until you were reduced to bones. You're pathetic. This was all about saving your own ass. You're a fraud, Harry. You go on and on about honor, but you're just a stinking cowardly fraud."

I exhaled deeply after unleashing my scalding diatribe and waited for him to react. Moments ticked away while I waited for his answer and then it came. He closed his eyes and slowly lowered his head in shame.

Chapter Eight-Seven

Gus was busily scoffing down huevos rancheros and home fries, Ma was elbows-deep in a plate of scrambled eggs and bacon, and Max was creating a Crayola work of art on his paper placemat—Sunday morning brunch with the family, what could possibly be better?

I grabbed Ma's mimosa and stole a sip.

"Hey!" she protested loudly. "That's off-limits."

"What can I say? I'm feeling my oats today." I cleaned the last bit of pancake from my plate. "I'm going back for more," I said, beaming as I wiped a smudge of chocolate off my upper lip. "The chocolate-chip pancakes were delish, but I'm not leaving without trying the Nutella-stuffed French toast." Best of all, the doctor told me that I could have one cup of regular coffee per day and I was saving that happy experience for last.

The clouds had departed and I was finally seeing that fabled silver lining optimists are always talking about. My future as an NYPD homicide detective teetered precariously on the opinion of the medical review board, but I had decided not to dwell on their pending decision because it was out of my control. So for the moment I was happy being with my family and sucking up every crumb of happiness life had to offer. "Can I bring something back for either of you?" I asked before setting off to pillage the buffet table.

"I'll take some of that Nutella French toast, babe. Thanks."

"What about you, Ma?" I asked. "How about a trough of oatmeal to keep the old constitution chugging along?"

"*Bah.* My constitution is just fine, you rotten kid, but I could go for one of those cannoli cronuts."

I bowed. "Your wish is my command." I handed Max a butter cookie with a cherry on top, which he reluctantly traded for his blue crayon. What can I say? The kid is a workaholic and utterly committed to his art.

I took my time at the buffet, surveying it one last time in search of delicacies I might've somehow missed. Of course, nothing had escaped my eagle eye on the previous visits I'd made, but I spotted the barista behind the coffee bar and had him whip me up a cappuccino made with real espresso, because I decided that I needed the bean more than I needed the stuffed French toast. The stuffed French toast looked heavenly, but God knows it wasn't as if I was never going to eat again, and I'd put on a few pounds from having been out of the gym for months. What with the pixie blond haircut and all, I was beginning to look like a generously enhanced porn star. Gus didn't seem to mind, but with all the cold showers he'd been taking, I was afraid we'd get an unkind letter from the EPA.

As I walked back to our table, I passed a family: a mom, dad, and two little ones. There was something about the shape of the dad's head and his black hair that reminded me of Yana. We'd been partners about a year, and though I initially struggled with our cultural differences, I had grown to care for him very much. It saddened me to think that he was gone and that his wife and two kids would have to forge forward through life without a husband and father. He was a good man who had paid for the sins of his brother.

It was something Yana once said to me that convinced me to go after his brother tooth and nail in the interrogation room.

He'd once told me how surprised the family was when Haruki joined the police department because he had always been a troubled child, the one who wasn't expected to amount to anything. It wasn't much of an indictment, but it was enough to swing my thinking, and I knew that there was a very thin line between being an undercover cop and being a dirty cop. It happens all the time—a policeman goes undercover and gets so corrupted and immersed in the dirty lifestyle that he loses his way for good.

There was also the report we'd received from the Japanese government, in particular the section that stated, "There was evidence that Daichi's brother had been betrayed by a spy, someone inserted into the family by a rival faction, who undermined Mirai's authority and was planning to assassinate them both." I had no trepidation about hounding Harry to the brink because I knew that he was most certainly that spy.

Harry was going to stand trial for the murder of Daichi Shiroo. I wasn't going to speculate nor was I interested in knowing in which country he'd be tried although I suspected he'd be sent back to Japan to stand trial. His career as a policeman was over, and I had more important matters to focus on than whether the courts would slam him with corruption and abetting charges in addition to murder. His brother was dead because of him and he'd have to live with that bitter truth all the days he remained alive.

Because of him, Daichi Shiroo had likely followed Yana and me that entire day, taking the opportunity to shoot us from the building rooftop when the opportunity best aligned with his murderous MO and skill set. My guess was that he'd followed us to the building where Serafina Ramirez had lived, watched us park the car, and decided he'd have an opportunity to shoot us from the roof of the building while we were returning to our car.

Whether Daichi had planned on killing me as well as Yana would never be known, and really, at this point it no longer mattered.

I returned to a table of smiling faces, with Ma's cronut and Gus' French toast. Not that he needed another, but Max got a second cookie as well. I mean, all was finally right with the world—Yana's killer was dead, I was on the mend and surrounded by loved ones, and with a little good luck I'd somehow manage to hold onto a career in law enforcement.

All told we spent most of two full hours with our derrieres firmly planted in comfortable chairs, gorging ourselves on food and drink. It wasn't until we were outside and a horse-drawn carriage came to a stop that I was forced to spill the beans.

"The hell is this?" Gus asked, sounding suspicious. "What did you do now, Stephanie?"

Ma was giggling as she hailed a cab and stowed Max and his stroller within.

I grinned mischievously. "Ma's gonna watch Max for a couple of days. I shot the wad on twenty-four-hour concierges, twenty-four-hour room service, twenty-four-hour hallway butlers, and an eight-thousand-square-foot spa. I booked The Plaza, babe. Let's *rock*."

"But what about—"

"The doc?"

"Uh-huh."

"I'm good to go. The doc gave me the all clear. I haven't had a seizure in two months and he said that you could ride me like one of Teddy Roosevelt's Rough Riders."

"Did he really?" Gus crossed his arms and looked into my eyes with a serious expression. "Were those his *exact* words?"

"Almost verbatim."

"You're sure we're not rushing this?"

"I'm fine," I assured him. "More than fine—I'm randy as a rabbit and ready to be ravaged."

The horse whinnied. "I guess all the talk about the Rough Riders got him excited."

"How do you know it's a him?"

Gus pointed at the powerful beast's underside. I turned and my eyes grew large. I continued to glance at the proud equine before kissing Gus. "Well, big fella, are you ready to climb aboard, or am I leaving with the horse?"

~END~

I hope that you enjoyed Compromised. Now is the best time for you to review the book, so please click on the hyperlink and post a review while your opinion is still fresh:
http://smarturl.it/g7s29m

For more information on Stephanie Chalice and Chloe Mather thrillers, and my other books, please visit my website: lawrencekelter.com.

Write to me at any time and sign up for my forthcoming newsletter: larrykelter@aol.com.

In the Stephanie Chalice Thriller Series

Full-Length Novels

Don't Close Your Eyes
Ransom Beach
The Brain Vault
Our Honored Dead
Baby Girl Doe
Compromised

Stephanie Chalice Novellas

First Kill: Prequel #1
Second Chance: Prequel #2
Third Victim: Prequel #3

In the Chloe Mather Thriller Series

Secrets of the Kill
Rules of the Kill
Legends of the Kill
Carnage of the Kill (Winter 2015)

Other Full-length Works of Fiction

Counterblow
Kiss of the Devil's Breath
Palindrome
Saving Cervantes
Season of Faith

About The Author

I never expected to be a writer. In fact, I was voted the student least likely to visit a library. (Don't believe it? Feel free to check my high school yearbook.) Well, times change I suppose, and I have now authored several novels including the internationally best-selling Stephanie Chalice, and Chloe Mather Thriller Series.

Early in my writing career, I received support from none other than best-selling novelist, Nelson DeMille, who reviewed my work and actually put pencil to paper to assist in the editing of the first book. DeMille has been a true inspiration to me and has also given me some tough love. Way before he ever said, "Lawrence Kelter is an exciting new novelist, who reminds me of an early Robert Ludlum," he told me, "Kid, your work needs editing, but that's a hell of a lot better than not having talent. Keep it up!"

I've lived in the Metro New York area most of my life and rely primarily on locales in Manhattan and Long Island for story settings. I do my best to make each novel quickly paced and crammed full of twists, turns, and laughs.

Enjoy!

LK

Made in the USA
Middletown, DE
14 July 2015